Sigrid Undset

IN THE WILDERNESS

Sigrid Undset was born to Norwegian parents in Denmark in 1882. Between 1920 and 1922, she published her magnificent and widely acclaimed trilogy of fourteenth-century Norway, *Kristin Lavransdatter* (composed of *The Bridal Wreath*, *The Mistress of Husaby*, and *The Cross*). And between 1925 and 1927, she published the four volumes of *The Master of Hestviken* (composed of *The Axe*, *The Snake Pit*, *In the Wilderness*, and *The Son Avenger*). Ms. Undset, the author of numerous other novels, essays, short stories, and tales for young readers, was awarded the Nobel Prize for Literature in 1928. During the Second World War, she worked with the Norwegian underground before having to flee to Sweden and then to the United States. After the war, she returned to Norway, where she died in 1949.

ALSO BY Sigrid Undset

KRISTIN LAVRANSDATTER

The Bridal Wreath (VOLUME I)

The Mistress of Husaby (VOLUME II)

The Cross (VOLUME III)

THE MASTER OF HESTVIKEN

The Axe (VOLUME I)

The Snake Pit (VOLUME II)

In the Wilderness (VOLUME III)

The Son Avenger (VOLUME IV)

IN THE
WILDERNESS

IN THE WILDERNESS

THE MASTER OF HESTVIKEN, VOLUME III

SIGRID UNDSET

VINTAGE BOOKS

A DIVISION OF RANDOM HOUSE, INC.

NEW YORK

First Vintage Books Edition, July 1995

Translated from the Norwegian by Arthur G. Chater.

Library of Congress Cataloging-in-Publication Data
Undset, Sigrid, 1882–1949.
[Olav Audunssøn og hans born. I. English]
In the wilderness / Sigrid Undset. — 1st Vintage Books ed.
p. cm — (Master of Hestviken ; v. 3)
Originally published in Norwegian as pt. 1 of Olav Audunssøn og hans born (2 v.).
ISBN 0-679-75553-5
1. Middle Ages—History—Fiction. 2. Norway—History—1030–1397—Fiction.
I. Title. II. Series: Undset, Sigrid, 1882–1949. Master of Hestviken ; v. 3.
PT8950.U506213 1995
839.8'2372—dc20
94-42543
CIP

Manufactured in the United States of America
10 9 8 7 6 5 4 3 2

IN THE
WILDERNESS

PART ONE

The Parting of the Ways

O N a day in spring Olav was out with one of his house-carls spreading dung on the frozen soil of the "good acre."

The fields that faced north still gleamed and glittered with ice, but from above on the Horse Crag water trickled and ran. And on the sunny side, across the creek, the cliff was baking—the Bull rose out of the sea with a flickering reflection of the ripples on its rusty-grey rocks. Brown soil showed under the pines over there, and the thicket on the hillside toward Kverndal was hung with yellow catkins.

Out in the creek Eirik was rowing—the lad's red kirtle shone sharply against the blue water. Olav stood for a while leaning on his spade and looked down at the little boat. 'Twas ever the same with Eirik—he took such a time! He had only had a few sheep to ferry across; sheep and goats were now turned out in the wood on that side. Today there was good use for the boy at home.

There came a tripping of feet on the rocks behind Olav's back—the great bare rocks that rounded off the "good acre" toward the fiord. There stood Cecilia with the sun behind her so that its rays shone through her fair, curly hair, lighting it up. She sat on the rock and slid down, crying out to her father and holding up a bunch of coltsfoot.

Olav turned and waved her off.

"Come not too close, Cecilia—you will be all besmeared." He lifted her onto a stone. The little maid dabbed her posy into his face and looked to see how yellow she had made her father with the pollen. 'Twas not much, for Cecilia had already pulled the flowers to pieces, but she laughed none the less and tried again.

Olav caught the faint scent, fresh and acrid—the first of the

3

year's new growth. The winter that lay behind him had been as long as the Fimbul winter.[1] But now he felt with a zest all through him that his boots were wet and heavy with earth. Even here in the shadow of the rock the ice shield covering the ground had shrunk away and exposed a strip of raw mould along its edge. The manure that lay spread over the field steamed with a rich smell, and from the waterside came a powerful springtime breath of sea and tar and fish and salt-drenched timber.

The little sailboat that he had sighted just now off the Bull was making this way. The craft was unfamiliar—no doubt some folk who were going upcountry.

He wiped the worst of the dirt from his fingers and led Cecilia back over the rocks.

"Go away to Liv now. You must not let the child run so far from you, Liv—she might fall over."

The serving-maid turned toward him—"such fine weather"— with a great smile on her face. She sat sunning herself; the garment she should have been mending was flung aside into the heather.

Olav turned from her with distaste and went back to his work. The boat now lay alongside the quay; the strangers were walking up in company with Eirik. Olav made as though he had not seen them until they stopped by the fence and greeted him.

They were two men of middle age, tall, thin, with keen, hook-nosed faces and merry, twinkling eyes. Olav knew them now, he had often seen them in Oslo, but never spoken with them; they were sons of that English armourer, Richard Platemaster, who had married a yeoman's daughter from the country west of the fiord and had settled in the town. What business these men might have with him Olav could not guess. But he went with them up to the houses.

When the Richardsons had been given a meal and they were sitting over their ale, Torodd, the elder, set forth their errand: he had heard it hinted that Olav was minded to make an end of his trading partnership with Claus Wiephart. Olav answered that he knew nothing of it. But, said Torodd, he had heard in the town that this year Olav Audunsson had withheld his goods and not allowed Claus Wiephart to sell for him.

[1] In Norse mythology the Fimbul (i.e., mighty) winter, lasting for three years, precedes Ragnarok, the death battle of the ancient gods.

'Twas not so either, replied Olav. But he had made a funeral feast for his wife here during the winter, so that much had been consumed in the house, and with the death of his wife he had also been hindered in his work in many ways.—Olav thought he could now see whither they were tending. And perhaps it might be worth considering, to find another trader for his wares.

Then said the other brother, Galfrid: "The matter is thus, Olav, that my brother and I have business in England this summer. And we know you to be a skilful shipmaster, and you are acquainted with that country from your youth. We have never been there, though it is the home of our father's kinsfolk. Now we have been surely told that you purpose to make a voyage this summer—"

While he was speaking Eirik had come in at the door, with a chaplet of blue anemones in his hand. Olav knew that the hazel thicket on the other side of the creek was now blue with these flowers. With such childishness as plucking flowers this long lad idled away his time on a bright and busy day of spring.

Eirik stayed by the door, listening intently and only waiting for his father to send him out of the room.

"Who told you that, Galfrid?" asked Olav.

It was Brother Stefan—that barefoot friar who had been hereabouts so much during the winter. The Richardsons were free of the Franciscan convent, as one of their brothers was a monk there. And there they had heard that Olav of Hestviken had thoughts of faring to foreign lands this summer, though doubtless he had not yet made any bargain about a ship.

Olav kept silence. But how the friar had got hold of this he could not guess—he did not recall having spoken of it to a soul. Go away—ay, God knew he had wished he could—but still he had not thought of *doing* it. He owned neither ship nor freight, and to seek out an opportunity of sailing with other folk had seemed somehow too troublesome a matter. Moreover there was enough to be done at home now, seeing how everything had been neglected during the long years of his wife's sickness.

But when an opportunity was offered—! He felt his heart contract in his breast as a hand is clenched to strike the table, the moment he fully realized that he *could* get away from everything. Far away—for a long while—Yes, oh yes!

"I said no such thing to Brother Stefan—" Olav shook his head. "Maybe I let fall something—I do not remember—I may have said

I might have a mind to see the world again, now that I am a man without ties—"

Then he became aware of the boy standing there, all ears, and he bade Eirik go out. Eirik came forward quickly and flung his chaplet about the little crucifix that hung on the wall within the bed where his mother had lain. But having done so, he had to go out.

How Brother Stefan's long nose had sniffed out these thoughts that he harboured—that was nevertheless more than Olav could make out.

In the course of the afternoon the men had reached so far in their colloquy that Olav took the two strangers and showed them what wares he had for sale. It was not much—less than a score of goats' pelts, three otters' skins and a few other skins of game, some barrels of oak bark. He would have to take with him all his store of fish and herrings—his house-folk could be content with fresh fish this summer. He had also some oak logs and barrel-staves he had intended for his own use—but if he himself were absent, they would only lie unused.

Late in the evening Liv came in and asked her master to go with her to the byre; there was a cow that was to calve, but the dairy-woman had fallen so grievously sick, said Liv—and besides, it was not her work to see to the cattle.

The night was moonless, cold, and still as Olav came out of the byre again. Now he had to go and wake old Tore, ask him as a favour to watch in the byre tonight, for it was of no use to let Liv be there alone. Lazy she was and thoughtless. One would scarce have believed it, but not even while they were struggling to tend the poor beast that lay there lowing plaintively—not even in the dark and narrow byre could the girl leave him in peace. She was after him like a kitten seeking to be caressed—time after time he had almost to fling her from him so that he might use his hands freely. She had taken the idea, Olav guessed, that now she would be his leman and mistress of the house. And however he let her see that it was bootless to aspire to *that* dignity, it made little impression on Liv.

He was secretly ashamed before his own house-folk—they must be laughing behind his back and watching whether the girl would

coax him the way she wanted in the end. He thought he saw it—
Liv playing the lady here with the keys at her belt. Oh no.—He
did not care to go in even with Tore, when he had roused the old
man.

There was ice on the top of the water-butt as Olav plunged
his arms into it and rinsed his hands. He listened and gazed out
into the darkness as he bethought himself whether anything had
been forgotten.

It was still now—the merry purling of little brooks on the slope
was frozen into silence and there was only the faint splash and
ripple of the sea beneath the cliff—and over in Kverndal the murmur of the stream. The stars seemed so few and so far away tonight—there was a slight mist in the air.

The calf was full-cheeked and long-eared—looked promising;
that was so far well; he had lost three calves this spring. And not
one cow-calf had he had yet.

In the northern sky above the dark back of the Bull pale flickers
of northern lights came and went—like a dewy breath over the
vault of heaven. They were not often seen here in the south. At
home in the Upplands the lights flashed half across the sky; and
when as children they used to tease them, by whistling and waving
linen cloths at them, there was a crackling sound and long tongues
shot down toward the earth and back to the sky. Once when they
had stolen out behind the outhouses and stood there flapping one
of Ingebjörg's longest wimples, Arnvid had come upon them, and
then he had beaten them. It was a great sin to do so, for it meant
storm when the northern lights were disturbed.

Here in the south the lights were usually but pale and faint.—

Olav gave his shoulders a hitch in his reeking clothes—'twas
still four days to washday and Sunday.

Instinctively he went quietly as he crossed the yard: the little
ice pockets made such a crackling, and he was loath to break in on
the low murmuring sounds that came up from below, as from the
depths of the night.

Within the room a little lamp was burning at the edge of the
hearth.

Olav had given the two strangers beds in the closet, and seated
on the edge of Ingunn's bed he undressed—slowly, with a pause
after each garment. He rose to pinch out the wick.

A whisper came from the northern bed: "Father!"

After a moment Olav answered in a hushed voice: "Are you awake, Eirik?"

"Yes. When shall we sail, Father?"

Olav was silent. But Eirik was so used to his father's seeming not to hear, or answering like the echo when one shouted toward the Bull—after a pause and as though across a distance.

"Father—take me with you! I shall stand you in good stead"— Eirik spoke in a loud and eager whisper—"I shall serve you as well as a full-grown man. I can do the work of an able-bodied man, ay, and more!"

"You can indeed." Eirik could hear that his father was smiling, but then there was neither anger nor refusal in his voice.

"May I go with you, Father—to England this summer?"

"None has yet said that I go myself," said Olav soberly.

He blew out the little flame, pinched off the burned wick, and dropped it into the oil. Then he got into bed. Something fell down and touched his neck in the darkness. It was soft and cool, reminding him of young, living skin, among the coarse, rough wool and sheepskins of his bedclothes. It was Eirik's chaplet. Olav groped for it and hung it in its place again. It had reminded him of her body—her shoulder so slight and soft and cold, when the coverlet had slipped off while she slept and he drew it up and spread it over her again.

Of course he would go—he was firmly resolved on that in his inmost heart, and he would suffer nothing to come in the way and hinder him. Only for appearance' sake he still let it seem uncertain whether he would accept; it would not do to acknowledge that he had let himself be persuaded so easily by two perfect strangers—nay, that he had seized their offer with both hands.

But he would not stay here at Hestviken the whole summer, now that he espied a means of escape. No matter that this little old hoy that the Richardsons' grandfather owned was a wretched craft—and that he himself was no more of a seaman than that they might easily have found many a better one. *Once* before he had been in England, some fifteen years ago with the Earl—so it was but little he knew of that country; a great lord's subalterns cannot stir far abroad. But as the Richardsons had not questioned him of it— He knew nothing of these two, but he could see that they were untried men and not over-wise. And by degrees he had been forced to admit that he himself would never be a good tradesman. It made him angry when he saw he had been cheated. But he had accustomed himself to say nothing and put a good face on it; 'twas bootless for him to wrangle with folk who were sharper than himself in such matters. He had not even thought of dissolving his partnership with Claus Wiephart—he might fall into the hands of others who would shear him yet closer.

These Richardsons looked as if they themselves might stand to be shorn. In that case there would be even less profit in throwing in his lot with them. Howbeit—

He missed her who was gone so sorely that he could not guess what it would be like to live here without her in all the years that were to come. He went about as one benumbed with wondering.

He could remember the thoughts he had sometimes had in her last years: that it would be a sin to wish her to lie on here and suffer torment to no purpose. But now that she was gone—ay, now he remembered that shred of saga that Brother Vegard had once repeated to them while they were children, of King Harald Luva, who sat brooding three years over the corpse of his Lapp wife. He was bewitched, the monk had said. Maybe—ah yes, but maybe 'twas not all madness either.

As far back as he could remember, he had been used to think of her as much as of himself, whatever he were doing or thinking. When two trees have sprung up together from their roots, their leaves will make *one* crown. And if one falls, the other, left standing alone, will seem overgrown. Olav felt thus, exposed and grown aslant, now that she was gone.

He knew full well they had been joyless years, most of them, but his memories of the happiness they had shared were far clearer and more enduring. It was as with the lime trees here on the hills about the inlet: they made no great show to the eye, but in summer when they blossomed, the whole of Hestviken seemed laden with the scent of them, so that one almost felt its sweetness clinging to the skin like honey-dew. In all the years he had been away from here, as boy and as man, fostered among strangers or an outlaw in other realms, this scent of lime blossoms had been the only thing to remind him that he owned lands that were his—all else about them he had forgotten.

And even in the saddest days of their life together she had been his—the same as that little Ingunn who had been so sweet and fair when she was young, so slight and supple to take in his arms, with the scent of hay breathing from her golden-brown hair when he spread it over him in the darkness. He had often loved her with the same gentle goodness as one loves a favourite faithful, innocent animal—a handsome heifer or a dog. And at other times he had loved her so that his body trembled and quailed in anguish when he recalled it now and remembered that it was done, had been done for many a day before she died. And nevertheless she was the only woman of whom he cared to recall the possession. He could not think of the others without feeling a chilly aversion to the memories creep over him.

Now he had lost Ingunn, and when he thought of the last night before she died, he knew it was his own fault that he had lost her entirely. He was well aware of what had befallen him. When he was plunged in the most helpless distress and sorrow, about to lose his only trusty companion in life, God, his Saviour Himself, had met him with outstretched hands to help. And had he but had the courage to grasp those open, pierced hands, he and his wife would not now have been parted. Had he but had the courage to stand by the resolve he had taken at that meeting with his God —whatever might have been his lot in this world, whether pilgrimage or the headsman's sword—in a mysterious way he would have been united with the dead woman, more intimately and closely than friend can be united with friend while both are alive on earth.

But once again his courage had failed him. He had stood looking on when God came and took Ingunn, carried her away alone.

And he was left behind as a man is left sitting on the beach when his ship has sailed away from him.

And to bide here at home in Hestviken after that—it was the same as waiting for the days and nights to pass by in an endless train, one like another.

No, he would not turn away the Richardsons' offer, that was sure.

From out of the darkness came the boy's wide-awake voice: "The Danes, Father—they lie out in the English Sea and seize our ships, I have heard."

"The English Sea is wide, Eirik, and our vessel is small.—Best that you stay at home this year, for all that."

"I meant it not so—" Olav could hear that the lad sat up in his bed. "I meant—I had such a mind to prove my manhood," he whispered in bashful supplication.

"Lie down and go to sleep now, Eirik," said Olav.

"For I am no longer a little boy—"

"Then you should have wit enough to let folk sleep in peace. Be quiet now."

His father's voice sounded weary, only weary but not angry, thought Eirik. He curled himself up and lay still. But sleep was impossible.

He would be allowed to go, he believed that firmly—so firmly that when he had lain for a while thinking of the voyage, he felt quite sure of it. He was certain that they would fall in with Danish ships. They have a much higher freeboard than ours usually have, so at the first onset it might look bad enough. But then he calls out that all hands are to run to the lee side and hold their shields over their heads, and then, when all their enemies have leaped on board, they come forward and attack them. His father singles out the enemy captain—he looks like that friend of Father's they met in Tunsberg once: a stout, broad man with red hair and a full red face, little blue eyes, and a big mouth crammed with long yellow horse's teeth.—Then Eirik flings his shield at the stranger's feet, so that he slips on the wet floor-boards and the blow does not reach his father—yes, it does, but his father takes no heed of the wound. The Dane stumbles and his hauberk slips aside so as to expose his throat for an instant; at the same moment Eirik plies his short sword as though it were a dagger. Now the Danes try to escape on board their own ship. The ships' sides creak and give as they crash against one another in the seaway, and while the men hang sprawling, with axes and boathooks fixed in the high, overhanging side of the Danish vessel, the Norwegians lay on them with sword and spear. "Methinks 'tis no more than fair," says his father, "that Eirik, my son, should take the captain's arms—but if ye will have it otherwise, I offer to redeem your shares from this booty." But all the men agree: "Nay, 'tis Eirik that laid low this champion single-handed, and we have saved the ship through his readiness."

"Are you the young Norse squire, Eirik Olavsson from Hestviken?"—for the tale has spread all over London town. And one day when the governor of the castle rides abroad, he meets him. The White Tower is the name of London's castle; it is built of white marble. And one day when he has gone up to have a sight of it—this castle is even greater and more magnificent than Tunsberghus, and the rock on which it stands is much higher—the governor comes riding down the steep path with all his men, and some of them whisper to their lord, pointing to the lad from Norway—

Nay, stay behind in London when his father goes home, that he will not, after all. Not even in play can Eirik imagine his father leaving him and going back to Hestviken, and the life here taking its wonted course, but without him. In his heart Eirik harbours an everlasting dread; even if of late he has been able to lull it to sleep, he goes warily, fearing to awake it—what if one day he should find out that he is not the rightful heir to Hestviken? Even if he lies here weaving his own story from odds and ends that he has heard—the house-carls' tales of the wars in Denmark, the wonderful sagas of old Aasmund Ruga—the boy does not forget his secret dread: if he should be renounced by his father and lose Hestviken. Then let him rather play at something else—at strangers who make a landing here in the creek; his father is not at home, he himself must be the one to urge on the house-folk to defend the place, he must rouse the countryside—

But in any case his father shall soon have proof of what stuff there is in this son of his. He shall have something to surprise him, his father. Then maybe he will give up walking as one asleep, taking no heed of Eirik when they are together.

But the next day Olav set Eirik to bring home firewood for the summer, and his father said he was to have it all brought in today. The snow still lay over the fields here on the south side of the creek, but tomorrow most of it might well be gone.

The going was good early in the morning. Anki loaded one sledge while Eirik drove home the other. But as the day wore on, it grew very warm, and even before the hour of nones Eirik was driving through sheer mud a great part of the way.

Eirik spread snow along the track, but it turned at once to slush. Olav went higher up and spread snow on the fields there; he called down to the boy to drive round under the trees. But this was many times farther, around all the fields—and Eirik made as though he had not heard.

When Olav looked down again, the load of wood had stuck fast at the bottom of the slope leading to the yard. Eirik heaved off billets, making the rocks ring; then he went forward, jerked the bridle and shouted, but the horse stood still. "Will you come up, you lazy devil!"—and back went Eirik, dragging at the reins. Then he threw off more wood.

The sledge was stuck in a clay-pit at the bottom of the rock under the old barn, where the road from Kverndal turned up toward the yard. The sun had not yet reached this spot, so the rock was covered with ice, but water trickled over the surface. Eirik took hold of the back of the sledge and tried to wriggle it loose. But the horse did not move. The boy strained at it all he could, stretching to his full length over the ground; then he lost his foothold in the miry clay, dropped on his hands and knees, and some billets of wood slid off the load and hit him on the back—and there was his father standing on the balk of the field beside him. Fear at the sight of him gave Eirik such a shock that he was on the verge of tears; he plunged forward, tore at the reins, and belaboured the horse with them: the horse floundered, threw its head about, but did not move from the spot. "Will you come up, foul jade!" Quite beside himself, seeing that his father did nothing but stand and look on, Eirik struck at the horse with his clenched fist, on the cheeks, on the muzzle. Olav leaped down from the balk and came toward him, threateningly.

Then the horse put its forefeet on the frozen surface, slid, and looked as if it would come down on its knees. But at last it got a foothold, came up to the collar—the sledge with its lightened load came free—and dashed at a brisk pace up the slope.

On reaching the yard Eirik turned and shouted back to his father, with tears in his voice: "Ah, you might have lent us a hand—why should you stand there and do nothing but glare!"

A flush spread slowly over Olav's forehead. He said nothing. Now that the boy shouted it at him, he did not know how it had been—but he *had* simply stood and glared, without ever a thought that he might give Eirik a hand. A queer, uncomfortable feeling came over Olav—it was not the first time either. Of late it had happened to him several times to wake up, as it were, and find himself standing idly by—simply staring without a thought of bestirring himself and doing the thing that lay to his hand.

Up by the woodpile he heard Eirik talking kindly and caressingly to the horse. Olav had seen this before—such was the lad's way with both man and beast: one moment he was beside himself with sudden passion, the next all gentleness, imploring forgiveness. With a grimace of repugnance Olav turned away and walked up again across the fields.

The Richardsons returned to Oslo, and Eirik guessed that his father had made a bargain with them. But now he dared not ask whether he would be allowed to go too. What deterred him was that not even this last misbehaviour of his had sufficed to drive his father out of his sinister silence. When Olav suddenly appeared beside the sledge, Eirik had been so sure that now he would be given a thrashing—he winced already under his father's hard hand. But afterwards he felt it as a terrible disappointment that nothing had happened. Blows, curses, the most savage threats he would have accepted—and returned, inwardly, at any rate—and felt it as a relief, if only it put an end to this baneful uncertainty—not knowing what to make of his father.

Olav would sit of an evening staring straight at Eirik—and the boy could not tell whether his father were looking at him or through him at the wall, so queerly far-away were his eyes. Eirik grew red and unsteady beneath this gaze which he could not read. Sometimes Olav noticed his uneasiness: "What is it with you, Eirik?" There was a shadow of suspicion in his voice. Eirik found no answer. But it might chance that he collected himself, seized upon something that had happened during the day, and poured out his story, usually of how much work he had performed or of some remarkable thing that had befallen him—when he came to speak of it to his father, everything became far more important than he had guessed at first. Most commonly it fell out that long before Eirik had finished he found that his father was no longer listening—he had glided back into his own thoughts. But the worst was when his father finally gave the faintest of smiles and said quietly and coolly: "Great deeds are common when you are abroad." Or "Ay, you are a stout fellow, Eirik—one need only ask yourself to find that out."

Yet Eirik did his best, when talking to his father, to remember everything as it had happened and to say nothing beyond that. But when his tongue was set going, it came so difficult to him—before he knew it he was relating an incident as it might have happened, or as he thought it ought to have happened. Another thing was that the house-folk egged him on to tell everything in the way that was most amusing to listen to. They knew as well as Eirik that he tricked out his truthful tales with a few trimmings, but they agreed with him that so it ought to be, and not one of them betrayed a knowledge that Eirik was apt to tell a little more than the truth. It was only his father who was so cross and dull of apprehension and always required to be told everything so baldly and exactly.

But one day his father should be forced to say it in earnest— that Eirik was a brave fellow. Of that he was resolved.

For that matter, Eirik now gave a good account of himself, for his age, both on the farm and in a boat. He had not much strength in his arms, was slender and lightly built, but tough and tenacious, so long as he did not trifle away his time and forget to do what he had been set to. But, for all that, the house-carls were glad to have Eirik working with them—he was of a kindly and cheerful humour so long as no one provoked him, but then he was quick to anger. He had also a fine, clear voice for all kinds of catches and decoy songs and working-chants.

This spring both Tore and Arnketil spoke to the master about him, praising his industry and handiness. Olav nodded, but seemed not to see the expectant look on the boy's face. And much as Eirik strove to please his father and serve him—well, sometimes Olav did remember to thank him. And at other times he appeared quite unaware of it when Eirik gave him such help as he could; he accepted it without looking at the boy or giving him so much as a nod.

Then Eirik's anger flared up. He turned over in his mind something he would do simply to vex his father—*then* maybe he would remember to chastise him at any rate. But when it came to the point he did not dare—for that would end all chance of his going on the voyage to England.

In the week after Whitsunday, Olav Audunsson sailed up to Oslo, and ten days later the Richardsons' little hoy lay alongside the quay at Hestviken. The freight that Olav was to take was soon loaded, though he had charged himself with some trifles for Baard Paalsson of Skikkjustad; skins and pig-iron. Apart from this,

Olav had not been able to get hold of any goods in the country round at this unfavourable time of year. The very next day Olav's boats towed the hoy out of the creek; they came out into the fiord and hoisted sail. It was a bright, calm morning of early summer.

Eirik had been on board, helping to stow the cargo and talking to the men. There was not a strip of plank or boarding, not a block or a rope's end, that he had not pried into and handled.

Toward evening the boy sat on the lookout rock gazing after the little craft, which was now sinking out of view far away to the south. He went down to the quay, cast off his own boat, and rowed away under the Bull.

Some way up the headland there was a green ledge, and in the middle of it lay some great rocks. On the biggest of these grew three firs; Eirik called it the King. One could crawl in between these rocks; underneath the King there was a little hollow like a cave, and here he had a hiding-place.

On this side of the Bull there was only one place where one could land from a boat and climb up by a cleft in the rock. Otherwise one had to row round to the north side, or else up to the head of the creek. And toward the water this ledge ended in a sheer drop. Eirik had thought many a time that if a man were surrounded by his enemies up on that ledge, he could leap out, swim a long way under water, and save himself, before the others found the path down to their boat.

But this evening he was so sad and heavy of heart that there was no solace in the thought of these things. He crept into his cave and took out his possessions, but felt none of the old thrill and joy of ownership when he sat with them in his lap. He had not had them out more than once before this year—and then he had overhauled his treasures with the same intense delight as of yore.

There were two wooden boxes, turned on the lathe. The little one he had used for collecting rosin in summer, but now it held nothing but some scraps of little birds' eggs that he had kept because they were redder than most. In the other box he had the bones of a strange fish. It had been caught in the nets one day, several years ago; neither his father nor the boatmen had seen the like of it before, and so Olav ordered them to throw it into the sea—it looked likely to be poisonous. But Eirik saw that it had fallen between the piles of the old pier; when the men had left the waterside he rowed out and fished it up. There was no knowing whether it was dangerous to keep its bones, or whether there might be some hidden virtue in them; therefore he had always counted them very valuable. Until now—and now even he thought they were only trash.

He also had a leather bag full of smooth and barbed flints. Under an overhanging crag above the mouth of the stream in Kverndal he found plenty of these in the gravel, but he only kept the finest, those that looked like arrow-heads. His father said they *were* arrow-heads—the Lapps had used such things in heathen times, long before the Norsemen came and settled Norway. But Eirik thought there might well be something queer about them— perhaps they were thunderbolts. He had also found a bone fish-hook up there one time—a fine hook, with barbs and an eye for the line. He had thought of using it some day, when the fish would not bite; then the others would marvel at him, pulling up fish by the heap when no one else had any. But now he had lost that hook.

For all that, his dearest possession was the horse. It was roughly whittled from the root of a tree, and was not much bigger than his hand. Eirik did not know where it had come from—he had brought it with him from the place where he was fostered as a child, he believed; and he had a notion that it had been found under a rock, beneath which mound-folk dwelt—it was a gift from them. He had given away his childish toys long ago, for he saw that he was too big to play with such things without disgracing himself. But the horse seemed to be more than a toy, so he kept it up here under the King Rock.

Eirik knelt on the ground looking at the horse. It was dark and worn; one of its hind legs was so short that it stood on three, and it had an eye on only one side of its head, which stood out, a knot that had been cut away. It gave it such a weird look.

He took it up and placed it on the flat white stone that belonged to it. With closed eyes he walked backwards three times withershins about this altar, crooning softly the while:

"Sun sinks in the sea, carrion cumbers the foreshore,
Down go we to our doom, Fakse my fair one. . . ."

But having accomplished this, he did not care to make the sign of the cross backwards—that was sinful, and foolish besides. He had a misgiving that the whole game had always been foolish.

He could never really have expected to see it turn into a copper horse with a silver bridle. But he had believed in a way that one day something wonderful must happen, after he had sung that ugly spell over it.

Jörund Rypa would think it a foolish game. He was always afraid that Jörund might come upon him while he was thus employed. It was not very likely—Jörund had kinsfolk who lived far up the parish and sometimes he came to stay with them, but it was scarcely to be imagined that he would show himself out here on the farthest rocks of Hestviken. Nevertheless Eirik was always afraid Jörund might come upon him. He felt in himself that Jörund would make nothing of it, would only think he was faddling here like a little child—and he could well believe that Jörund would bear the tale of it and make mock of him. Yet Jörund Rypa was, of all the lads of his own age Eirik had met, the only one of whom he wished to make a friend. But Jörund had not been in the neighbourhood for more than a year now—his home was in the east, by Eyjavatn.

Eirik sat with his hands clasped about his knees and his chin resting on them, gazing over at the manor.

It was now flooded by the evening sun, and the creek below was still as glass, so that it could not be seen where the land came to an end and the reflection began in the deep shadows under the foreshore, but below the quay with its sheds another quay stood on its head in the water, and deep down in the creek he saw the image of the sun-gilt rocks on the hill and the row of turf roofs, already slightly yellowed by the sun, and the meadows and all the fair strips of plough-land where the corn was now coming up finely and evenly—but across this mirrored Hestviken a bright wavy streak was drawn by the current.

The constant sound of bells from the wood under the Horse Crag came nearer. Ragna was calling the cows home: the herd came in sight at the gate at the brow of the wood. The line of roan and dappled cows moved forward along the edge of the top field.

Again a breath of distasteful memory crossed the boy's mind. Just before his father went to Oslo he had sent him on an errand to Saltviken. Up on the hill he had met the cattle, and then he had gone and stuffed the cow-bell full of moss—not for any reason, it had just occurred to him to do it. But Jon, the herdsman, had gone on about it and complained to the master when he came home in the evening. And once more the devastating thing happened that his father was moved neither to wrath nor to laughter by his prank; he only muttered something about child's tricks and looked unconcerned.

There went Liv up the path from the quay—she had been to the shed again, with Anki no doubt. Eirik moved uneasily. His body was hot and tingling, he felt guilty and ashamed. Though indeed *he* had done nothing wrong—he could not help it if she said such things to him, and it only made him angry and ashamed when she tried to take hold of him and hug him in the dark. What did she want of him? He was not yet grown up, and she had men enough without him, the ugly trollop.

But he could not get it out of his thoughts, for he guessed that she hung about his father too. And then it all came back to him, all the evil he had had in his mind when he found out about his father and Torhild Björnsdatter—his dread and his despair, not knowing whether he were sure of his right to his father and to Hestviken, and a miry flood of foul and evil thoughts and visions, and a mortal hatred that made his cheeks go white and cold when he thought of how he hated.

His father's fits of silence, which lasted from morning to night, the tired, drawn look of his mouth, of his eyes with their thin, filmy lids—even the way he rose to his feet after a rest, to go back to his work, as though laboriously collecting his thoughts from far away—all this filled the child's mind with insecurity. He guessed that he was living under the same roof with a pain of such a kind that it must strike him with terror if he ever saw it laid bare. And he hated, he raged against anything in the world that prevented him from ever having peace and happy days. And at the same time the boy could see that his father was still a handsome man, and no old man. The house-folk openly discussed what maidens and widows might be reckoned a fit match, both in the parish itself and in the neighbouring districts—little joy as Olav had had of his wife for many years, they doubted not he would marry again as soon as might be.

Had not this Liv been such a loathsome creature, it were almost better—for his father could never *marry* her. Many men were content to keep a leman in their house. But then he recalled the time when Torhild was here. No, his father must *not* bring any strange woman to dwell at Hestviken—he would not have anyone going about here, keeping the stores and dealing out the food, whispering in his father's ear at night, asking a boon or giving a word of advice, making mischief for him and Cecilia with their father, and filling the place with her own brood the while.

From here not much more was seen of the houses of Hestviken than the row of turf roofs on the slope under the crag. The shadow crept higher and higher up the hill, but the sun still shone on the roofs and the black cliff behind, with green foliage brightening the crevices. Up on the back of the Horse the red trunks of the firs were still ablaze.

All at once the tears burst from his eyes. His love of the manor smarted like homesickness; his grief at his father's leaving him was overwhelming. The relish had gone out of all his former joys. Eirik gave himself up entirely, he lay on the ground weeping so that the tears ran down.

There was a rustling sound on the edge of the cliff above him. The boy started up, burning with shame. A sheep thrust out its black face among the bushes—there was a white gleam of sheep behind it. Eirik scrambled up and chased them away. A good thing it was not men. Or Jörund—

Slowly he came down again. There stood his wooden horse, a wretched little toy. He snatched it up, ran forward to the brink, and threw it over.

It was now just dark enough under the cliff to prevent his seeing what became of it—whether it landed on the rocks below or in the water. For an instant he stood as though spellbound—now he had done it! Then he turned and ran, sobbing with remorse. He slid, leaped, tumbled almost, down the steep path in the cleft, to where his boat lay.

Eirik reached it and cast off. "Oh nay, I must find the copper horse again"—so intent was he that the faint gurgling of the water against the bottom of the boat troubled him. As noiselessly as he could, he poled and rowed along under the cliff, staring and listening intently in the shadows. *There* was something black floating among the rocks—he raked it toward him with an oar. No, it was only a stick of wood. And there—no. What if he searched all over the beach tomorrow—it was so small.

"Dear, holy Mary, help me, let me find the copper horse! I will give my three pennies to Helga with the tooth, next time she comes.—*Ave Maria, gratia plena Dominus tecum*—"

There it was! On the other side of the boat, a little way out. It was almost a miracle that it had not drifted in among the stones of the beach, and then he would never have found it. The boy drew a deep breath of happiness when he held the wooden horse in his wet hand. Now that it was so late he dared not go up again and hide it in the cave; he stuffed it into the folds of his coat.

Then he seized the oars and rowed briskly across to the other shore.

The quay was deserted when he came ashore. In the wood above, the thrush was singing—Eirik had to stop and listen to it. Then he went at a run up the path to the houses, he was so beside himself with happiness. And every now and then he had to stop to listen to the song of the birds.

All was still at the manor. As the lad opened the house door the thought struck him: now he was to lie alone in this house the whole summer. He had slept alone there now and then for a few nights, when his father was from home, and never been afraid, but now he felt his flesh creep a little.

The smoke-vent was not closed. Some food was left for him on the bare, clean-swept hearth. But the room had a cheerless look in the pale twilight. Eirik made haste to close the door leading to the black hole of the closet. He would close the outer door too, before sitting down to his food. But on coming to the doorway he could not help staying a moment to listen—how the birds sang tonight!

Out on the meadow a dark shadow stirred. Eirik whistled softly —the dog dashed up, but stopped a little way off, wagging his tail and not daring to come nearer. Eirik coaxed and coaxed—"Come along, King Ring—what have you been doing now?" The rascal was a most mischievous beast; his life had long been threatened daily both by Olav and by the servants, but none had yet had the enterprise to make an end of him.

At last King Ring took courage and slipped through the door, crouching down and rubbing his head against the boy's calf. Eirik hastened to bolt the door, and as he stooped in the darkness, the dog nearly knocked him down as he whimpered affectionately and licked his face with his hot tongue.

Sitting on the edge of the hearth, he ate cold porridge and sour milk and shared the wind-dried meat with the dog. Now his only thought was that it would be fine to have the living-room to himself this summer.

He hid the copper horse under the pillow in his bed. King Ring jumped up and lay down over his feet.

"—And when the ogress comes in and gropes about in the dark for this Christian man, he whistles for his white bear—"

Eirik drew his legs up closer under him and thought it all over again from the beginning. There is a man—and this man is himself, as it might be—who has wandered all day through wild forests; late in the evening he comes to a house. It is deserted, but he finds food and a bed prepared, and he goes to rest. In the course of the night he hears a great noise, and in comes an ogress—she is so tall that she reaches to the roof-beams and as broad as she is high. And she sniffs and scents the blood of a Christian and gropes and searches, for she wants to take the man and roast him on the fire. But then he whistles for his dog—

Sleep began to creep over Eirik; his thoughts were confused. He took it up again—through wild forests all day long, he and the white bear—and then there came in an ogress—first they came to a great house in the depth of the forest—he saw it all as large as life, the little clearing and the empty house.—Then sleep overcame him and quenched all visions.

2

CALMS and contrary winds delayed the *Reindeer's* voyage southward along the shore, and only on the twelfth day after their departure from Hestviken were the men able to stand out to sea. But once in open sea they had a good breeze and by the third morning Olav made a landfall on a high, mountainous coast that he took to be Scotland. He had heard that there was war between the English and the Scottish Kings; therefore he chose to bear off to sea again. They stood off and on for the best part of a day, and then the wind became more northerly. Now the men put on their shirts of mail and steel caps, for the southern sea between England and Flanders was never peaceful and safe for trading voyagers.

Since his life had been spent far up country until he was grown up, there was always something adventurous about the sea and a sea-voyage for Olav Audunsson; and though his body was tired out, his heart felt wonderfully fresh and rested. He had watched through the long, grey summer nights, always with mind and senses calmly alert, directed toward sea and sky—it was as though he were sailing away from the very memories of endless wakeful nights, when he had lain imprisoned at the bottom of a dark bed in the pitch-dark cave of the closet. They sank beneath the horizon at his back like the very coast from which he had steered. The weather had been fair almost all the time—the steady wind whistled in the rigging and bellied out the sail; the long, heaving ocean waves lifted the little hoy. For an instant it seemed to hesitate and think about it before plunging into the hollow—then a foaming at the bows, a little flying spray, a glimpse of grey-green water along the gunwale, the full note of the ocean as it raised its waves and drove one before another—the three big waves that came again and again after a certain interval. Clouds covered the whole vault of heaven, pale grey, drifting unhurriedly across the sky, now and again a pale gleam of sunshine falling on the sloping wet deck. Toward evening the weather often cleared a little; over on the horizon there was a glitter of sunlight on the sea. Then the bank of clouds closed in, reddened by the sunset behind them.

His sleep in the daytime refreshed him through and through, lying in a barrel, with the fur lining of his cloak wrapped warmly about his cheeks. The rushing of the waves, the sighing and creaking of the ship's timbers, the cries of the crew, rattling and heavy steps on deck—all these sounds reached him as he lay feeling the vessel lifting under him, gliding and sinking. Under the wide vault of daylight, where wind and wave flowed freely, filling his head with a loud, monotonous roar, he could fall asleep as easily as a child.

He felt young; it was as though the wind and the sea had washed and scoured him to this sensitiveness of body and soul— that afternoon when at last he stood on the vessel's poop as she was borne by wind and tide up the London river. The land on both banks was low and green—marshy meadows, cornfields on the rising ground, thick forest farther off on low hills undulating one behind another, till the farthest were lost in the pale blue haze of distance. Feeble gleams of sunlight broke through bright rifts in the clouds; somewhere in the west a cluster of pale rays fell upon the ground, saturated with moisture: the sun was drinking up rain.

It was not unlike Denmark. But Olav had never scanned those coasts, from which his mother had once come, with the same joyful expectation as he now felt. And England was much more populous. Innumerable towers and spires of great churches showed up inland above the woods. And they had sailed past many strong houses, built of white stone, enclosed by walls and watchtowers.

And when one of the men in the bows called out that now they could see the town, Olav leaped down and ran forward under the sail.

Through the light mist ahead he could make out towers and pinnacles, an innumerable multitude close together. And the darker grey streak that lay low down over the river, that must be the famous London Bridge. Olav forgot all else and gazed ahead.

Torodd Richardson came up to him. He had been talking to the pilot whom they had taken aboard at the mouth of the river. That was London's castle, the mighty fortress with four towers and a surrounding wall rising straight out of the water—that was the White Tower itself. And the long ridge of a leaden roof they saw on this side of it was St. Katherine's Church. The highest of all the spires on the rising ground was St. Paul's.

It was nevertheless the sight of the bridge that impressed Olav most deeply, for it was like nothing else that he had seen. It was the greatest marvel—built on huge arches that stood in the bed of the stream; what was more, it was of stone, and there were houses upon the bridge all the way. South of the river stood St. Olav's Church, said Torodd, and thither they must go to mass tomorrow; perchance they would meet fellow countrymen there. In former days, when the Norwegians sailed their own merchandise to London town, this had been their church. Nowadays they seldom came so far south. The *Reindeer* was the only vessel that had sailed hither from Oslo this year, but there might be men from Trondheim or Björgvin in town.

Olav listened in a way to the other's talk while gazing and waiting—he knew not for what.

. . .

They were late in going ashore next morning. The sun was already up when the six men from the *Reindeer* crossed London Bridge.

It gave Olav a queer feeling to think that this narrow street between the clothiers' shops lay over a broad river. The tide rushed upstream in a wave that was sucked out to sea again: he had noticed it in the little haven where they had put in the night before; there was more difference between ebb and flood here than at home in Hestviken. But men had been able to build up these heavy pillars of stone in the midst of the rapid current and throw a bridge over it. The thought made him strangely happy.

In many places the street was so narrow that only a little strip of sky could be seen between the houses. But farther along the bridge there was a break in the row of houses, so that wagons might pass each other. The Norwegians went out to the parapet to look down into the river.

The sun was above the woods in the east, and the air was filled with a bright haze; the sunlight glimmered in snow-white patches on the stream. The water ran through the arches with a rapid, steady roar; it was strange to see this strong stone wall rising straight out of the river. Unconsciously Olav raised his head and looked back at the town. Behind the thin mist, towers and spires shone in the morning sun. And all at once an immense flock of pigeons flew up from some place within there, circled about in a great ring, and turned, with the sun shining on their white and sea-blue wings.

A rowboat worked its way up against the stream, the sun glistening on the blades of the oars, twelve or fourteen pairs. It was not quite like any craft Olav had seen before, but it reminded him of a longship. Olav would have liked to stay and watch it go under the bridge, but Galfrid reminded him that the morning was far spent and mass would soon be over in all the churches.

There was not much traffic on the bridge so late in the day. But now they had to step into a shop door to make way for a company that came toward them: in front went a tall, large-limbed old man with an iron-shod staff in his hand and an armorial device embroidered on the bosom of his cloak. After him came two young maidens in trailing gowns, bearing their trains over their arms and holding books and rosaries; they wore wreaths of flowers in their fair, flowing hair and were beautiful as the morning, both of them. They were followed by an old serving-woman and two young pages, who carried the damsels' cloaks, and one of them had in his arms a lap-dog that yelped and jingled the bells on its collar.

Meanwhile a young man had appeared in the shop behind them; he chattered and tried to show his wares—took hold of Olav's coat and held before him a particoloured surcoat, half yellow and half blue. But when he found that the strangers were in no mind to bargain—or did not understand his speech—he pulled a face and laughed scornfully.

On the battlements over the southern gate of the bridge were some human heads stuck on stakes. On arriving in the open space beyond, Olav and his companions stopped to look at this. Immediately a little humpbacked old woman hobbled forward on crutches; after her came a young boy who crept on boards under his hands and knees—he had no feet. They pointed and chattered. Torodd Richardson was the only one of the party who knew a little of the language of the country; he interpreted for the others: the four nearest heads were those of great lords from the north country, rebels.

Olav Audunsson nodded in serious approval. There was nothing gruesome in this sight. He looked up, thoughtfully. The sun shone upon bare, greyish-yellow skulls, the morning breeze faintly stirred some tufts of hair. The flesh had rotted away, or the crows had pecked off what they could—there was not food for a bird left on any of the heads. A strange peace was upon these noseless faces that stared straight into the sun with unblinking eye-sockets. They looked iridescent, striped with black and greenish mould, but calm.

Olav had never before seen the heads of executed men close at hand. Often enough he had sailed past the Wheel Rock at Sigvalda, but had never landed on it. And the gallows hill outside Oslo lay in a quarter he had never had occasion to visit; nor had there ever been anything to take him thither, for it had never chanced that any was to be hanged when he was in the town.

But there was no horror in this sight, nothing that cried shame and dishonour over the dead. They looked like men of valour on guard over the gateway, waiting patiently for something, with faces turned toward the sun and the fresh morning breeze.

Olav was the first who remembered to make the sign of the cross; half-aloud he began to pray:

"Pater noster qui es in cælis, sanctificetur nomen Tuum, adveniat regnum Tuum—"

"Opera manuum Tuarum, Domine, ne despicias," the beggars took up the response, and said it together with his shipmates.

"Requiem æternam dona eis, Domine, et lux perpetua luceat eis."

Olav and Galfrid gave alms to the beggars, and then they hobbled off, this way and that. The thought struck Olav that these were the first words he had understood of folks' speech in this country—the prayer for the souls of the beheaded men.

The portreeve's officers had assigned the *Reindeer* to an anchorage west of the bridge—a little square-shaped dock at the riverside. None but small vessels lay there and most of them seemed to be English. The water was turbid and muddy; at low water the slimy bank was exposed. But the harbour itself was well compassed about on three sides with a quay and warehouses; the upper story was supported on pillars, so that the place resembled a cloister in a convent. These quays were astir all day long; more than a score of men were regularly employed in loading and unloading goods and in ferrying folk across the river. Torodd had found out that they had better not use the ship's boat to take them to and from the shore; the ferrymen did not like it, and it was foolish to set them against one. So they made a bargain with one of them that he should row the *Reindeer's* men ashore and back every day and have five English pence a week for it. It was dear—but it had not taken Olav long to perceive that he was unlikely to reap any great profit from this English voyage.

Oaken timber, furs, and hides they had here in abundance—there was no need to carry such things over the English Sea, and not much was to be got for fish at this time of the year. The otter and marten skins and Baard's iron were the only wares he was able to sell with any profit. It vexed him somewhat that he had known so little of how things were in the outside world. But he did not regret the voyage.

Nor had he any need to feel ashamed in the presence of the Richardsons—they were no shrewder merchants than he. But their chief business in this voyage was not trade. It was their brother, the Minorite friar, who had moved them to go. When he was in England some years ago he had found a kinsman, a rich priest in the west country, and this man had taken so kindly to his sister's grandson that he promised to give the Minorites of Oslo a great quantity of costly books and mass vestments at his death. News had been brought last year that the priest was dead, and now the Richardsons were to see to taking up the heritage; the Franciscans' house here in London would help them and send men with them into the west. At the same time their brother had obtained for them the charge of buying silk yarn, gold wire, flax, and velvet in England, both for the convent of nuns in Oslo and for the Queen's household.

The Richardsons were to lodge with their kinsmen here in London, a man named Hamo, who was by craft an armourer. Olav was also bidden there as a guest. But in the narrow street where Hamo's house lay there were smithies in every yard, and in the alleys about were taverns and stews—noise in the daytime and racket and shouting all night. Moreover he would have to give great gifts to everyone in the house at his departure. So Olav chose rather to stay on board with a young lad and an old man whom folk called Tomas Tabor, because in wintertime he went round in Oslo playing the tabor at banquets. The other two mariners stayed with the Richardsons up in the town.—Another thing was that Olav thought he slept so well under the open sky. It often rained at night, so that the water streamed in upon them where they lay under the poop, but in spite of that he preferred it to sharing a warm bed with a strange bedfellow.

Every morning early the waterman fetched him and one of his companions and set them ashore. By his second day in town Olav had already found out that the preaching friars had a great convent here, and thither he went to mass—St. Olav's was so far out of the way, and he was not very eager to meet fellow countrymen either. They followed the river westward through a narrow street that ran behind the warehouses; here was a rank, raw smell in the cold depth between the lofty gabled houses. At last they came to a little green space among heaps of stones and rubble, beside which grew bushes and flowers; the town wall had here been pulled down and moved out farther to the westward to give the Dominicans room to build. The convent lay close up to the new wall, and the church was still in building—it's outer walls stood naked and unadorned. But it was exceedingly fair within, built with pointed arches and a very lofty roof with crossed ribs. The morning light poured in full and clear through the lofty, narrow windows, which were not yet filled with pictured glass.

Olav sought out a place so near to the altar that he could hear the words of the priest saying mass. The Latin had a somewhat different sound from that of Norwegians, but not so much so that he could not recognize the passages proper to the saint of the day:

Me exspectaverunt peccatores, ut perderent me: testimonia tua, Domine, intellexi: omnis consummationis vidi finem: latum mandatum tuum nimis. Beati immaculati in via: qui ambulant in lege Domini—[2]

This was the office for a virgin martyr; but they also sing *Beati immaculati* over little children when they are carried to the grave. With hands clasped over his breast brooch and his chin resting on them Olav stood gazing at the priest's red chasuble. The gospel that followed had once been taught him by Asbjörn All-fat.

In illo tempore: Dixit Jesus discipulis suis parabolam hanc: Similie est regnum cælorum thesauro abscondito in agro: quem qui invenit homo, abscondit, et præ gaudio illius vadit, et vendit universa quæ habet, et emit agrum illum—[3]

He was always reminded of Arnvid Finnsson when he was in this church. The priest before the altar became as it were Arnvid —though when he turned toward the people he bore no resemblance to Arnvid, who had never attained to his heart's desire, of being ordained priest.—*Et vendit universa quæ habet, et emit agrum illum*—ay, that must be what Arnvid had meant by the counsel he gave him, when they met for the last time.

Another morning they celebrated the memory of a saint whose name Olav had never heard before—he must have been an Englishman. But this was a martyr too:

In illo tempore: Dixit Jesus discipulis suis: Nolite arbitrari, quia pacem venerim mittere in terram: Non veni pacem mittere, sed gladium—[4]

Gladium—Olav had always thought that word sounded so finely. And he saw that it could not be otherwise: when God Himself descended into the world of men and appeared as a man among men, it had to be, not peace, but a sword. For God could

[2] Psalm cxix, 95, 96, 1.   [4] St. Matthew, x, 34.
[3] St. Matthew, xiii, 44.

not intend to be as a sorcerer who puts man's will to sleep; He must needs come with a war-cry: for or against Me! God's peace —that must be like the peace that comes when the raging of the storm is past and the fight has been fought out—as indeed Saint John the Evangelist had seen in his visions; Bishop Torfinn had spoken of it.

In these early morning hours, when he knelt here during mass, the memories of his mornings in the church at Hamar were so near and living—though it had been winter then and dark outside, when he accompanied Asbjörn All-fat to the northern gallery. Asbjörn said his mass there at the altar of Saint Michael. It was so cold that he could see the priest's breath as a white vapour against the red flames of the two candles on the altar. No others ever came up there—and sometimes they were so early that the scholars were still asleep; therefore Asbjörn had taught him to serve as acolyte at the mass. When Olav did not remember to answer at once, Asbjörn whispered the first words of the response; with scarcely perceptible nods and pointings he signed to the young man to move the books or bring the ampullæ and the holy water.

His heart had been filled to the brim with a deep, solemn joy when he was permitted thus to assist at the sacred act, the eternal sacrifice, which was here carried out on the border between night and day. Here, in the secret chamber at dawn, he had felt safely in harbour—after his long, rough voyage through the tempest of his own and other men's uncurbed passions. He had pretended to be careless of the storm—but he had been so young; in secret he trembled with weariness. And he had not come through unsoiled: his heart was surely as turbid as the tarn north in the woods, when on the melting of the snows all the grey and rapid streams had emptied themselves into it. And no sooner had it cleared a little after the flood than the spruce forest round its banks came out and powdered the brown bog-water with yellow. But here at the foot of the altar he felt the Spirit of God as a cleansing wind—the mawkish pollen was blown away: once more his life would be bright and open as the tarn, reflecting the sheer blue and the sun and the clouds on their passage across the sky.

"Lord, Lord—'tis long ago! I am no more a young man. But even in autumn, when the ice has already begun to form around the rocks, and the tarn is choked with withered reeds and green scum—even then Thou canst send a wind that breaks up the half-formed ice and sweeps the surface clean so that it lies still and bright and blue for a while—before winter comes and imprisons it in ice."

These thoughts were scarcely formed, but the images haunted Olav as he knelt with bowed head and a corner of his cloak held up before his face. Everything was present to his memory, nothing would he attempt to deny. Nevertheless he was calm, full of confidence.

Now the little mass bell rang; the priest bowed low over the altar table, kneeling. Now he rose again, holding aloft in his hands the sacred body of our Lord, wrapt in the humble garment of the bread.

Olav looked up and worshipped: "My Lord and my God!"

Whether he would or would not, never could his heart cease to love God, he now knew. Whatever he might do and however he might try to drown the voice that made complaint in his inmost being: "Lord, Thou knowest that I love Thee!"

Nor had he forgotten that here he was, a traitor and a fugitive from God's host. For years he had done wrong, and never because he knew no better. But yet he did not now feel the gnawing pain of a sore conscience, which had tormented him so long, whenever he prayed or appeared to pray. Now every prayer he uttered was like kneeling down and quenching his thirst at a fountain.

Behind him in space and time he recalled all the years at Hestviken as a period of sickness—the memory of one long fever. The pain and ache had come from within, all the evil, all the nightmare visions had been bred within himself. Now it was as though the door were thrown open, light and refreshing coolness flowed in upon him from without.

He now felt whole again. The sea, the breezes, the nights on watch with senses directed outward, had washed away the close and fusty heat and cleansed him of his scalded sensitiveness.

It was not that he now thought less of his sin, but that he himself bulked far less in his own eyes. While he was brooding at home in Hestviken, silent and despairing over the loss of his soul, it had seemed to him there was so much he must throw overboard if he would find peace with God—*his* honour, *his* welfare, *his* life perhaps—these had been such great things. But now that he was in a place where he saw more of the glories and riches of this world than he had believed could be collected in one spot—now all that he called his own suddenly appeared to him so little—a man ought to be able to fling this from him as lightly as he would hang up his harp on the wall, when the trumpet summoned him to arms.

By God, there would always be men enough left upon earth. But each man's *soul*—that was a thing no man could take hold of, weigh and measure by the standards current among men. And in the end God collects all souls and weighs them with a weight that is His secret.

So he listened in calm meditation to the only voice that spoke to him in a tongue he understood—here in the foreign land, where all other voices shouted at him as though there were a wall between him and them. The voice of the Church was the same that he had listened to in his childhood and youth and manhood. *He* had changed—his aims and his thoughts and his speech, as he grew from one age into another—but the Church changed neither speech nor doctrine; she spoke to him in the holy mass as she had spoken to him when he was a little boy, not understanding many words, but nevertheless taking in much by looking on, as the child takes in its mother by following her looks and gestures, before it understands the spoken word. And he knew that if he journeyed to the uttermost limits of Christian men's habitation—folks' form and speech and customs might indeed be strange and incomprehensible to him, but everywhere, when he found a church and entered it, he would be welcomed by the same voice that had spoken to him when he was a child; with open hands the Church would offer him the same sacraments that she had nourished him with in his youth, and that he had rejected and misused.

And Olav felt like a man who has come home to his mother—from distant voyages that have brought him more of wounds and losses than of honour and profit. And now he sits alone with her, listening to her plain, reasonable speech and hearing her wise counsel: "If thou hast been the loser in every conflict thou hast essayed, be yet assured that not even the most hapless man has lost the fight that has not yet been fought."

Outside, the morning sun shone so fairly upon the little green before the church—this summer it scarcely rained but at night. After mass Olav and his companion strolled northward through the streets that led up to St. Paul's churchyard.

The houses here were much higher than in Oslo and they were

built of timber, with daubing between and boarded gables. But here and there the rows of houses were broken by strong stone halls surrounded by walls; watchmen with sword in hand stood at the gates. A green courtyard could be seen within, where men-at-arms exercised themselves in archery and games of ball.

There were trading booths along the walls of the churchyard, but if anyone stopped for a moment to look at the wares, a man instantly appeared to pounce upon the customer. Such was never the custom in Oslo—except among the Germans of Mickle Yard, where it was young women who stopped to look. But otherwise a man might go in everywhere, look around the shop, turn over and handle everything that was exposed for sale—the owner feigned not to see, scarce looked up from his work as he answered any question that was put to him. But here the prentices ran out into the street after folk. And here was a vast deal of noise and shouting.

The church bells rang incessantly above their heads—bells here and bells there, the deep booming of great bells and the busy tinkling of little chimes. Then for a while all the bells began to peal together in an immense chorus of resonance. With the conventual churches and all the small parish churches Olav thought there must be far more than half a hundred churches in London. At least ten of them were as great as the Halvard Church in Oslo; St. Paul's was greater than any other church he had seen.

In the east by the town wall stood the convent of the Franciscans, and in the open place before it the corn market was held. Huge wagons with teams of oxen and great heavy-limbed horses made the market-place and the streets about it difficult to move in. Olav and Tomas Tabor walked about for hours looking at this fair show of wealth. Even now in the middle of summer the great bulging sacks stood ranged along the pavement—untied, so as to show the good golden corn. The dust from it hung over the place like a light mist. The cooing of a multitude of pigeons was heard as an undertone through the din and the hum of voices.

The town wall was also worth looking at closely, with its strong towers and barbicans before the gates. There were prisoners in some of the gate towers, and they let down little baskets from the loop-holes, so that people might give them alms. The guards at all the gates were picked men, excellently clothed and armed.

The convent bells rang for the last mass; the sun was now high and it began to feel warm. Olav and his companion were sweating: they wore shirts of mail under their tunics; the Richardsons had told them they must always do so here. The soil, fed with the offal of human habitation for hundreds of years, gasped out its stench, but from the gardens behind the houses, enclosed by stone fences or convent walls, was wafted the sweet scent of elders and roses, the hot, spicy breath of pinks and celery. And now the smell of food, roast and boiled, poured out of open doors—it was getting on for dinner-time. The two strangers increased their pace through the lanes leading down to the river; they felt the suck of hunger under their ribs.

Black swarms of crows and jackdaws whose nests were in the church towers swooped down as soon as any offal was thrown out. There was a sickening stench from the blood that ran out of the slaughterhouses, making the gutter in the middle of the street run red. But when they came into the street of the brewers they were met by the sweet steam rising from the warm grains that were thrown out, and they had to drive off the pigs that were gobbling them, before they could pass. It was good to feel hungry and to buy bread on the way, two smooth, round, golden-brown loaves.

The ale-keg lay waiting for them in the ferryman's boat; he had offered to fetch the ale for them every morning and would not take pay for it beyond what was agreed. But then he took toll of the keg. Olav and the men swore a little and laughed a little when they shook it after coming aboard.

They brought their sheepskins out on deck into the sunshine, and produced from their chests butter, dried meat, and cheese. Olav made the sign of the cross on the loaves with his knife and divided them. Then they flung themselves down on their sleeping-bags and ate and drank in silence, for they were both hungry and thirsty. The ale was excellent. And then this new-baked bread that they ate every day over here—they agreed that there was no need to waste money on fresh meat in the taverns when they had that.

Olav got on well with his two shipmates; they were men of few words, both of them. A good thing that chatterer Sigurd Mund, as they called him, had gone with Galfrid.

After the meal Olav and Leif stretched themselves on their bags. Tomas Tabor sat down to play on a little pipe he had bought in the town. The thin tone of it, rising three notes, trilling down again, and leaping about the scale, the same over and over again, sounded, as Olav lay half-asleep, like a little maid at play, climbing about a stairway—at times he could plainly see Cecilia.

Toward evening Olav took the ship's boat and rowed on the river. The finest of all views of the town was from the water; there was a movement on the stream like that of a great highway. From the stately houses on the Strand, west of the city, came great barges, flying swiftly along under ten or twelve pairs of oars; across the water came the music of minstrels and pipers playing to the lords and ladies on board.

A little lower down, the walls of a castle rose out of the river, with strong water-gates and a wharf outside, and lofty gabled halls behind—*Domus Teutonicorum*. Olav fixed his eyes on the castle as he drifted past in his little boat. It booted little for folk of other lands to contend with these merchants of Almaine; bitterly he reflected that no doubt the day would come when they would found their hanse on Oslo wharves too. But it was a fair house, this of theirs, as everything that bears witness of strength is fair in its way.

He turned and rowed up against the stream. Now he passed the south-western water-tower of the town wall and could see the whole western sweep of the wall from the outside, with the towers and barbicans before the gates. Soon the roofs of the Knights Templars' *præceptorium* appeared above the trees.

Olav had never been out there, but Galfrid said he ought to go on a Friday morning. Then they carried out into the field an immense red cross, and while a priest preached to the people, the knights stood around, clad in mail with drawn swords in their hands, the points raised to heaven; they stood as though cast in bronze. And their priest must be the most powerful of preachers, for the people wept and sobbed, both men and women.

Olav's thoughts were busied, half toying, with this monastery of warriors. He had heard that the Pope had given their Grand Prior the same right of loosing and binding as he had himself. Before a man was admitted to the brotherhood he had to confess all the sins he had committed in his life, both atoned and unatoned— and of the severe penance he had to undergo the world heard no more than it hears of what is done in purgatory. They had strange customs, folk said—he who would enter their ranks was compelled to strip naked and lie thus for a night in an open grave in the floor of the church, as a sign that he was dead to all his former life.

He had seen the Templars ride through London more than once; they were clad in chain armour from the throat to the soles of their feet, with a red cross on their white tunic, which they wore over the shirt of mail, and on their white mantle; their great battle-maces also bore the sign of the cross. He had heard of the warrior monks before, but never seen them.

Then there were the anchorites. There were so many of them here in London; some dwelt in cells within the town wall and some in little houses that were built against a church with an opening in the wall between, so that the hermit might see the altar and the ciborium that held the body of the Lord. Some had a lay brother or a lay sister to do their errands for them, but many, both men and women, had caused themselves to be walled up, that they might share the lot of the most wretched prisoners. One of them dwelt in the wall close to a dungeon—till the day of his death he was to live there in a cold, black hole into which the water dripped, in his own stench and in his sour and mouldy rags; he was crippled and paralysed with rheumatism. And this man's life had been distinguished by great holiness even as a child and while he was living as a monk in his convent. When men who were to suffer punishment were led past the orifice of his cell, the anchorite cried out: "Be merciful, as your Father in heaven is merciful!"

Of late years Olav's thoughts had now and then been drawn toward the monastic life—whether it might be the end of his difficulties if he adopted it. But not for a moment had he believed it in earnest. Whatever might be God's will with him, he was surely not called to be a monk. Of that he had the most certain sign—for it was not the hardships of the monastic life that he shrank from. On the contrary, to let fall from his shoulders all that a monk is bound to renounce, to submit to the discipline of the rule—for this he had often longed. Nevertheless no man was fit for this unless God gave him special grace thereto. But now Olav had roamed long enough as an outlaw on the borders of the realm of God's grace to perceive that when once a man of his own will surrenders himself to God and accepts what is laid upon him, God's power over him is without limit. And in the long, sleepless nights he had often thought: "Now they are going into the choir in their convents, men and women, standing up to serve their Lord with praise, prayer, and meditation, like guards about a sleeping camp." But it was all the things that were included in the rules for the relief and repose of man's frail nature that *he* could not think of without distaste: the brotherly life, the hours of converse, when a monk has to show humility and gentleness toward his fellows, whether he like them or not, whether he be minded to speak or be silent; to have to go out among strangers or to serve in the guest-house when the prior bade him, even if he would rather be alone. He had seen that this was beyond the power of many monks, who were otherwise good and pious men; they grew sour and cross with strangers, quarrelsome among themselves. But this was a sign that these men were not fitted for the monastic life. "One may carve Christ's image as fairly in fir as in lime," Bishop Torfinn had once said to Arnvid, on his expressing a wish that he could be as calm and good-humored as Asbjörn All-fat; "but never have I heard that He turned fir into lime, like enough because it would be a useless miracle. With God's grace you may become as good a man as Asbjörn, but I trow He will not give you All-fat's temper, for all that."

But now he saw that the life of a monk had other paths than those he knew at home in Norway. There were paths also for those who were not fitted to associate with strange brethren. Warfare with the discipline of the convent behind that of the warrior, like a hair shirt under the coat of mail—in the Holy Land the Templars' hosts had been cut down many a time to the last man. In the Carthusians' monasteries each monk lived in a little house by himself; they met only in church. And now he had seen some other monks, the Maturines—their white habit resembled that of the preaching friars, but they bore a red and blue cross on their breasts. They collected alms, wherewith to cross the sea and redeem Christian men from slavery among the Saracens. And when they had no more money, the youngest and strongest of these monks gave themselves in exchange for sick and weary prisoners.

It had not yet come to any fixed purpose with Olav, but it made him thoughtful. The world had widened to his vision, and he now saw that that other world which stretched its curtain over the earth from one end to the other was without bounds. And now, when he saw himself standing beneath this immense vault, he felt

so small and so lonely and so *free*. What mattered it if a franklin
from the Oslo fiord never came home again? He might be stabbed
any evening on the quays here—they might be plundered and
slain by pirates on the Flanders side this autumn, they might be
wrecked on the coast of Norway—every man who put to sea on
a trading voyage knew that such things might easily happen, and
none stayed at home on that account. Strange that he could have
thought it so great a matter, as he tramped over his land and
splashed about his creek, that he should rule the manor—indiffer-
ently well—if he had to murder his own soul to do it.

That might yet be while *she* was alive. But now—Arne's daughters and their husbands would take charge of the children and of
the estate if he sent home a message this autumn that he would
not return.

London's church bells rang—time to put out fires. Olav rowed
downstream again. He put in at a little wharf just below the western water tower. The old man who took his boat was so thickly
covered with beard and dirt that he seemed overgrown with moss.
Olav exchanged a few words with him—he had picked up a little
English now. Then he made his way through the lanes, where
children ran and shouted and refused to obey their mothers who
called them in, up to the Dominicans' church.

He said the evening prayers and a *De profundis* for his dead,
and then found himself a seat on some steps that led to a door in
the wall. With his chin in his hands he waited till the monks
should come into the choir and sing complin.

The lofty windows darkened and grew dense; dusk collected
under the vaulting and filled the aisles. A single votive candle
burned before one of the side altars, but up in the choir the
golden lamp alone hovered like a star in the twilight. Outside the
open doors the fading daylight paled in a grey mist. Folk came
strolling in to hear evensong; the echo of their chattering whispers
murmured incessantly through the lofty pillared church; their
footsteps rang softly on the stone flooring. Then came the hushed
but penetrating beat of many footfalls in the choir, the clatter of
seats being turned up; the tiny flames of the candles were lighted
on the monks' desks, throwing their faint gleam on the rows of
white-clad men standing up in the carved stalls. And down in the
body of the church there was a rustle of people rising and drawing nearer, while a hard, clear, man's voice began to intone and

was answered by the chant of more than half a hundred throats, the first short sentences and responses—till the whole male choir raised the song of David on sustained, monotonous waves of sound.

Olav sat down again when the psalm began. Now and again he sank into a half-doze—woke up as his head dropped—then the veil of sleep wound about him again and his thoughts became entangled in it. Till he grew wide awake at the notes of *Salve Regina* and the sound of the procession descending from the choir. The people moved forward into the nave as the train of white and black monks advanced, singing:

"*Et Jesum, benedictum fructum ventris tui, nobis post hoc exsilium ostende. O clemens, o pia, o dulcis Virgo Maria!*"

Olav strode quickly down toward the wharf; it was dusk outside now, bats flitted like flakes of soot in the darkness. He must be aboard the *Reindeer* before it was quite dark—the other evening the river watch had called to him from their boat. To his very marrow he felt the good this evening service had done him. It was the same as he had heard in Hamar, in Oslo, in Danish and Swedish ports—in good and evil days he had always attended evensong, wherever he found a convent of the preaching friars. He had also heard the singing of nuns one evening here in London—for the first time in his life. He had never chanced to enter the church of a women's convent before, but Tomas Tabor had taken him one evening to a nunnery. Marvellously pure it had been to listen to— but nevertheless it did not stir the depths of him in the same way. The clear, sharp, women's voices floated like long golden streaks of cloud on the horizon between earth and heaven. But they did not raise themselves above the world over which the veil of darkness was falling as did the song of praise from a choir of men on guard against the approach of night.

Tomas Tabor appeared at the gunwale as Olav came alongside. Now it was dark already, he complained, and Leif had not yet come—likely enough he would stay ashore again tonight, and tomorrow he would make the same excuse, that he could not get a boat in time. Olav swung himself over the gunwale.

"You must refuse him shore leave, Olav! He cannot be so steady as we thought him, Leif!"

"It seems so." Olav shrugged his shoulders and gave a little snorting laugh. The men walked aft and crept in under the poop.

"I trow that serving-wench out at Southwark has clean be-witched him."

They snuggled into their bags and ate a morsel of bread as they lay.

" 'Twill end in the boy getting a knife between his shoulder-blades. That place is the haunt of the worst ruffians and ribalds."

"Oh, Leif can take care of himself—"

"He is quick with the knife, he too. You must do so, Olav, you must forbid him to go ashore alone."

"The lad is old enough; I cannot herd him."

"God mend us, Master Olav—we ourselves were scarce so wise or heedful that it made any matter, at seventeen years—"

Olav swallowed the last mouthful of bread. After a while he answered:

"Nay, nay. If he cannot come back on board betimes, he must not have leave. And he should have had his fill of playing now, enough to last him a good while."

Presently: "I think we shall have rain again," said old Tomas.

"Ay—it sounds like it," said Olav sleepily.

The shower drummed on the poop above them and splashed on the boards; the hiss of raindrops could be heard on the surface of the river. The men shuffled in under cover, as far as they could come, and fell asleep, while the summer shower passed over the town.

Torodd and Galfrid were tarrying in the west country, it seemed—perhaps they had not found it so easy to get their hands on the heritage of Dom John. Olav was as well pleased one way as the other—and the days went by, one like another.

3

ONE EVENING Olav had been sitting half-asleep in his corner of the church. When he heard the scraping of feet in the choir, he stood up and went forward into the nave.

Right opposite on the women's side was a statue raised against one of the pillars, of the Virgin with the Child in her arms and the crescent moon under her feet. This evening a thick wax candle was burning before the image; just beneath it knelt a young woman. The moment Olav looked at her, she turned her face his way.

And now his breath went from him and he lost all sense of himself and where he was—but this was Ingunn, she was kneeling there, not five paces from him.

Then he recalled the time and place and that she was dead, and he knew not what to believe. It felt as if the heart within him stood still and quivered; he knew not whether it was fear or joy that made him powerless, whether he was looking on one dead—

The narrow face with the straight nose and long, weak chin —the shadow of the eyelashes on the clear cheeks. The hollows of the temples were darkened by a wave of golden-brown hair; a transparent veil fell from the crown of the head in long folds over the weak and sloping shoulders.

Even as he drank in the first vision of her charm, Olav saw that perhaps this was not she—but that two persons could be so like one another! So slender and delicate from the waist down to the knees, such long, thin hands—she held a book before her, and her lips moved slightly—now she turned the leaf. She knelt on a cushion of red silk.

A sobering sense crept over him that it was not she after all. As when one wakes from a heavy sleep and recognizes one thing after another in the room where one is, realizing that the rest was a dream—so now he realized little by little.

His poor darling, she had not been able to read a book. Nor had she ever had such clothes. As he looked on the rich dress of the strange woman, a bitter compassion with Ingunn stirred within him—there was never anyone to give *her* such apparel. He remembered her as she had been all the years at Hestviken, in bad health and robbed of her youth and charm, poor and unkempt in the coarse, rustic folds of her homespun kirtle. *She* should have been like this one, kneeling on her silken cushion, rosy-cheeked, fresh and slim; her mantle spread far over the stone slabs, and it was of some rich, dark stuff; her kirtle was cut so low that her bosom and arms showed through the thin golden-yellow silk of her shift. Half-hidden in the folds at her throat gleamed a great rosary— some of its beads were of the color of red wine and sparkled as her bosom rose and fell. She was quite young. She looked as Ingunn had looked as she knelt in the church at Hamar, childlike and fair under her woman's coif.

The strange woman must have felt his continual stare—now she looked up at him. Again Olav felt his heart give a start: she had the same great, dark eyes too, and the uncertain, hesitating, side-long glance—just as Ingunn used to look up at those she met for the first time. She had never looked at *him* in this way—and a vague and obscure feeling stirred in the man's mind that he had been cheated of something, because Ingunn had never looked upon *him* for the first time.

The young wife looked down at her book again; her cheeks had flushed, her eyelids quivered uneasily. Olav guessed that he annoyed her with his staring, so he tried to desist. But he could think of nothing but her presence—every moment he had to glance across at her. Once he met a stolen look from her, shy and inquisitive. Quickly she dropped her eyes again.

The procession came down from the choir, and the sprinkling of holy water recalled him wholly to his senses. But truly it was a strange thing that here in London he should chance to see a woman who was so like his dead wife. And young enough to be her daughter.

He remembered that he had not yet said his evening prayers, knelt down and said them, but without thinking of what he was whispering. Then he saw that she was coming this way—she swept past so close to him that her cloak brushed against his. When he rose to his feet, she was standing beside him, with her back turned. She had laid her hand on the shoulder of a man who was still kneeling. Behind her stood an old serving-woman in a hooded cloak, carrying her mistress's cushion under her arm.

The man stood up; Olav guessed he must be the strange woman's husband. Olav knew him well by sight, for he came to this church nearly every day. He was blind. He was young, and always very richly clad, and he would not have been ugly but for the great scar over his eyebrows and his dead eyes. The left one seemed quite gone—the eyelid clung to the empty socket—but the right eye bulged out, showing a strip under the lid, and this was grey and darkly veined as pebbles sometimes are. His face was pale and swollen like that of a prisoner—he looked as if he sat too long indoors; his small and shapely mouth was drawn down at the corners, tired and slack; his black, curly hair fell forward over his forehead in moist strands. He was of middle height and well-knit, but somewhat inclined to fatness.

Olav stood outside the church door and watched them: the blind man kept his hand on his wife's shoulder as he walked, and after them came the serving-woman and a page. They went northward along the street.

That night Olav could not fall asleep. As he lay he felt the slight rocking of the vessel in the stream and heard the sound of the water underneath her—and through his mind the memories came floating—of Ingunn, when they were young. Sometimes they gathered speed, came faster, wove themselves into visions. He thought he had opened his arms to receive her—and started up, wide awake—felt that he was bathed in sweat, with a strange faintness in all his limbs.

It was too hot in his barrel; he crawled out and went forward on deck. It was dripping wet with dew; the sky was clear tonight above the everlasting light mists that floated over the river and the marshy banks. A few great stars shone moistly through the haze. The water gurgled as it ran among the piles of the wharf. A man was rowing somewhere out in the darkness.

Olav seated himself on the chest of arms in the bow. Bending forward over the gunwale, he gazed out into the night. The outline of the woods in the south showed black against the dark sky. A dog barked far away. Dreams and memories continued to course through him; it was their youth that rose from the dead and appeared to him. All the years since then, his outlawry, the time of disaster that came and shattered all his prospects, all the afteryears when he had tried to bear his own burden and hers too as well as he could—they seemed to drift past him, out of sight, as he headed back against the stream.

At last he started up—he had fallen asleep on the chest, and now he was chilled all through. Now he would surely be able to sleep if he crept in again and lay down. Outside, the day was already dawning.

He grunted when Tomas Tabor came and waked him. Today Tomas could take Leif with him to mass; then he would stay aboard.

In the course of the afternoon Olav made ready to row ashore. It was warm now in the daytime; he could not bear his haqueton under his kirtle, the one he had brought with him was so heavy, of thick canvas padded with wool. There could be no great danger in going undefended—as yet he had had no quarrel thrust upon him in the town—and it made him so bulky and awkward. Olav girded himself with a short, broad sword before putting on his kirtle, which was split over the left hip so that one could easily get at a concealed weapon. It was a rich kirtle, reaching to the feet, of black French cloth with green embroidery, light enough for warm weather. Ingunn had made it for him many years ago. At that time he had much more need of suitable working-clothes; not often had he had use for this handsome garment, but it was finely sewed and finished. Olav chose a brown, hoodless cloak bordered with marten's fur and a black, narrow-brimmed felt hat with silver chains about the crown. He pressed it down, so that his greying silvery-golden hair waved out under the brim on every side. But—though he would not admit it to himself—when he took the pains, he still looked a fair and manly man, and few would have guessed that he was as old as seven and thirty winters.

He rowed straight in to the town and strolled through the streets and alleys. But as soon as the bells began to ring for vespers, he made straight for the church of the Dominicans. Just after him came the blind man and his wife and their two servants.

Olav had now forbidden Leif to leave the ship after nones; instead he sent him ashore with Tomas Tabor every other morning. In this way he himself could only attend mass every other day, but it would be too bad if the young man met with a mischance out there in Southwark. And it would bring trouble on them all if one of their ship's company came to any harm ashore.

The blind man came to mass at the convent church every morning and on most days to complin as well. She was always there at vespers and sometimes with her husband at evensong.

Olav did not know who these folks might be or where they lived, nor did he ever think to find it out. It was only that a change had come about in his mind: all the thoughts that had been habitual with him for years, all the daily doings and cares and all that belonged to his life as a grown man had been flooded by a fountain that had sprung up in him. It was beyond his own control—in all these years, when he had thought of his youthful memories, he had not recalled them in this way. Now they were not things of the past—he walked in the midst of them; it was as though everything was to happen now for the first time. Or it was as when one lies between sleep and waking, knowing that one's dreams are dreams, but seeking to hold them fast, struggling not to be wholly awake. And every day he came hither to see this blind man's wife, for at the sight of her these clear, dreamlike memories flowed more freely and abundantly; the image of the rich young wife became one with the sweet, frail shadow of the young Ingunn.

And she was no longer angry with him for looking at her—she vouchsafed him this, he had noticed. One evening he entered the church, walking fast, and bent the knee as he passed the high altar. The scabbard of the sword he wore under his kirtle struck the pavement hard, driving the hilt against his chin. He must have cut a ridiculous figure—and when he looked round at her, he saw that she was bursting with suppressed laughter. Olav turned red as fire with anger. But after a while, when he looked round again, he met her eyes, and then she smiled at him—and then he had to smile too, though he was both vexed and angry. After that he kept an eye on her; she followed her book diligently, but all the time little secret smiles played like gleams across her lovely face.

After the service he stood outside the church as she came out, leading her husband. She saw him, bowed slightly—Olav did not know whether it should betoken a greeting or not, but before he had time to reflect, he had bowed in return, with his hand on his breast. Afterwards he was vexed with himself—if only he had known whether she had meant to greet him or not!

The next day he took his station outside the church door at the time folk began to come to vespers. She came, with her usual company; Olav bowed—but she made as though she did not see him and went in. Then he was angry and ashamed and would not look over to where she was; he tried to join in the singing and not think of other things. But presently he felt that *she* was looking at him—and as he met the glance of her great dark eyes, she smiled, a bright and gentle smile that was like sunshine.

And after that they exchanged glances and smiles as though they had been old acquaintances, though they had never said a word to each other, and Olav did not know so much as her name.

. . .

Olav never thought that his shipmates must have remarked the change that had come over him. He was not himself aware that he had put a distance between him and the two seamen. Until now they had lived together as companions and equals; that Olav was the master of Hestviken, and Tomas a minstrel in Oslo in winter-time, while Leif was the son of a widow who served in the house of the armourer—this difference was so familiar and obvious that it concerned them no more than that Olav was fair and middle-aged, while Tomas was old and grey, and Leif a boy, red-haired and freckled. But now Olav moved among them without being aware that he scarce noticed them—as the young son of a lord instinctively and without premeditation puts off his childhood's familiarity with the serving-men of the manor from the day he first divines the path that lies before him and feels that he is destined for another lot than theirs.

Each time Olav was going into the town he put on his long kirtle; he shaved himself regularly and one evening he went to a haircutter. But the others made as though they did not see such things, and Olav never thought whether they saw it or not. He was not himself aware that he had become as it were another man and was acting more as became a lad of twenty than a landowner of wellnigh two-score years.

Torodd and Galfrid had returned to London and it could not be very long before they would be ready for the homeward voyage. Olav thought of it with a twinge of reluctance; he did not feel that he was ready to leave England, and his vague thoughts of letting them go home without him stirred within him. The idea he favoured most was that of entering an order, the Maturines for choice, and setting out for the lands of the paynims.—But he was not yet ready for that. Just at this time it was as though he had grown deaf and dumb to the voice that had spoken so powerfully to him—but that should not be for long. Only there was something else that he must think out first—he was not very clear about it. But he had already known as it were a fore-taste of the peace that results when a man has surrendered himself to God. So he knew that he would make that surrender in the end.

Two young Englishmen had bespoken a passage in the *Rein-deer*—they wished to make a pilgrimage to St. Olav in Nidaros.

They were good seamen both of them; so the Richardsons had no need of him as a shipman.

And now the summer was already far spent.

Three weeks had gone by since he saw the strange woman for the first time. One evening she did not come to evensong. As Olav left the church after the service, someone caught him by the mantle. He turned round—it was her servant, the old woman in the hooded cloak. She said something—he did not understand a word. And yet he knew. He nodded silently and followed the old nurse.

Olav had never been outside Ludgate before. He remembered as he crossed the drawbridge that in an hour the curfew bell would ring, and then they closed the gates, and he wore no armour under his kirtle and no other weapon than the little sword he had hidden in its folds. But even these thoughts were not able to raise their heads above the frenzy that flooded his soul.

Here under the western wall ran a little stream that came in from the country and flowed into the Thames, foul and stinking with the refuse that was thrown into it over the city wall. There were but few buildings before this gate, and the ground was marshy along the banks of the brook. But a few steps and they were on a path that led through the swamp. There were little ponds, shining white, and beds of rushes and brushwood on both sides. The low land farther out was dotted with farms and groves and church towers, and the sky, arching wide overhead, was covered with fleecy clouds, streaked with yellow from the setting sun behind.

The path brought them back to the little stream. The woman said something and pointed to a cluster of houses beyond the meadows. Olav saw the gables of a stone-built mansion among trees and the roofs of outhouses. But they did not approach the place on the side where the stone hall stood; they followed a paling over which hung green thorn bushes, and Olav could smell that the cattle-yard was inside. Then along the bulging wall of a long mud house with a thatched roof. There was a gate in the wall, and the woman unlocked a little wicket in one side of it. A strong, rank smell of pigs met his nostrils, and between the outhouses the passage into which they came was so miry that he walked almost ankle-deep in greasy, black slush.

They went across a little field in which linen was laid out to bleach, and the woman let Olav into a garden through a gate in a wattled fence.

The grass was already bedewed under the apple trees, and in the cool air floated the scent of fruit trees and dill and celery and of flowers whose names he did not know, but all seemed bathed and cooled by the evening air. Here in the garden the daylight had already begun to fade.

The woman led Olav to a corner of the herbary, where bushes grew in a ring; she said something. He guessed that he was to wait here, while she left him and was lost among the apple trees.

Close by grew a cluster of tall white lilies that shone in the gathering dusk and breathed out their heavy, over-sweet scent. Then he saw that the lilies stood at the entrance to an arbour which was half-hidden among the bushes. Olav went a few steps toward it and looked in. Just inside the entrance hung a wicker birdcage; there was a bird in it and it hopped silently up and down between two perches. Within the arbour he saw that there was a bed prepared.

His heart hammered and hammered in his breast; he stood motionless. A moth fluttered against his face, making him start.

There she came across the grass among the fruit trees; she walked with bent head, holding up her light gown before her with one hand. Her cloak was thrown back over her slender shoulders, and Olav saw that she wore nothing but the thin yellow undergarment—with a gasp and a thrill of happiness he knew that in a moment he would clasp her tender, pliant body under the thin silk.

She bore a silver goblet in the other hand. Now she stood straight before him, bending her head yet deeper. Then she raised the cup and drank to him. Olav accepted it and drank—there was wine in it, so sweet as to be mawkish.

He handed her back the cup. The young woman paused for a moment with it in her hand; then she let it fall on the grass. And now she raised her face and looked into his. The great eyes, the wide nostrils, and the half-open mouth were like chasms of darkness in the pale oval. Olav took a step forward and threw his arms about the slender, silk-clad wife.

She sank into his embrace, with her ice-cold fingers clasped about his neck. Olav bent the crown of her head to his lips; first of all he would drink in the scent of her—and found with a shock of aversion that she smelt of unguent, a luscious, oily scent. Nevertheless he kissed her on the hair, but the mawkish smell of her ointment filled his senses with repugnance, as though he had been deceived; he had thirsted for a breath of young hair and skin.

Unconsciously he turned his head away. He knew well enough that rich ladies used such perfumes to anoint themselves with, but he disliked it. Although he felt how she clung to him in abandonment, him who for years had not held a woman in his embrace, yet as he stood there with his arms full of her, his senses were cooled by the thought that this was an unknown.

No, this was not she—and it was as though he heard a cry coming from somewhere without; a voice that he heard not with his bodily ears called to him, aloud and wild with fear, trying to warn him. From somewhere, from the ground under his feet, he thought, the cry came—Ingunn, he knew, the real Ingunn, was striving to come to his aid. He could tell that *she* was in the utmost distress; in bonds of powerlessness or sin she was fighting to be heard by him through the darkness that parted them.

The woman hung upon him with her arms clasped about his neck and her head buried in his shoulder. Olav was still holding her, listening, as he gazed over her head, feeling his own desire, not quenched, but as it were dissolved in foam, far away from this one. Ingunn called to him, she was afraid he would not understand that this stranger was one who had borrowed her shape, seeking to drag him under.—"No, no, Ingunn, I hear you, I am coming—"

He strained all his senses to catch clearly this ringing cry of distress which did not reach his bodily ears, even as he did not see with his bodily eyes the form that struggled beneath folds of gloom. Now it grew fainter—

Olav gently loosened the strange woman's hands from his neck and drew back from her a little. She followed, and now she looked up—his head swam as he met her timid, gentle, animal look. She was so like that he was sick with desire to kiss the living lips, though he knew it was a stranger who looked at him beseechingly and cravingly from the depths of those eyes that were so terribly like. But he felt as if he must use his utmost force to tear himself away from her; it was like the temptation of his worst nights, when he could not help thinking of the fiord—of plunging into its waters and being free of it all.

"No—Ingunn, I hear you. Help, Mary!"

As he gave way, she threw herself into his arms, like a wave striking a ship's bows, and unconsciously he raised himself on his toes as he shook himself free of her. The touch of her long, white hands was the last he felt. He turned and walked quickly away.

Behind him he heard a low, long-drawn whine—and then cries, howls of scorn and rage. He swung himself over the fence—his kirtle caught in it a moment. "Now they will come after me," thought Olav; "she will call her servants now—" He ran across the bleaching-field and between some cattle-sheds and reached the palisade. It was twice the height of a man, at least.

How he got over he did not know, as he stood outside in a little dry field among haystacks—he had a feeling that he had pushed something against the fence, and instantly he seemed to recall having done the same once before—made his escape over a fence.

"That was that." He had said it aloud, standing ready to run, as he listened whether any sound came from within the enclosure. He was on a different side of the mansion from that to which the woman had brought him. Olav heard nothing; then he ran straight across the fields, taking the nearest way to cover.

Passing through the grave, he found a track that led by some mud cabins and down to the marshes about a little river. He did not know exactly where it was—it was down in a valley, but he followed the path along the river, thinking meanwhile that now the gates would be shut, darkness was falling fast. He could not enter the town, and could scarcely reach the *Reindeer* tonight. Well, there was no help for it. He passed his hand over his forehead and noticed that he had lost his hat. Well, well, so be it.— Here was a plank bridge, and when he came up the slope on the other side, he could see the light town walls and the high, pale watchtowers in the dusk. He continued to follow the ill-marked path across the fields to the northward—down toward the Thames the land seemed to be all swamp.

How far and for how long he had walked he did not know, but he thought he must be somewhere to the north of the town. Pools of water shone here and there in the darkness, and from some place came the baying and howling of great deep-voiced hounds.

Olav knew that the townsmen's hunt had its kennels somewhere out in the country. But it had an ugly sound in the dark.

To the left of the path he made out a piece of rising ground on which tall trees grew—there was a faint glimmer of dead leaves underneath them. Olav's senses grasped, without his being aware of it, that the ground here would be as good and dry as he could expect to find. He went up the slope—the brambles caught and tore his clothes. Then he came on something like a suitable hollow and lay down, wrapping his cloak about him as well as he could.

Now he felt that he was bathed in sweat, soaked and bemired almost to the waste, both kirtle and hose. Olav drew his sword and lay on his side, holding it under him. He fell asleep at once.

He woke in pitch-darkness, choking with horror, and thought he had cried out. Struggling with the tangle of his dream, he knew not where he was—he lay on the bare ground, and around him was a blackness that stirred and flickered, and he was wet and icy cold, and his heart was ready to break with despair and remorse and guilty feeling. He was lying in withered leaves.

Then memories dawned on him—of his adventure and of his dream, interwoven. At the same time as he recalled how he had come to be lying out in the woods, he remembered his dream too, and slowly the horror ebbed away—even now it seemed gruesome to recall it, but it was only a dream. And he had not done it, no, not even in his dream could he remember that *he* had done anything to the young child. That three-edged dagger of his he had not even brought with him on the voyage; it lay at home in his chest.

He had thought he stood by a bed—in the dark, and in a forest, as it seemed—a bed that was full of withered, wet, and earthy leaves, and half buried in the leaves lay a naked human body. The leaves covered it to the waist and covered the upper part of the face. He was not sure whether it was a boy or a girl, but he thought it was a little girl—the smooth, childish breast was so white and looked so soft—and under the left pap there was a triangular wound, as if someone had thrust in one of those daggers with a three-cornered blade up to the hilt. A little blood had oozed from the lowest lip of the wound—but it was one of those ugly, silent wounds which hardly bleed at all—the blood runs inward, suffocating the heart.

And the mortal horror of it had been that he had thought this was his work, and he was not able to bear it.—He tried to take the dead child up in his arms; he must bring her back to life. Yet he could not remember having dreamed that he thrust the dagger into the child. And it was but a dream.

A wind was blowing, with a sighing in the tree-tops and a rustling of leaves. He lay shivering and tried to distinguish things about him in the dark. A little animal was stirring among the dry leaves. His dream still troubled him; and he could not guess what it might mean—he had never wronged any *woman* that he knew of, save Torhild; but this was a little girl. He remembered plainly the face of the dead child among the leaves: the chin was short and broad, the lips full, the hair dark and reaching no farther than the shoulders. He could not recall having known any child like her.

It could not be Cecilia, his fair-haired child. A warm feeling of relief went through him: there could be no danger threatening her.

But his thoughts would not leave the dream. It was either a sorcery of the evil powers or a warning that he was unable to interpret—as yet. And he thought of that adventure in the garden the evening before—was that real or glamour? She had been so like Ingunn that it could not be true—and he had felt that Ingunn herself was there, quite near him, wailing in the fires of sorrow and impotence. And all at once he saw it—*if* she had not been able to make him hear, if she had been forced to witness it, in the place where she was, bound with fetters of gloom and death and powerlessness—that he yielded himself to the pixy or whatever she was—

It was as though something went to pieces within him. Sorrow and tenderness flowed over, hot as blood, and filled his being, thawed and relaxed every fibre—*so* near had he been to working her destruction—after he had striven, all the years she had lived, to sustain her as well as he could.

Then it flashed on him that he had called on Mary for help—and he wondered at it; for it was years since he had asked anything of *her*. It had seemed that he must think himself above seeking help there, when he wilfully defied her Son. He had said his Ave as he had been wont to do from childhood, in order to show her such honour as was her due, but never with the thought of gaining anything. And now he had called upon her, as a lost child calls for its mother.

Olav turned over on his other side and settled himself with his face buried in his arm so as to shut out the darkness. *Salve Regina, mater misericordiæ*—he would repeat the anthem over and over again until he fell asleep and had no other thought in his mind. "Ay, Mary, now I will come and pray for grace with our Lord."

By turns he slept awhile, woke again, slept, and tossed in a riot of disconnected dream-visions, and over them all was a vague horror—each time he awoke with a stab of pain at the heart. But each time he settled himself again, summoning all his will to the same end: the prayer that was to be his shield that night.

And then at last he woke and felt that the sun was shining and that he was rested. And there still lingered in his mind the aftertaste of a morning dream, giving sweetness and security beyond compare.

He was penetrated all through by the raw cold of the ground, but he lay still, gazing about him in the woodland, where the dew glistened blue and white in the brightness of the morning. The drops lay thick on every blade of grass. The bushes with the dark, hard, spiked leaves shone like burnished steel. A blue haze lay among the trees, round which the ivy twined its green curtain. And the dream ran on in his mind like the soft and milky morning light.

He had thought he lay in a woman's lap, with his head against her heart, and from his feeling of deep sweetness, free from desire, he knew who she was, and said it: Mother! He did not recall the look of her face—did not recall it now—but in his dream he thought he had recognized her, though he had been but a tiny witless infant when she died.

Arnvid had also been dimly present once in his dream, in a long, white garment—the habit of his order, no doubt—and Arnvid had spoken to his mother; but they had talked as it were over his head, as though he had been a child in swaddling-clothes that his mother held in her lap. Bishop Torfinn he had also seen. Their figures were all illumined as clouds are by the sun behind them, but this refulgence did not shine upon him; and he knew that it was not the sun, but a knowledge, or a vision, that was theirs; but he had it not, he only saw the reflection of it in them.

A little church bell began to tinkle not far away. Olav got to his feet, stiff with cold. He was in a sorry state, with kirtle rent and soiled. He brushed and picked off leaves and litter. If he had only had a cloak with a hood to it—he took it off and carried it over his arm; thus his going hatless would be less noticed.

Olav followed the sound of the bell; the path led down along the edge of the beechwood. On rounding the corner he looked involuntarily to the westward—but instantly thought it would be of little use to look for *that* manor-house: it would scarce be there today. The little church where the bell was ringing stood on a mound on the other side of a brook. He made for it, sure that there he would find the solution of all that baffled him.

It was a bare and poor little house and the air was musty and raw within; Olav guessed that mass was not often said here, and the mass that was now being celebrated was for the benefit of the ten or twelve poorly clad men who stood near the altar with a banner in their midst—it was no doubt some little brotherhood and this was their feast-day. The men had made themselves trim according to their means. But the priest's chasuble was threadbare, the deacon and the choirboys seemed listless and comported themselves without grace or dignity, while the priest hurried through the service, as though his only thought was to get it over.

Any message to himself he could not find, other than that he stood there, poor and a stranger, among these poor men who took part with him in the perfunctory office. It became clearer to him than before, how little a middle-aged man counts for in this world when he is stripped of all the added worth that goods and kindred bring. And he would learn this more and more thoroughly the farther he strayed from his home—he saw that now.

He had learned it once before, he remembered—in his youth, in the years when he was an outlaw. A clear, cool bitterness seized upon him. Was it for this he had come home, and was it for this he had dwelt all those years with his only dear one as in a dark house—that God should now lead him out, lock the door behind him, and send him roaming again?

He *saw* his manor, as in a vision—more clearly than he had ever seen it with his eyes. The wharf and the sheds with the water of the fiord lapping about the piles, the long row of sun-scorched turf roofs and dun gables up on the hillside and the wall of the Horse Crag behind, his cornfields among bare grey and reddish rocks, the hills around, grey and weather-worn, with wind-bent firs toward the fiord, meadows inland along the valley, and then the forest. The domain was not so great but that he had seen greater, but it was *his;* from here his fathers before him had gone out into the world, and hither they had returned. If all else in his life had turned out otherwise than he had expected, he had won back his patrimony and maintained it; he would leave behind no less than he had received. There were boats now, great and small, by the wharves; there were fields and meadows that he had cleared anew on the mossy, alder-grown land toward Kverndal.

The poor men advanced to the altar in a body. Now he saw the image on their banner: Jesus bending under the cross, and a man walking behind and helping to bear it, Simon the Cyrenian. So it was a guild of porters. A deacon made a sign to Olav, thinking he belonged to the fellowship. Olav shook his head and knelt down where he had been standing, by the door.

And in the poor vesture of the host our Lord descended and gave Himself to His poor friends—he was the only one present who dared not to go forward to the table. For years he had known that when he needs must go, at Easter, he went as Judas went to the Last Supper. As a child he had never been able to understand that Judas dared, for he must have known that God knew what he had done. Now he himself was in the same case as Judas Iscariot: he moved among his even Christians, and they reckoned him a good Christian, even as the apostles had reckoned Judas their fellow as they sat down with him at table that evening. And his only thought had been that in the midst of the company he was alone with Him who knew of his betrayal.

Such a man had he become. Yet his spirit had once been as a young field, full of the good corn that had been sown in it: the heritage of his ancestors, loyal men and unafraid, who did not cast their eyes backward after their lost happiness so long as they could keep their honour bright. But he had so ordered his life that now it had become as the lost fields he had found when he came home to Hestviken, overgrown with weeds and scrub.

Olav looked up. On the wall opposite there was painted a picture of our Lord sitting at the marriage feast in Cana. And near to Him stood Mary; she motioned with her hand to the servants, while her eyes looked straight into those of the man kneeling by the door:

"Whatsoever He saith unto you, do it!"

Olav knew not whether he had heard the words from without or within himself.

"Then clear me, Lord, as the husbandman clears his field with fire and with sickle—take back Thine inheritance, that it may bear increase for Thee!"

Once again he saw Hestviken as in a magic vision. A vision of a grey sea, flecked with silver over the glittering waves, and beyond it the coast sinking in a blue-grey mist. And he saw himself, so puny and alone, as a man standing on a rock in the outermost belt of skerries. In solitude he waited for Him who walks upon the glittering waves as a husbandman walks over his fields, and checks the storm as a man checks his horse. And the man on the skerry was free, so free as none can conceive, save him who has been stifled in the darkness through the long night of deadly sin.

Among the torch-bearing acolytes the priest advanced along the line of poor workmen. Each time he took a host from the ciborium Olav prayed softly: "Thou rich Christ, have mercy upon me!" Thou rich Christ—never till now had he reflected why men called God so. Now he knew it. "Lord, I am not worthy that Thou shouldst enter in under my roof, I am poor and naked, I own nothing wherewith to do Thee honour; but Thou enterest into an empty house, Lord, and fillest Thy creature with blessings.

"Then it may be that Thou wilt take me into Thy service again. Am I too old to learn to read and sing Thy praises? Then I am surely young and strong enough to be sold in exchange for an outworn slave in the land of the blacks."

He became aware of someone tapping on the wall close beside him. A half-grown boy was chipping off plaster with the key and seemed impatient to lock up. The church was empty. Olav rose to his feet and went out.

Down through the fields they passed, the brotherhood, the priest and his assistants. The blue silken banner showed up against the yellowing wheat. The boy locked the church door and darted after them. Olav followed slowly, bareheaded in the sunshine.

The ship's boat was gone when he reached the landing-place in the west of the town; he had to go on to the hithe where they lay and find a ferryman. He laughed on seeing Olav, and said something. Olav guessed the meaning, if not the words, joined in the laugh, and shook his head. He was strangely cheerful and light-hearted—as though in face of a new departure.

On board he found the Richardsons. Olav saw that they had been talking about him—and they looked at him with sly merriment, coming home so late in the day, ragged and without his hat. But they ignored it, and so did Olav.

The Richardsons had come to get the others to join them in a pilgrimage. There was a sanctuary somewhere in the woods north of London, with a miraculous image of our Lady; this had once been hidden in a hollow oak when the vikings were harrying the land, and found again in that place. Tomorrow was the feast-day.

Olav was glad. He had already thought that from tomorrow he would attend a church of Mary; he cared no more to think of the Dominicans' church.

4

IN the afternoon of the next day Olav stood on the green outside the place of pilgrimage—he was looking for his companions.

In the yellow rays of the declining sun the dust hung like a mist over the trampled grass—the place swarmed with folk who were now taking their departure. An immense cross came swaying along, carried in the midst of a body of men in penitential garments; they sang the litany as they marched, stirring up fresh clouds of dust with their feet. For a long time the notes of their singing floated after them like a streak through the drone of voices and the thunder of hoofs, the plaintive whining of fiddles, and the sombre throbbing of harps.

The beechwood surrounded the place like a wall, and the foliage shone with a dull gleam in the sunshine against the blue-grey sky—it was a hot day. At the bottom of the slope a fair was being held in a meadow by the stream: the smoke of bonfires rose above the copsewood; oxen and sheep were being roasted whole down there, and the shrill cries of the vendors cleft the hum and uproar of folk who were now beginning to be drunken and frolicsome.

A few people were still moving in and out of the church; but that morning the men from the *Reindeer* had barely been able to press their way in to the mass, and they had seen nothing, so

packed was the great church. And it had taken a long time to elbow their way into the chapel where stood our Lady of the Oak.
At least a hundred candles were burning in there, like a wall of
living flame; the shrine gleamed with gold and silver. The image
was black as pitch, the face was long, stiff, and hard under the
golden crown, and the child peeping out under the mantle of
gold brocade was like the stump of a root. But it was very ancient
and venerable. There was no time to say any long prayer within
the sanctuary, such was the press of folk.

Afterwards, when they were to share their provisions, they had
bought cider—it was mighty good and their heads were a little
mazed with it. Then they lost one another in the crowd down in
the fair-field. Olav and Tomas had kept together longest, but then
Tomas would stand listening to a minstrel so long that at last Olav
was tired of waiting and went on. Now he stood at the edge of
the forest looking out, if he could see any of his companions in
the swarm that drifted hither and thither on the green.

He felt within his kirtle for the packages he was carrying over
his belt. They were gifts that he would send home—a last greeting.
Embroidered velvet gloves for Signe and Una, a rosary of corals
and gold beads for Cecilia, a dagger for Eirik. Though Eirik
would now inherit all his arms—except Kinfetch; he must remember to send a message home that the axe was to descend in
Cecilia's branch of the family.

The thought was like stirring up a wasps' nest. He turned away
from it, looked about him; no, he could see none of his company.

From somewhere in the wood behind him he heard singing; it
sounded like ballads. Olav turned and followed the woodland
path—if they were dancing he would be certain to find Galfrid in
any case, and Leif.

After a while he came to a great open space in the forest. Upon
this plain stood a band of dancers, getting their breath; people lay
on the grass under the trees, eating and drinking. A little child
ran toward Olav, stumbled, and fell. Olav picked up the little boy,
who was howling, and tried to comfort him. He stood looking
about him with the child on his arm, when a stout, good-looking
young woman came running up. Olav smiled faintly and shook
his head at her flood of words. With a sudden gesture he pressed
the boy to him and kissed him before handing him to the mother.
It was like taking farewell of something.

The dancers formed a ring again—they were only men, who went arm in arm and broke into a wild and stirring tune. Olav went forward, forcing his way through the crowd looking on.

The strange, resounding, and provocative dance inflamed him through and through: it was fighting they sang of, and it seemed like something he had heard before—his heart stirred as the grave-mould stirs over a dead man who wakes and struggles to come out—and when he saw the look on the faces of those around him, his excitement grew. Old men stood leaning forward, beating time with their heads, glowing with passion. Big, portly matrons listened with hard faces, as though the song had to do with disasters they themselves had suffered. Even Olav felt that he knew something of it, but could not come at what it was—

—And all at once he had it! The river, Glaana, rushed down in flood, cold in the shadows, while the sun still blazed on the pinnacles of the keep—the castle stood on a little island, cleaving the stream. And he stood in the water-meadow watching the Earl's retainers, the lads from the Cinque Ports, as they danced and sang of the battle between English and Scots. *That* was the song, by God!

Memories that he had never recalled for years rushed up from the depths within him, like prisoners from a dungeon. A stream of rapid visions—furious hand-to-hand fighting, torchlight flickering over wild sword-play in a narrow gateway that sloped away into darkness—and then he was in a boat, rowing in the pale evening light outside the island walls of Stockholm, and facing him in the stern sat the Earl, short and broad as the door of a loft, invincibly strong and shaggy and warm as a he-bear, bright in his crimson velvet cloak, with his clear amber eyes laughing at war and adventure—oh, Lord Alf, Lord Alf, my liege!

The chain of dancers surged past him, and there was no end to the wild, ringing song. The men hung together, hooked arm in arm, leaning backward with their shoulders, and the chain swayed; the fiery faces of the singers could be seen through the clouds of dust each time they leaped high and stamped hard as they came down. Then a sudden jerk to the right all round the ring, and back they came charging toward the left.—His memories still sped through Olav's mind: of men with whom he had been friends in a cool and pleasant fashion, each man for himself within the iron shell of his coat of mail, but covering one another with shield and sword. Oh, to hell with all women, they cling all too closely to a man! The glare of flames among the dark timber gables of a city street. And himself, a lad of twenty, fully armed, standing in a doorway—a young serving-maid, whose name he had forgotten, seeking to drag him in and hide him. He laughed, snatched a kiss and tore himself away, rushed up the street, sword in hand, to where he heard the trumpets of the Danish King's men—and he was wild with an angry fear lest the Earl's men should let themselves be driven down to their ships without attempting resistance.

Olav's hands clenched upon the borders of his cloak—his spirit was in a violent uproar: to think that he could forget all this! And now it came back, his vision of the manor on the hill above the creek, but strangely paled and faded now; it was fraught with memories of ill health and contention with a dense, grey, overmastering force, and of a sick woman who crushed the youth and manhood out of him and who grew ever paler and more faded in spite of sucking his strength dry. And, with a sudden break, whatever feelings these memories had brought him hitherto—they now sickened and revolted him—Jesus! had he not been as one bewitched—or thrust into hell?

The song ended in a resounding roar and the thud of half a hundred feet that struck the ground at once. Olav drew a deep breath.

The ring of dancers broke up and the crowd of onlookers scattered. Olav moved about, uncertain what to do with himself. Then he ran against someone—looked at him and saw that it was the blind man from the church of the preaching friars.

For a moment they stood and stared at each other—so it seemed to Olav: the wan, sightless face, contracted with misfortune or bitterness, seemed all agaze. Olav's only thought was that he had been clumsy. Then a change came over the stranger's face, as though awakening from an evil dream. A smile broke out on it as he felt before him with his hands and spoke a few words.

"*Cognovis me?*" whispered Olav doubtfully.

The stranger—he was not much more than a lad, Olav now saw —replied at once in the same language, but he spoke it so quickly and fluently that Olav did not understand a word.

"*Non capio bene latinum,*" muttered Olav awkwardly.

The other smiled courteously and began again more slowly, in fewer words. Olav grasped so much: that he was parted from his company, and now he asked Olav to lead him somewhere—to the church. With hesitation Olav accepted the young man's proffered hand and felt with aversion how clammy it was. Then he let the other take his arm and led him toward the path by which he had come.

The young man tried to enter into conversation—in Latin, English, and French, a little of each. Olav understood him to say that he knew him from the Dominicans' church.

"*Non es—*" he sought the word for "blind." He stole a look at the other's ruined eyes. No, he must be stone-blind. A shock went through him—then someone had pointed him out to the man. "*Non es cæcis?*" The tension filled him with something like joy. Now he must be on guard.

It was dark in the forest; cautiously Olav led the blind man over roots and stones in the path—watching intently for any sign of men lurking in the undergrowth. And it had chanced unluckily that he had the stranger's left arm locked in his right—or had the other managed it of set purpose? Olav was ashamed to change now. But he kept an eye on the man's sword-hand.

He was waiting all the time for the flash of a dagger—or for someone to burst out of the thicket—and the way could not have been so long as he went to the sports green, nor the path so narrow—and dark it was here in the wood. But to the blind man's questions he replied calmly that his name was Olav; he was a Norseman and a merchant. He would have told him too where he lay with his ship—it were well that the man should know he had no thought of hiding—but when he tried to explain it, he could not make himself clear in the foreign tongue.

And all at once they were out of the wood. Olav led the blind man up toward the church, which now gleamed faintly in the fading light. And a dull, oppressive fear came over Olav—it was not with dagger or armed men the stranger would attack him. But into the church with this man he would not go!

Then a serving-man came running down toward them and called out on seeing his master. The latter at once dropped Olav's arm, took him by the hand, and thanked him for his help. Olav was dumb with surprise. The young knight turned to his man, laid a hand on his shoulder, and allowed himself to be led away, as he turned once more and greeted Olav with a parting "*Vale!*"

Olav stood still; it was now so incomprehensible that he felt almost disappointed. He followed the stranger with his eyes. Before the gate of the little priory by the church a company was getting into the saddle. And in a little while they came riding past him.

There were several men of rank in velvet, with gold chains on their breasts; they had excellent horses and costly gear. The blind man rode on a black stallion, which was led by a page. The serving-men who followed were armed and equipped for a journey, and in the rear came several horses laden with merchandise. Olav guessed they had come from far away.

And now it dawned on him that the blind man must have been away from home for some days. So she, the wife, had sent for him while she was alone.—He recalled the arbour in the secret corner of the garden, the young woman who came with perfumed hair, naked under her thin silken robe—neither pixy nor phantom as he had made himself believe—only an unfaithful wife.

In a surge of passion Olav felt as if he himself were the man betrayed. His rage was red and hot as lust—he could have seized and killed her with his bare hands. And he was dazed the while by a strange, unreal feeling—this had happened to him once before.

Then the rush of blood ebbed back, the red mist faded from his eyes. He felt the ground under his feet once more and saw everything about him with a strange distinctness. The beeches were bathed in a pale, subdued light, and the sky above was whitish, with a few bright shreds of cloud; the grey stones of the church flushed faintly in the afterglow. The place was now almost deserted, and a scent of dew and dust arose from the trampled grass. And Olav saw the cold, clear truth of it: that this game in which he had here been involved—he had taken part in it once before. But this time he was himself the thief.

He took the front of his cloak in both hands, as though he would tear off his bonds. But from the innermost chambers of his soul—now that at last he had been forced to open a crack of the door—the darkness spoke to him, a voice without words. This was the *meaning* of what had lately befallen him. Another man's wife had been offered to him, so that he had but to reach out his hand to take her. And he himself had had no other thought—until that cry had warned him, from heaven or from purgatory.

Had he not been *snatched* away, as a child is snatched from the fire by its mother, he himself would now have been a wedded woman's paramour.

Olav began to walk swiftly, as though he would escape from these thoughts. He strode across the fair-field. Embers still glowed upon the ground in the increasing dusk; in one place a fire was burning brightly. Many people still lingered here, and all seemed drunken. Olav walked on rapidly; he entered another wood by a well-marked path that led downhill.

In a kind of desperate resentment he struggled to drown the voice—"in the devil's name, I did not *touch* the woman. I have behaved like a fool, making eyes at an English bitch, because I thought she was like my wife." And he might well be angry, at his age, for being caught in the woman's snares—"but I had no such thought in my mind, and did I not make off at once, when I saw what she would with me?" And that the blind man had known him could hardly be a miracle; for he had often seen that blind men—beggars and aged folk—seemed to see with their whole body: they had the scent and hearing of dogs.

But all his striving to drown the voice within him was of no avail—*he* had violated no man's honour indeed, but he had not regarded it in this way as he led the blind man through the wood; then he had been sure that the other sought his life, and justly. And again he knew that he had been guilty in accompanying the strange lady's messenger—or an old, drowned guilt had floated up into the daylight.

As he hastened down the wooded path in the growing darkness, over stock and stone and bog-hole, sure of foot as a sleep-walker, it was borne in upon him that this darkness into which he hurried farther and farther was his own inner self, and presently he would have entered its deepest and darkest secret chamber. Soon he would be driven in, with his back against the last wall; but he knew withal that he would fight and defend himself to the utmost. And he understood—

First God had spoken to him face to face—that was in the night when he was to lose Ingunn. In that hour, when he was forsaken by his only friend, God had spoken to him from the forsakenness of the cross. In that night, when his grief was such that he could have sweated blood, God had appeared to him, bedewed with the blood of the death agony and the scourging and the nails and the thorns, and He had spoken to him as friend to friend: "O all ye that pass by, behold and see if there be any sorrow like unto my sorrow!" And he had seen his own sin and sorrow as a bleeding gash upon those shoulders. Yet he had not been strong enough to come.

And God had spoken to him a second time. He had spoken to him in His holy Church, as soon as Olav was so far healed of grief's fever that he could compose himself and listen to calm words. Yet he had voluntarily delayed on the road—nor was he any longer sure that he had obeyed the call. Unless—

But now this last thing had befallen him, so that he was forced to see what manner of man he was and what was his sin.

All at once he stood as it were outside and looked upon himself—as one stands behind a fence and looks at a man labouring in a barren, weed-grown field.

The man toils about a bramblebush, trying to clear it away, and tears his flesh and his clothes on it. But the weeds, the coarse and noxious growth of tares and thistles, he seems not to see. Yet it is not the bramble that has choked all the good seed in his corn-field: it may bulk large as it stands in full bloom, but it does not seed and scatter everywhere; one may clear it out once for all if one will take the trouble. And there it stands flowering, rank in its unprofitable beauty, and no one will *despise* it.

He had only been willing to acknowledge his great sins. For indeed they were blood-red transgressions against the laws that prevail in the kingdom of heaven. That he had always known, but at the same time he had known that among men it was accounted otherwise. And according to the law that held good among the men with whom his birth entitled him to rank himself, he had done no more than his duty—vindicated his right and his wife's honour.

Even if it came out, this thing that he had done in secret, the murder, the dastard's deed—it was not so sure that his memory would be tarnished with dishonour, even if his head had paid the penalty on the block. Not *one* man of all those he reckoned as his equals would judge him to be a dastard—if they knew all. Olav saw now that this knowledge had lain somewhere far back in his soul, always.

Young as he had been, he could not escape doing wrong, since his fate was tangled in the coil of other men's wrongs and misfortunes. But all the evil that followed was due to the attempted betrayal of him and Ingunn by those who should have defended the two children's rights. Up to the last and worst evil, his false confessions, the sacrilege that burned his mouth and heart—foot by foot he had been driven to all this, since he had had to take his own and his foster-sister's cause into his own hands, and as a raw youth he had grasped it mistakenly.

He had never before thought it out clearly in this way, but within himself he had always known, in the midst of his distress, that God, the all-seeing, saw this much more clearly than he did—that his greatest sins were the sins of others no less than of himself. And inextricably bound up with the burden of his own misdeeds he bore the burden of others.

So he had bowed low and smitten his breast when the deacon said the Confiteor in the mass; he was willing to confess: "not one of these men standing about me is guilty of such black misdeeds as I." In the mirror of God's justice he saw himself sunken so much deeper than these others, as the reflection of the oak in a pond sinks deeper than that of the undergrowth around it. And even in a human view he must have seen himself standing like an oak above the brushwood.

But in this unearthly light which now shone into his darkness, what he had secretly wished to preserve from God's hand appeared to him at last: the pride of the sinner, which is even harder to break than the self-righteousness of the righteous.—"Be it as it may, I am innocent of the sins of a mean man."

Twice had Jesus Christ spoken to him out of the sweetness of His mercy—and he had shrunk away like a timid hound. Twice had the Voice spoken: "Behold, who I am, behold the depth of my love!" Now it said to him: "See then who *thou* art. See that thou art no greater a sinner than other men. See that thou art as small a sinner!"

The sword sank into the most hidden roots of his being and pierced him. *Non veni pacem mittere, sed gladium. Qui invenit animam suam, perdet illam, et qui perdiderit animam suam propter me, inveniet eam.* Olav saw that these words were truth, such as he had never dreamed of before, and when he understood their meaning, it was like sinking beneath the ice-cold waters of the very ocean.

He laughed with pain as he ran through the dark forest.

He had behaved as though he were afraid of losing his life—
he who had long been so tired of life that if it had not been for
Ingunn's sake he could never have borne it for a day. He would
not go back to it—he lost nothing if he now chose obedience,
poverty, chastity, nay, the lot of a slave and a martyr's death at
last, for all that he must renounce he counted nothing worth, but
what lay before him promised gains beyond measure—adventures
and travels in distant lands, and at the last peace and God's forgiveness, and admission to the ranks of His soldiers again.

But now he tardily understood that then he must choose, not
between God and this or that upon earth, not even his worldly
life, but between God and himself.

The path brought him to an open glade; it led high up along
a slope, where the trees had been cut. Above him he now saw a
wide stretch of the sky, dark and strewn with stars. Below him
lay a little valley, he could see that he was looking down over the
tops of trees; a sound of running water came from somewhere in
the darkness.

Unconsciously he slackened his pace. The light, cooling breeze
fanned his cheek; Olav wiped the sweat from his forehead. And,
feeling that he was walking on high ground with open, airy space
about him on every side, he had a sudden instinct that he was
being led out into the wilderness; he walked here all alone in
a foreign land and knew not whither he was going. Here was
no familiar place or thing that might help him to escape seeing
what he would not see; folks' speech, which he did not understand, could not break in and drown the Voice that he would
shun.

Olav halted abruptly. He seemed to absorb strength from the
gloom around and from the raw, cold earth under his feet, so that
he felt his ego swell and grow in black defiance: "Why dost Thou
deal thus with me? Other men have done worse—and more con-
temptible—deeds. But Thou dost not drive them from home and
peace and persecute them, as Thou drivest and persecutest me."

The voice that replied seemed to dwell in the very stillness under the wide, star-strewn heaven and the forest that rustled faintly
in the night breeze and the hushed murmur of the brook in the
valley.

"Because thou dost yet love Me, I seek after thee. Because thou dost long for Me, I persecute thee. I drive thee out because thou dost call upon Me, even as thou fliest from Me."

The path descended steeply, leading into the thick of the woods. Olav stopped again, threw himself down at the entrance of the dark gap that penetrated the foliage, and sat with his head buried in his arms.

Visions came swarming upon him without his being able to hinder them. Once he complained aloud. Was it to see this that he had been brought back to the very starting-point, his youth? In secret he had been proud of his youth: "After all, I was overborne by force, I was compelled to stand alone, none helped me—whatever I have done or left undone, was not the sin of an ignoble man."

Was there none who helped him? Now he descried a little light low down, a lantern stood on the floor in a dark stable, and there were two young men. He recognized the face of Arnvid Finnsson, stricken and perplexed—it was he himself who had wounded his friend with a lie. Ay, *that* sin was his own and none other's. Now he saw that this was surely the first sin he had committed deliberately and wilfully: when he cast his guilt upon the shoulders of his friend, who, he knew, never refused to take up another's burden.

"No!" He whispered it breathlessly. This he would not have—let it be good for monk and priest, but *he* would not be imprisoned in this cell of self-knowledge they talked of; let it be their concern alone to watch the mirror that reflects God's light and man's darkness.

But he could not protect himself—the light that shines in darkness continued to burn, and in it he saw the thousand things that he had wilfully forgotten.

Had none helped him? They had helped him, those of whom he had asked help, Arnvid and the good Bishop, Lord Torfinn. They were the men he had loved and looked up to as his superiors—of his inferiors he had never asked anything. But of the friendship of these two he had availed himself as fully and eagerly as any of his inferiors had availed themselves of him. The difference was merely that *he* had never thought of calling any man his friend and equal who came to him as a suppliant. Out of a pity that was both proud and lukewarm he had given his gifts.

But the men who took *him* under their protection when he came to them in his need had received him as a younger brother.—Humiliation overwhelmed Olav like a landslide—he was painfully crushed beneath the rocks.

"Nay, God, I will not have this. Ingunn, help me," he prayed in his distress; "you must bear witness for me—Ingunn, I was never false to you?"

Again he felt with overpowering clearness how near she was now. Death only hid her form, like a darkness. But he heard her answer close beside him, out of a sorrow so deep that it made the living seem like children who lacked understanding:

"I witness for you, Olav, and every soul to whom you have shown pity witnesses for you of your good deeds. They are many, Olav—you were designed to render abundantly to God. But your deeds have become as withered stalks of corn, tainted in root and ear—they have so long been choked by the tares."

He *saw* them before him, sick and wan, ears that bore no corn to ripeness. His inmost will had driven them on—that will which God had given him for ruling and protecting. But this will had been overpowered by whims and desires and perversity and unwise impulses, as vassal kings overpower their rightful sovereign lord. He had been sustained by the secret pride that his sins in any case were not those of cowardice and ignominy. And now he saw that these great sins were a load that he had allowed others to put upon him, because he had never been strong enough to admit it when he had taken a false step through weakness and cowardice and thoughtlessness.

By tricks and by honest dealing, by a little lying and a little truth combined, he had gained advantage for himself from the few men he had met in the world whom he had reckoned good enough to call his friends, to love and respect. He had never dared to tell them the truth about his own conduct, because he wished to have their respect—and because he needed their help. He stood in debt to his friends—he who had always looked down with pity on every debt-burdened wretch.

It was not true, that which he had said to Bishop Torfinn, and to all his friends, so often that he himself had almost forgotten what was the truth. It was a lie that he had asserted his right to his betrothed merely because miscreants sought to take away their rights. Oh no, he had not been a strong-willed, resourceful grown man who took Ingunn and made her his, reckoning that, if there is dispute about a thing, he is best placed who has that thing in his possession. The truth was otherwise, humiliating—and at the same moment he was bathed in the sweetness of all these memories of his youthful love, now that at last they leaped up, naked, from beneath all the lies under which he had tried to hide them. He had been but a boy in those days at Frettastein, and he had had no thought of either right or wrong when he took to himself his young bride, dazed and wild with desire to possess her full sweetness and charm. He had thought no more than a child who grasps for everything it wants, without heeding, as it runs forward, whether it may fall.

Behind his closed eyelids he saw a cleft in a scree; under the rocks at the bottom of it ran a beck; red rosebay waved on the face of the precipice. Before him walked Ingunn: he saw her long, supple back in the red kirtle; she was plaiting her thick, dark-yellow hair, and he thought her so fair that he followed her as one bewitched. Before them the firs stood erect on the rocky cliff, and by the pale-blue radiance of the summer air he could see that the hillside dropped sheer beyond. He walked behind and looked at her, with mind and senses filled with secret memories of their meetings in her bower at night, with pride in being the master of her loveliness. And when they came to the end of the glen, where the lake lay far below under the dark, wooded heights —there was a little grassy slope between great shivering aspens— he ran up, embraced her from behind, and turned her face toward his own. Hers was pale, bedewed with warmth; as soon as he took her in his arms he felt that she grew weak and trembled in her everlasting animal docility.—This was before he knew that Steinfinn was to die, and before he had ever suspected that any man could hold their betrothal to be aught but a binding, irrevocable bargain.

In all these years he had never dared fully to recall to mind how it had been to feel nothing but the youth within him and all the world's beauty in a young maid. His longing caught him by the throat and made his eyes burn in their sockets.

Olav rose from the ground and let his arms drop. He gazed out at the patch of starry sky, black velvet powdered with gold, that lay above this unknown country in which he had lost himself. Unconsciously he caught a whiff of smoke from a fire somewhere in the night.

He divined that now he had wellnigh unravelled the whole skein of his life's misfortunes to the end of the thread. "Cleanse thou me from secret faults, O Lord," he had learned in his morning prayers—in all these years, when he recalled that psalm, he must have thought upon his own evil deeds. Now he saw that what he had tried to conceal, from both God and men, was that he might have gone astray from weakness, from childish thoughtlessness and blind desire—*that* he had sought to deny at any cost: even if he should take upon himself the guilt of far worse deeds, charge himself with a burden of sorrow so heavy that it broke him down, then rather that. If only it might look as if he had acted with premeditation and accepted his sorrows knowingly and of his own free will.

"—And preserve thy servant from the power of strangers: let them not have dominion over me; so shall I remain unspotted—" "Let me not submit to my enemies," he had meant. And then it had been nothing but his own sheer nature that kept him from submitting to his enemies, he would not bend to men for whom he had no respect or who opposed him; to such he had always shown his stubborn obstinacy and his mute, cold defiance. It was toward his friends he was weak and submissive, even to falseness and dissembling; it was when he first became aware of his love for his child bride that his whole being was inflamed and bent aside from uprightness, melting and leaning over like a heated candle.— *That* should have been the object of his prayers: courage, so that he dared acknowledge his blushing; strength, so that he ventured to act rightly and speak the truth without heeding the judgment of those he loved.

But in all these years he had believed himself to be a hard and stubborn, steadfast man; he had himself chosen the bitter lot of Cain, and he had chosen it of necessity, since he was to be the master and protector of the frail, weak-minded wife to whom he had been bound as a child.—And yet he had had to do violence to himself many a time before he could act as a hard man—gag the voice of his own conscience: do we not know how ready a man is to do wrong blindly when friendship and love are at stake, when joy and pleasure call?—He had said to himself he was playing for a high stake—and he had not been playing, he had merely shuffled the draughtsmen like a witless child. He had not *chosen* the lot of Cain; he himself had never known *when* he made a choice.

Olav clenched his teeth; it was as though another had pronounced this judgment upon him, and he would still defend himself, deny it. But the memory of that evening in the garden came back to him: old as he was, it required no more than a false air of youth, and he let himself be carried away, ran to grasp at the first shadow that played before his eyes. True, he had not thought of sinning—he had thought of nothing. As for the blind lad at whose side he had heard mass day after day, he had not remembered his existence.

His mouth filled with water—as in his boyhood when he chanced to see anything that was alive with maggots.

Weak, hasty, short-sighted, sleek-skinned, and spiritually yet a babe—a man of near forty winters—Olav laughed despairingly. No, that judgment he would not accept.

In a fleeting vision he recalled the dream of his former night in the woods: a bed of leaves in the midst of the darkness, a naked white body lying in it, the slain child—as he had seen in pictures of a deathbed: the soul leaving the dying man's mouth in the likeness of a little child, and angels and devils contending for it.

He trembled in extreme terror. Again the feeling came over him that he had had as a child on seeing maggots. And in the wild horror that seized him now that he saw what he had concealed from himself beneath his manifest sins, the temptation awoke—simply to throw more leaves over the murdered child, hide it completely, and fly.

And as though the words were spoken without him he heard: childish, soft, heedless—such a character he would scarcely be given by the neighbours at home. Weak—he? The memories roused by the fever of the dance returned, and now they seemed like a troop hastening to his succour. He could not judge his whole conduct as a grown man by the headlong follies he had committed on finding himself, a lad bereft of kinsfolk, charged with a cause that called for great resourcefulness if a full-grown man were to bring it to an honourable issue. Nor by the years he had spent at Hestviken, tied to a wife who was able neither to live nor to die. He had always been different in those periods of his life when he

71

had been able to act with free hands. Surely he need not call himself white-livered and soft-hearted for disliking his uncle Barnim's fatuous and useless cruelty. Nor weak because it went against the grain to slay Teit; it was, as that youth himself had said, far too like hunting flies with a falcon. Had he not been just as brave, just as eager for the sword-play, as the boldest among the Earl's men—a trusty comrade, well liked by his fellows, a friend with most, not too good a friend with any, loyal to defend his neighbour, cautious whom he trusted—? "God, my lot might have been so cast that I could lead a man's life, perform manly deeds like my forefathers, achieve my meed of honourable exploits—Thou didst set me where I had to fight with sickness and misfortunes black as hell, till I felt myself sink to the knees in mire. Does it make me a coward if I know myself that I was oft afraid, though no man saw me flinch?

"Did I run blindly after my own desires when I renounced pardon, manor, and wife at the moment when all were within my reach, for the sake of following my banished lord in his outlawry?"

But at the bare thought of the Earl his heart began to quiver with the old, ardent loyalty—oh, nay! If at any time he had blindly followed his own desires, it was when he rejoined the Earl. At that time he had *forgotten* Ingunn almost—he knew he was bound to her; never would he abandon his claim that their relation that autumn had been a lawful one, the consummation of an agreed marriage; but he had not remembered his love for his wife. Of his affection for Earl Alf he had never spoken to a soul—fate had given him a woman for his only trusty friend, and how should *she* be able to grasp anything of a squire's affection for his lord?

Olav drew himself up in agitation. About him loomed the trees; black and immensely high, they hid from him the starry heaven. He had a feeling that he was in flight, carrying himself off as booty into the woods. Here the path dropped so steeply that every moment he was in danger of falling headlong—it was dark as a badger's hole under the huge masses of foliage, and the track was full of big stones and twisted roots. Olav guessed that he must have left the broad, beaten path that he had followed at first. This gave him a strange feeling of relief—now he was forced to have a care of his feet, and he had to think of where he was, and whether perhaps he might reach some habitation where he could obtain a lodging for the night. In this country one could not enter the first house one came to along the road and ask for shelter, as at home.

Once, when he had to stop to empty his shoes of all the earth he had got in them, he came across the same smell of smoke as he had noticed before when he sat on the ridge. It must be the smoke of a watch-fire—'twas not likely that folk would keep the hearth-fire burning in any house so late at night. So it seemed there were men abroad in the wood. Olav took his sword out of the slit in his kirtle and let it hang in readiness. With his wonted caution he tried if it were loose in the scabbard and then walked on, slowly and quietly, holding it in his left hand.

The path swung out round a sort of promontory where the slope of the valley was bare of trees. Right under him, farther down, he saw a fire burning among the brushwood.

The discovery filled him with unreflecting joy; none could tell what sort of men might frequent this place. But Olav rejoiced at the prospect of meeting no matter whom, if only he might escape from solitude.

Now he saw the flame through the trees, heard the crackling of the fire. It lighted up a little clearing under the wooded slope on the farther side of the river, casting a red reflection on the black, running water. Between him and the fire he made out the dark forms of two men and heard voices.

The path led down to a little plank bridge and across to the meadow. The men lying about the fire did not hear his approach as they had just thrown an armful of dry faggots into the blaze. They were three young fellows—dressed as men of the people, none of the worst sort, seemingly. So he called to them.

They started up. Olav held his cloak wrapped about him with his left hand. As he stepped into the light of the fire it struck him that it would have been just as wise if he had first taken off the two gold rings with gleaming stones that he wore on that hand, but now it was too late. He greeted the men and asked, as well as he could, if this was the way to London.

As far as he could make out from their answer, it was not—the men pointed in the direction of the stream and over the hill. It was evident that the road to town ran on the high ground toward the south-west, but the men thought he would not be able to find it in the dark and he had better stay with them till daylight. Olav

73

nodded and thanked them. Then they threw him some armfuls of leafy boughs they had cut. Olav spread them out and lay down by the fire.

It did him good—now he felt that he was ready to drop with tiredness and hollow with hunger; he had eaten no more than once that day, and that was many hours ago. So he wished these strangers would offer him something, but they did not; it seemed they had eaten their supper. Now they tied up the mouths of their bags again and stretched themselves on their beds of leaves, two of them. The third was to sit and watch. So Olav did not care to ask for food.

They lay chatting for a while, as well as they could. The men were from the west—nor was their speech like that of the London folk, Olav heard. To their questions he replied that he had been to the pilgrims' church, he had lost his companions, he was a Norseman. But the conversation flagged. Then one of them began to snore, and soon after, Olav also fell asleep.

It was still night when he awoke, but the darkness seemed to have thinned; dawn was not far off. He had slept heavily and dreamlessly, but cold and hunger waked him. The fire had almost gone out, and the watchman seemed to be asleep.

Olav got up noiselessly and went down toward the river. At any rate he would have a drink of water. He knelt down and filled his hand—then he was on his feet again with a bound: he felt that someone was behind him. No time to draw his sword—he flung himself upon the man and felt the knife slash his cheek; it was lucky he did not get it in his eye. But he had got a good hold of the other and gripped his head under his arm, so that the man's cries were half-stifled. "The knife," thought Olav, but could not let go; so he raised his knee and drove it into the fellow's ribs, scarcely noticing that he got a stab in the thigh as he tried to wrest the knife away. But this gave the stranger a chance to close with Olav; and, locked together, they rocked and wrestled in the darkness, each trying to throw the other into the river. The man's smell and the firm, hot hug of a flesh-and-blood opponent filled Olav with a deep sense of voluptuous joy. He put forth all his strength—it was like pressing back the iron-bound gates of a castle against the assaults of the enemy.

Now he heard that the others were on their feet. At that moment he got a hold and succeeded in throwing his adversary; his body crashed into the bushes. Olav drew his sword and ran to meet the other two, with never a thought that he was running into danger and not away—there they were! In the dark he knocked aside a weapon—an axe, no doubt—struck and felt that he got home, and well; there was a cry and something fell in a heap. His second blow found nothing but the empty air, and he ran on. The plank bridge was too far, so he took a run and leaped out into the stream.

He splashed a stroke or two, then found bottom. When he stood up, the water came to his middle, but the bottom was muddy and he sank into it. Then he got hold of something—overhanging branches and then a root; the turf broke away under his knee; mould and gravel or whatever it was rolled down into the water. A moment later he was standing on the other bank. They were howling and roaring yonder.

Olav threw off his drenched cloak and wound it about his left arm, broke into the thicket, and forced his way through the undergrowth, with his bare sword in his right hand. Only now did he notice that he had cut it in wresting the knife from the first robber; the blood poured from it. Now and then he stopped a moment to listen—they must be on the plank bridge now. It seemed they had no great heart to pursue him; perhaps they guessed it was too uncertain in the dark and the thick underwood—a cursed wood it was, nothing but thorns and brambles.

Olav made his way on up the slope protecting his face as well as he could with the cloak about his left arm.

Arrived on the high ground, he presently came upon a broad road that seemed to lead down the valley. The sky was growing lighter now and the stars were fewer and paler, the woods swelled darkly against the first signs of dawn.

Again he stood and listened—he heard nothing of any men now, no sound but the tiny rustling of some small animal low on the ground among fallen leaves; here were tall trees, beeches. Olav walked on, more slowly, and now he felt the whole weight of his soaking kirtle beating heavily against him as he walked—ay, he was wet from top to toe, and as soon as he had gone a little way at an even pace he began to shiver in his clothes, which clung to him, cold as ice.

It did him good in a way. Vaguely and with a strange indifference he remembered the rushing stream of inward experiences that had carried him along from evening till darkest midnight—what had afterwards befallen him, his fight with the robbers and his flight through the thorn thicket, seemed to have placed an enormous distance between him and his hours of revelation. It was clear to him that he had not seen these visions with any faculty that dwelt within himself; a light had poured in upon him from without; and it was clear to him that he had called troops to his succour against this power, and help from that quarter where a man never seeks it in vain when he would defend himself against the truth—that help had surely been given him. He knew too that if at that moment he had had the power to see clearly and understand fully what it was that he had done—understand not only with the head, but also with the heart—then he must have been a desperate man. But he felt nothing but relief, and the cold from his clinging wet clothes wrapped itself around him and made him calm, as one puts out a fire with wet sails.

He wiped his face and found that it was scratched by the thorns, and bleeding, and blood was running down the inner side of his right thigh. After a while he was going lame, but kept on walking—it was as though he could not check his pace. So he walked and walked, stupid at times with sleep.

A mist rose from all low-lying lands on the approach of morning; all at once the fog surrounded him, dense and white, hiding the blue of heaven and putting out the last of the stars. Olav had been walking half-asleep for some time and stumbling now and again in the deep ruts that scored the turf of the road. Now he was wide awake for a moment.

Within the moist and muffling fog the trees loomed huge, beyond their natural size. Through Olav's tired brain there flashed a last glimpse of that world of visions to which he had been admitted and from which he had fled. In an instant it was gone again.

The grass was soaked with dew, bent down and grey all over. The road led through a forest of great ancient oaks, and in the thick undergrowth every bush was wreathed in cobwebs, which were coated with dewdrops. Olav shivered as he stood—and when he moved on again, he felt his right leg heavy and painful and his hose stiff with blood.

After a while he came out into a field, where red-dappled cattle were grazing in the fog. Olav called to the old man who was herding them, but received no answer that he could understand. Again a while, and he was in a little village street, and now he could ask his way, so that he reached London just as the sun was breaking through and all the bells of the city were ringing. He entered by one of the gates on the east side—he had gone a great way round out in the country. Olav looked neither to the right nor to the left; half-asleep he limped through the town, ragged, bespattered, and torn about the face. Down at the hithe he found a waterman to take him off to his ship.

The others had come home the evening before. They seemed to be glad when Olav came aboard. He told them he had been surrounded by some men who tried to rob him, in the forest, but he had cut his way out in the darkness, and after that he had lost himself. Not much more was said about it. But when Galfrid was helping him and washing away the clotted blood, and Leif came with a bucket of water, the lad could not contain himself.

"So it was you, Olav, not I, that came home at last with a hole in his skin," he said with a sly smile.

"Ay, one never knows—" Olav shrugged his shoulders.

Galfrid bound up his hand and bandaged his thigh. The other scratches were nothing.

Olav stayed on board for the most part, during the week they lay by Thames-side. Then they sailed home.

5

Olav sailed home down the Oslo Fiord one morning with a fresh northerly breeze; it was a day of blue sky and sparkling sunshine, and the fiord lay dark, flecked with white foam. Every tree on the wooded slopes of the shore was bright and glorious; the wind tore the first yellow leaves from the tops of the birches. The surf creamed white over every skerry and around every islet with its yellow, sun-scorched grass among grey rocks—Olav thought the very spray that sprinkled him felt good and homely, different from the empty sea. Once more he sat steering his own boat; long enough had he been away from all that was his. All was well at Hestviken, said Arnketil.

Olav called to Eirik forward, who had stood up and was about to fall over the thwart as the boat dipped into the trough of a wave.

It was marvellous how the boy had grown. Eirik had come up to the town with Arnketil to fetch the master home, but Olav had had little leisure to talk to them, the few days he had to stay in Oslo, and moreover Eirik worried him with all the questions he asked about his voyage to England. Olav himself was not very well pleased with the way it had turned out; the profits were well-nigh swallowed up by the expenses, and he would rather have had no more talk of it. With some surprise Olav had remarked that Eirik offered to answer back, with sullen disrespect—evidently it had not been good for the lad to pass the whole summer with no one over him to keep him in order. But now, as he sailed home by the familiar channel, with Haa Isle and Hougsvik Sound ahead, he was more inclined to forget the boy's ill manners and to be friendly with him. So when Eirik came straddling aft and took his seat on the thwart facing his father, Olav nodded. Eirik burst into the story of a murder that had been done in the parish on the eve of St. James [5]—and he himself had had leave to ride with Baard of Skikkjustad to the Thing. Olav nodded unconcernedly— he knew neither the slain man nor the slayer; they were strangers who had served on one of the farms in the forest tract to the north.

And Beauty had had two calves, Eirik went on.

"That was news!" Olav gave a little laugh.

And Ragna had two sons on the eve of St. Cnut [6]—

"That was not so well," Olav commented with a smile. " 'Tis many children—and she is left alone with them." Ragna, the dairy-woman, had been left a widow at the new year, and she had a daughter already.

But Cecilia had done her best to make them fewer, said Eirik mirthfully, Cecilia was so fond of the little twins. And one day when Ragna was out, Cecilia had gone in to them, and then she had stuffed the mouth of one of them full of ferns to quiet him. It had almost cost the babe his life.

Olav shook his head with a little laugh.

His dogs rushed hither and thither along the quay, barking and whining with delight as the boat came alongside. Then he stood

[5] St. James's Day is July 25.   [6] St. Cnut's Day is July 10.

on his own wharf, shook hands with his own people, while the dogs jumped noisily about him, snapping their teeth and licking him in the face.

Liv pushed Cecilia forward. The child was dressed in a faded and outgrown red kirtle, but it shone in the sunlight, and her hair surrounded the white little face like a floating, radiant cloud. She looked healthy, though her skin was so white—it seemed but cold as grass and flowers are cold—and her immense eyes were a very pale blue-grey, or greenish like sea-water. She looked up at her father's face rather like a stranger, when he bent over her and spoke to her. Then Olav took his daughter's hand and led her as he walked toward the manor with the dogs around him and his household in the rear.

He took the path up the hill by the side of the "good acre." The corn was ripe, it made a good show, and Olav felt strangely relieved: there were not many weeds among it this year. It was as though his life were connected in a mysterious way with the crop of this field. But it ought to have been cut ere now, the gales had damaged it somewhat.

"They say you have brought great gifts for me, Father," whispered Cecilia, and these were the first words the child had spoken.

"Ah, if they say that, it must be so," replied her father with a smile.

In the evening he sat in his high seat, with hands resting on the smooth-worn heads carved on its posts, and neck leaning against the old tapestry that covered the logs of the wall. In his thoughts he went over all the things he had seen to and arranged in the course of the day, while his glances idly followed the flickering light of the hearthfire on the smoke-stained walls of the hall.

He was filled with a vague well-being and something like a hope of the future. It did not shape itself as a thought—but for the first time the husband realized without pain that *she* was gone. The very emptiness felt like the physical peace that sets in, when the wound is healed, after the amputation of a diseased and aching limb. Olav was himself scarcely aware of it, but he had lost the desire of thinking of Ingunn since that evening in the strange woman's garden. The shameful memory of that adventure had in a way infected those memories that lay beneath it.

Liv came in, swung aside the pot and its hanger, and made up the fire. Inconceivably ugly, thought Olav; inconceivable that the men cared to touch her—and yet they *had* done so, it seemed—

"You are late with supper for us tonight, Liv," he said, and the maid giggled with pleasure, as she always did if her master but addressed a word to her.

The door stood wide open for the sake of the draught; from outside came the sound of iron-shod heels on the rock. Then Cecilia's fair head appeared in the shadow of the anteroom door. Olav kept his eyes fixed on her as she climbed over the threshold. She went up to the hearth—the glow lighted up her red frock and fair hair, as she picked up a few grains that had fallen on the hearthstone and put them in her mouth.

"Come hither, Cecilia," Olav called quietly.

The child came and stood by his side.

"Have you put away my rosary, Father?"

"I have so." Olav reached out for her, trying to take her on his knee. But she slipped away from him, back to the fire.

The groats were bubbling and popping in the steaming pot. Olav looked forward to a meal of porridge and ale—hot food he had not tasted since he left home.

He took a turn in the yard before going to bed. The wind had dropped toward night, the fiord sighed back and forth in the shoal water under the hill. It was dark outside and the stars twinkled brightly; not unlikely there would be rime-frost toward morning. Olav walked up to the cattle-sheds. There was a muffled beating against the stable wall—he waited outside for a moment, then opened the door and went in. He went up to Ran, the mare, and spoke a few words to her—taking deep breaths of the warm, acrid smell of the stable.

Up behind the barn he paused again, listening to the faint autumnal murmur of the stream down in the valley and looking at the stars that blazed over the top of the black wooded ridge. To the westward he made out a faint whiteness along the beach where the sea broke against the rocks. Up the valley the ripening cornfields showed under the shroud of darkness.

God! he thought for an instant, looking at a great star that blazed just above the tops of the firs opposite. He recalled that starry night in England when he had been held fast and addressed by a Voice that no man can remember if he has chosen not to hear. He had chosen, and now it was as though he had fled and hidden himself, creeping beneath the corn that stood pale and ripe in the darkness; he stole down to the raw, cold fields and hid himself there.

It was true enough what they said of Hestviken, that it was a strangely dead place. Old folk said it was Olav Half-priest who had driven away all the elves and underground beings—save one— and that one he could not cope with. No one knew exactly what kind of being it was; its usual haunt was by the bridge over the mouth of the stream, and it appeared in the likeness of an immense badger with only three legs; it did neither good nor harm. Olav vaguely wished now that there had been more life about the manor.

Then he walked slowly down to the house again and went to bed.

Just as he was falling asleep a thought occurred to him—Liv. What if the people of the parish should take it into their heads that it was *he*? The thought made him wide awake and burning hot—he had always had such a violent loathing of the stumpy, toad-like, loose-living wench, and now he felt he would give he knew not what rather than that any soul should believe he had resorted to her foul couch. This time he would have to see to getting her married and away from the manor—Arnketil might be the likeliest to take her. Olav lay awake a long time, tormented by this sickening uneasiness.

Next day he spoke to Liv. The maid wriggled this way and that and tittered foolishly, but at last she agreed that the child was most likely Arnketil's. At first she seemed but middling glad when Olav said he would help them to marry. But then she changed her tone, was full of thanks and promises—he guessed she thought that now she and Arnketil were to be set over the servants of the manor. He told her curtly that such was not his intention; he would help them to set up house for themselves.

But how he was to manage this, Olav himself did not know; he could not turn out any of his tenants. Only Rundmyr stood empty.

Olav had carried on the farm there for Torhild Björnsdatter and her brothers and sisters ever since the maid came to Hestviken. One after another most of the fields had been left fallow, for he saw no means of manuring them; Olav used the land for hay, and the houses stood empty. Now and then the elder sons of Björn and Gudrid stayed there for a few weeks—they took after their mother, were unsteady and reputed untrustworthy. Egil, the eldest, was now over twenty; ever since Olav had abused his half-sister he had hung about Hestviken when he was in need of help—demanded this and that as though it were his due. He hinted that he was the son of a good man and therefore it would cost Olav dear to atone for the shame he had brought upon the family. Olav put up with it, though at the time he had paid fines in full to the brothers and made good provision for Torhild and the child—but Egil was certainly never under his half-sister's roof. Olav saw here another advantage in buying Rundmyr: he would no more have Egil idling about the neighbourhood.

But when Olav was alone with Arnketil, he somehow did not bring himself to speak of the matter. The man was a picture of poverty and simplicity: tall and scraggy, with loose-hung limbs, and his head, far too small, was set upon a long, thin, sinewy neck with a huge and prominent Adam's apple. It was impossible to tell his age from his begrimed and sallow face, but he could not be more than five or six years above a score, for he had not been fully grown when he first took service with Olav. So stupid was Arnketil that he must have lacked something of his full wits; nevertheless he was in his way a useful workman, and he had always served Olav faithfully—until he had taken up with this Liv, for she taught him both lying and pilfering; though the girl was scarcely more than half-witted herself, she was remarkably cunning in such things. So Olav thought it was a pity of the poor body and said nothing to him about his marriage.

But a day or two later Olav came in to supper tired and wet, and Liv was bearing round the bowls of food—since she had taken on herself the duties of mistress the table was seldom set up. Eirik had seated himself a long way down the bench by the side of Arnketil. There was some joke that amused those two so that they had to keep their eyes fixed on the cups they held in their laps; even then they spirted with sudden laughter now and again. Olav glanced angrily at them once or twice. At last the fun was too much for Eirik; he fell forward and the porridge spirted from nose and mouth with his bursts of laughter. Then Arnketil could not contain himself either; he laughed, swallowed a mouthful the wrong way, coughed and laughed, and coughed again so that the tears ran down his cheeks, and then Eirik laughed quite uncontrollably.

Olav turned round sharply. At that Eirik jumped up and darted from the room, roaring with laughter, while Arnketil dropped his porridge-bowl on the floor and let himself go, and Liv stood sniggering foolishly without even knowing what this unseemly merriment was about.

After supper Olav took Arnketil outside and told him his intentions about the marriage with Liv. Arnketil answered compliantly and seemed well pleased. Again Olav felt pity for him—God alone knew what sort of house this pair would keep at Rundmyr. But they would have to make the best of it now—help they could be given, if they needed it.

At night Olav lay pondering—whether he should let them stay at the manor after all. But then he thought—no. Liv had managed the house wretchedly enough while she was alone; if these two were to stay here, with their children, a cow or two, goats, and sheep, it would make far too much trouble. For he could not send away Ragna and her three children; she was an honest woman, widow of an upright man. And she brought luck with the cattle, so it seemed.

In the afternoon of the next day Olav took the lightest skiff and rowed across the fiord.

It was a longer walk over the hills than he remembered. Now and then he halted, uncertain whether he was on the right path, but he would not ask his way.

The day was calm, with a heavy, leaden sky, but now the eye of the sun pierced the clouds, lighting up the dark-green firs and giving a strange richness to the colours of the birch groves against the thick grey air. The yellow leaves of the aspens rustled gently; their foliage was already much thinned up here on the high ground, and the path was brightened by fallen leaves. A raw breath rose from the ground under the trees, as always in autumn, even when it was dry.

At last Olav recognized where he was. Beyond a great bog, with tufts of red heather and white bog-cotton around its pools, lay the farm to which Auken had belonged. Through an opening in the forest he came to a gate and saw the yellow timbers of the newly built houses standing on a rocky piece of ground, with small fields below, in which the corn stood in stooks.

The path ran by the edge of the cornfield, past some great heaps of stones. It turned a corner, and straight before him Olav saw a child, a boy of two with pale-yellow hair that curled over the neck. He was crawling among the stones and plucking wild raspberries; on hearing someone approach he turned round. The boy had been thrust into a pair of leather hose that were far too big for him, so that the thongs were crossed over and under his shoulders, and his homespun shirt hung out before and behind, looking ridiculous. But in spite of that he was a singularly handsome child.

Olav stood still, and the boy looked up at him, till his little berry-stained face puckered with coming tears. Olav looked about him, and now he caught sight of Torhild—she raised her head among the yellow corn in the field. She looked this way, then put down her sickle, took off the coif that had slipped down about her neck, and bound it tightly over her hair. She was dressed as Olav had always been used to seeing her when she was at work, in a grey homespun shift reaching to the ankles and held in at the waist with a woven belt. Her bare feet were thrust into rough shoes. She looked neither younger nor older than she had seemed in all the years Olav had known her, but as she came toward him with sickle in hand he thought her handsome, so strong and stalwart and upright was her gait.

They greeted one another in silence.

Torhild said: "This was unlooked-for—are you abroad in these parts today?"

"Ay, I had business on this side."

Torhild laid the sickle on a stone, bent over the boy, and lifted him up in her arms.

"He looks so queer," she said, as though excusing herself; "but we are so thick with snakes up here—I dare not let him go barefoot."

Together they walked up toward the houses.

On entering the living-room Torhild bade him sit down. "Maybe you are thirsty?" She fetched a bowl of ale, with a head of froth on it, and drank to him. "I am brewing now for Michaelmas."

As he sat there, Olav recognized the faint and delicate scent of

withered garlands that Torhild had always been used to hang up
indoors in summer to keep away vermin. Meanwhile Torhild had
passed behind the foot of the bed: she slipped a green kirtle over
her working-dress and put on the belt with copper mounts which
she wore on the minor holidays. Then she sat down to dress the
boy, asking the while after the folk at Hestviken, how Eirik and
Cecilia were thriving, and what was the state of the crops.

Olav replied that he had been out of the country this summer.

"Ay, so I have heard. You have been on a long voyage too. And
it was to be expected—that you should wish to see something of
the world, now you are a free man."

Torhild set food before her guest, and while he ate she stood
aside with the boy on her arm.

Once Olav could not help saying, as he looked around: "He is
big for his age, the boy—two winters old?"

"Folk say he is big." The mother bent her head and stroked
her cheek against the child's. But now the boy began to kick and
struggle, he wanted to get down, and she put him on the floor. He
went up to the strange man and stood for a moment looking at
him. But then he remembered something more important, stumped
away to a corner, and sat down to play with a toy.

Olav bade Torhild be seated: " 'Tis with you I have come to
speak." She took the dish of food and set it aside. Then she sat
down on the edge of the hearth facing him, looking down with
her hands in her lap as she listened to Olav's proposal.

"As to this I must consult with my brothers," she answered
when Olav had finished. " 'Tis so that you may rightly look to
me to meet your wishes in this matter; you may look for that with
all of us. But I wonder, Olav, if it be wise of you to lodge such
folk as Anki and Liv in a cabin so near to your house."

"I have thought of that myself. You mean, they are somewhat
uncertain. But from year's end to year's end 'twill not be more
but that I can bear the loss without being brought to beggary.
And I can see no other way to deal with them."

Torhild then promised that she would advise her brothers to
consent.

Afterwards they went out to look over the place. Torhild took
her milking-pail—she had two cows and a fine heifer grazing just
outside the fence in the wood. While she was milking, Olav stood
leaning on the fence and looking at her; they exchanged a few

words about the cattle and the weather and such things. The boy Björn came up and tried to climb on the fence so that he could see his mother; Olav took hold of him and helped him up; he kept hold of him while he and Torhild talked as before.

From out of the wood came three half-grown children with a sledge-load of dry leaves; the two boys pulled and the girl pushed behind. They were Kaare and Rannveig, Torhild's youngest half-brother and sister. Olav gave the children good-evening; they had been reared at Hestviken.

The third was a tall, thin, fair-skinned boy with lank hair and a long, low chin; he had a foolish look, but Torhild said he was very useful to her. "He is my foreman, is Ketil." He had been found by the cross on the highway north of here fourteen years before, as a new-born child, and the old people, who took him in for the love of God, were now dead; thus he came to be at Auken.

They walked back toward the houses, and Olav declared that such fine corn as this of Auken he had not seen anywhere that year.

"Then I must send you a box of seed-corn, Olav," said Torhild with a little smile. "If you will accept such a gift from me."

"Thanks, but that is too much."

The children sat at their meal when they entered the house. Torhild told them they must sleep in the byre tonight: "—for we have a guest from far away."

They went out at once, and Torhild took out of her chest a pillow and two coverlets woven with stars, with which to deck the bed.

"You must not trouble yourself for my sake," said Olav in a low tone. "I must needs return to Hestviken tonight."

Torhild stood with her back to him. She was silent for a moment; then she said:

"The path down to the shore is none too easy. And it will soon be dark."

"Ay. Maybe it were better not to stay much longer—"

"No. If it is so, that you must cross the fiord tonight—then surely you must go now."

Olav stood up, took his cloak and his spear. He came forward and gave Torhild his hand, bidding her farewell.

"There is a shorter road here—I can go with you."

Torhild lifted the child from the floor, where he was rattling some stones in a wooden cup, and laid him in the bed. Then she went out with Olav.

The curious dark-blue colour of the day had faded to grey twilight and a few drops of rain were falling; but when Olav bade her go in again, Torhild answered that the wet would come to nothing. She walked before him southward across the fields to the beck that divided Auken from the main farm. On coming to the manor lands she waited for him and they walked side by side along the edge of a field that had been cut and lay pale with stubble under the grey sky.

"Whom have you taken, then, instead of Liv," asked Torhild, "to keep house for you at Hestviken this winter?"

"Nay, I have had no time to look about for anyone yet," said Olav. "But I dare say I shall find somebody."

Torhild was silent for a few paces. Then she said—and seemed a little short of breath: "Olav—what woman—of those you know —think you best fitted for this post?"

He said nothing.

Then she repeated more plainly: "Who, think you, would be most zealous for your welfare and serve you to the best of her powers, more faithfully than all other women?"

Olav replied hoarsely: "I know that, as you know."

They walked on in silence; then he said: "But you see it well enough too. It would scarce be long before— I will not ask you to return to such a—dishonourable lot."

Torhild said in a low voice: "I would gladly accept such a lot —with you, Olav."

Again they walked a little way in silence.

Then Olav said with warmth: "No. I will not have you suffer more ills for my sake than I have already put upon you. And you are best off here at Auken, you and the boy. I have seen enough today to know that you will hold your own here, Torhild."

"No doubt of that." He could hear she was smiling. "I am not ungrateful, Olav. But I know not—had it not been for her lying there sick and palsied, whom we had wronged—I know not whether I should have reckoned myself badly off that last winter I was at Hestviken."

Olav shook his head. A moment later they came to a gate at the brow of the wood.

"Now you cannot go wrong," said Torhild. "By this path it is much easier to find your way to the hard than by the path you came."

She held out her hand and bade him farewell.

Olav looked at the woman—in the last rays of daylight he dimly saw the fair oval of her face and the upright carriage of her high-bosomed figure; for aught one saw, she might have been quite young. Far below under the woods the fiord lay dark and lifeless under the heavy, autumnal sky; the farther shore was merged in the blackness of the raincloud.

With a thrill of desire he thought of taking her. Within the forest the fallen leaves showed up against the dark, rounded cushions of the heather; up at the house the hearth would be glowing cosily—the boy lying asleep. The thought of his homeward journey filled him with repugnance.

He knew that she was waiting as she stood there.

Then he quietly bade her farewell, turned, and went rapidly down the hill.

From time to time he stopped and was lost in thought on his way through the woods. It was quite dark when he came to the shore. He found the place where his boat was drawn up on the beach, was about to push it into the water, but paused, leaning against the boat, gazing into the night and listening.

Olav could not tell what had prompted him to leave Torhild—but he had had no choice. It was raining, he noticed all at once; he had not known when it began, but now there was a hiss of raindrops in the water of the fiord, a dripping and rustling in the foliage behind him.

As he stood there in the darkness, letting himself be soaked by the autumn rain, he felt to the roots of his being that he was bound to live alone, just as firmly as if he had bound himself by a monastic vow—only that it seemed as though his own will had had nothing to do with it. It *was* to be so, whether he would or would not. His life had now become like a journey in a trackless wilderness; he saw neither path nor trail, and he had to find his way alone.

He got the boat out; the scraping of the keel over the sand and the little hollow sounds as he put out the oars roused him. The rain still poured down. Now and again he looked over his shoulder at the other black coast, to see that he was not drifting too far down.

Torhild—he felt his heart contract at the thought of her. But it was a shame—the station to which her father had brought his daughter. Had not Björn Egilsson played away all his possessions, then married that Gudrid, begotten all those children to grow up as servants and vagabonds— As he rowed Olav worked himself up into indignation against Björn, who had left his daughter in such a case. From her birth and ancestry Torhild had had a right to look for a good and honourable marriage.

Olav was half-aware of a reversal of his own standpoint. When faced by a misfortune, he had never before tried to shuffle out of his share of the blame; he had never before been afraid to bear his own part and more, if a weaker sought to lay his burden on his shoulders. Now he was himself seeking someone to whom he could transfer the blame for wrongs of his own doing.

PART TWO

The Wilderness

ᴇᴀʀʟʏ in the spring, the year after Olav Audunsson's foreign voyage, a Thing was held at Haugsvik one morning, and Eirik was allowed to attend it with his father. But as they were going home, it fell out that the Rynjul folk went in Olav's boat, and Eirik was to follow in another craft.

Not till late in the afternoon did he come—in a little sailboat that was laden to the water's edge with half-grown lads. Ragna came in to her master and said that as many of the boys came from far up the parish, they might well want food and drink before setting out inland. Yes, said Olav.

The lads made their way indoors and Olav replied to their greetings with a nod. Then he went out, for he felt disturbed by all these strange children who hung about the benches looking ill at ease.

He was standing by the stable door when the band of youth came out again. But they did not seem to think there was any hurry about leaving; they stayed about the yard, nosing here and there among the houses, two or three together, prying and looking about them; others kept together in a bunch, chattering and laughing and bickering in a mild way; but it was all play and good humour.

Olav stayed where he was, for he had no desire to mix with this throng. It was cold, now the sun was down, and the sharp young voices carried far in the still spring evening.

Snow was still lying under the north walls of the houses, and presently the lads took to snowballing. Olav paid no great attention to them, but there was one who showed up among the other lads; he was the tallest of the company and handsome in a way, red and white like milk and blood, with long, smooth straw-coloured hair. Eirik kept close to this lad and helped him.

But after a while Olav saw that all the other boys had joined in attacking Eirik; they belaboured him with snowballs and barred his way to the drift, so that he had none to throw back. The tall lad stood looking on.

Then Eirik made a dash between the byres. The hollow behind the outhouses was still full of snow. Eirik jumped into it and began making snowballs, which he hurled at the crowd of his pursuers. And now Olav stepped behind the outhouses to see what would happen.

Eirik shook off the first enemies who leaped down on him; plunging through the crust so that he sank to the middle in the wet snow, he pulled himself out of the hollow and onto a ledge of the rock behind. From there he sent fistful after fistful of turf and loose stones at the heads of his assailants, who replied with snowballs. There was a great shouting at this—evidently the game was about to take an angry turn.

A snowball caught Eirik in the eye, making him duck and put up his hand. At that moment the tall fair boy who had stood aloof jumped up and threw his arms round Eirik. He flung him head-foremost into the snowdrift, and all the other boys threw themselves on him and ducked him in the filthy snow, yelling and laughing the while, as Eirik howled with rage, half-stifled under the heap.

Olav came a few steps nearer—the tall fair boy caught sight of him and said something to the others. They got up at once.

Eirik got onto his feet; he was bleeding at the mouth, and he turned to the tall boy, shrieking frantically:

"A dirty clown you are—call yourself a man! I—I helped you—" he was crying with rage.

Olav noticed that the tall fair boy looked strangely foolish now, as he blinked and turned away from Eirik's father. But all the other lads made haste to get out of the hollow. Olav followed slowly; on reaching the yard he saw the whole band of them up by the barn making for the east. They had neither taken leave nor thanked him for his hospitality.

Eirik stood just behind his father. He was still panting as he pressed a snowball, now against his swollen eye, now to his bleeding lip.

"Who was he, that fair lad?" asked Olav.

"Jörund Rypa." Eirik snuffled and swallowed; he was staring at the band as they disappeared in the darkness toward Kverndal.

"Jörund? Have they that name anywhere hereabouts?"

Eirik replied that Jörund came from a great farm to the east-ward, by Eyjavatn, but he had an aunt who was married at Tjer-naas and kinsfolk at Randaberg; he was often there.

Olav shook his head unconcernedly; he knew little of these folk and had never spoken with them.

After supper the men sat in the hall; they had brought in some saddlery and implements to put in order for the spring work of the farm. Once on waking from his own thoughts Olav heard his house-carls laughing and sneering, while Eirik poured out an im-petuous tale:

"—when they came and set on me all at the same time, what could I do? Do you think I could not have thrown every single one of them, if we had met on level ground?"

"Oh, ay, surely. You would have done that."

"And I kept them off me a long time—"

"But then you had such help from that brave foster-brother of yours, Eirik," laughed one of the men.

Eirik was instantly silenced. Olav saw that the boy's lips quiv-ered; he was pressing back the tears and trying to look uncon-cerned.

Olav felt with latent anger that there was something wrong in this—that the house-carls dared to taunt and slight the son of the house while his father was by. Eirik was no longer a little boy. So he put down what he had in his hands, stretched himself, and yawned:

"Nay, men—'tis already late. Time to go to rest."

When father and son were left alone in the hall, Olav came and stood before Eirik. The lad sat on the bench weeping quietly.

"You must have done with this now, Eirik—this childish boast-ing—so that the serving-folk think they may make a fool of you."

As the boy made no answer, but simply sat there struggling with his tears, Olav went on, rather more harshly:

"And you ought to be ashamed to cry because you got a beating!"

Eirik snuffled once or twice. "I am not crying because I got a beating!"

"What are you crying for, then?"

"Jörund—" Eirik swallowed. "We had promised each other

loyal fellowship for life—we took the oath of blood-brotherhood last autumn and—"

"What nonsense is this?" asked his father rather scornfully.

Eirik explained with sudden eagerness. They had met at church one Sunday in the autumn, and then Eirik had spoken of something he had lately heard: that it was a custom in old days for friends to bind themselves by an oath of blood-brotherhood. Jörund was willing. But every time they got so far as lifting the strip of turf on the points of their spears, it broke to pieces, and at last Jörund lost patience—and then Sira Hallbjörn came out, and he was very wroth when he saw all the holes they had dug in his calf paddock.

Olav shook his head in despair. "What folly!"

Eirik was standing with one foot on the hearth, close to the glowing embers, and a cloud of steam came from his shoe. The boy looked so melancholy with his tall, weedy body, his long neck, and the dark, curly head bent down—everything about Eirik was young and slight. Olav had a sudden desire to show the boy a kindness.

"Do not scorch your shoe—'twill be hard as a board tomorrow." Olav handed him a pair of his own shoes. "You may have the loan of these tomorrow—stuff straw in your own, so they may dry slowly."

Eirik thanked him cheerfully, and Olav began to pull off his clothes. Presently the boy cried out with a laugh:

"Father, I have outgrown your shoes now—look here."

It was true. Ah yes, his own feet were unusually small. And Eirik looked like being large-limbed.

Olav lay long awake; the thought of Eirik galled and troubled him.

In these last years—nay, ever since his relations with Torhild Björnsdatter took that unfortunate turn—he had shunned the boy, almost without premeditation. Eirik *was* there, but the less he thought of it, the better.

But this last winter it had seemed as if Eirik sought to thrust himself on his father's attention. At first Olav believed this was the result of the lad's having run loose a whole summer without any man's hand over him; now he must quickly find some means of quelling these loud-voiced ways that the boy had got into. But

Olav was startled to see, with great surprise and little joy, that he was no longer able to relegate Eirik to that outer sphere of his father's life to which the lad had so long been banished. It was clear that he would have to devote more care to the boy's training, cordially as he disliked the thought. He saw all the lad's faults and failings, and things could not go on as now—when their inferiors showed openly that they, too, saw them. Eirik had now reached an age when it was only seemly that he should mix with other men in his father's company. But then Olav would have to see that the lad was shown the respect due to their position.

But Eirik himself had little sense of how to behave himself. At home he mixed with the servants of the house: one day he was their familiar, childish and fatuous; the next he put on a proud and lofty air—but the folk only made fun of this before the boy's very eyes.

The worst thing, however, was that he haunted Rundmyr early and late. The place had become a vile den since Liv and Arnketil had gone there. Egil and Vilgard, his younger brother, were also housed there now, and they brought in others of the like sort. It came to Olav's ears that Eirik had actually joined in dicing with folk who came in from the highways, all kinds of vagabonds, both men and women. He took the lad to task for it, chiding him sharply. Then to Olav's unspeakable surprise Eirik turned insolent and answered back. Olav simply took hold of the boy's neck, forced his head down, and flung him aside—but he liked doing it no better, as he felt how weakly and as it were disjointedly the lad collapsed under his hand. And the expression of Eirik's eyes, at once cowed and malicious, aroused violent repugnance in Olav, though at the same time he felt pity for the weakling.

There was another matter that troubled Olav tonight. He had guessed well enough what Una had in her mind when she came down to the boats on leaving the Thing and asked him to take her with him. And he had been right—when they came ashore she had contrived to be alone with him by the boathouses. Then she told him in plain words: there were now other suitors for Disa Erlandsdatter. But both she and Torgrim would rather that Olav won the bride.

Olav thought he had given no very definite reply, but now he could no longer avoid making them a plain answer. And doubtless it would lead to some cooling of friendship between him and his kinsfolk when he showed so little appreciation: he saw clearly enough how kindly they had meant it when they as good as offered him Torgrim's rich cousin in marriage. And assuredly the whole neighbourhood had heard of the matter. Olav saw now that he ought to have let them know long ago that he did not wish to marry again.

They had every right to complain that he had rewarded their loyal spirit of kinship with disdain. Since he had been a widower there had been a revival of intercourse between him and his kinswomen, the daughters of Arne, and their husbands. And now too he remarked that his neighbours seemed to smooth the way for him; did he wish it, he could now come forward and resume the position that the master of Hestviken ought to occupy in the district. Together with his kinsmen by marriage at Skikkjustad and Rynjul he could acquire both power and honour in the hundred. And he liked both Torgrim and Baard—ay, Baard he liked better than most men.

It was the daughters of Arne and their husbands who stood in the background and induced people—those who had their boats and boathouses on his beach—to come forward and suggest that all the old questions that had been left undecided, as to the rights to the different estates, his share in the catches of fish, and such matters, might just as well be settled now. There were many things that Olav had let drift for years, because he felt lonely and overburdened. And his neighbours and others, who had been wont to make the lower road down to the creek, keeping away from the manor on the hill, now found occasion to visit his house and enjoyed such hospitality as had been shown in former days at Hestviken. Perhaps it was not unnatural—it had been reasonable enough that folk kept away from the house so long as its mistress lay there sick and disabled.

But now Olav was offered an opportunity of retrieving—ay, he might just as well be frank about it—he could now recover all it had cost him to be Steinfinn Toresson's foster-son and Ingunn's bridegroom. But he *would* not!

Disa was rich, of good family; her first marriage had added to her repute, and she had inherited Roaldstad and its wealth from her two little sons who had been drowned a year or two before in the breaking up of the ice. Her age agreed with his—some thirty years. And if she was not a lady of surpassing beauty, she was far from ugly, a shapely, kind, healthy, and cheerful woman. Never again would he be offered so good a match. If he did not grasp at her with both hands, it would be deemed by all that he did not desire his own welfare. And he liked the young widow, the little he had seen of her.

But he would not marry Disa Erlandsdatter. It was not the same as when he refused Torhild; that he had done under compulsion, he knew not of what. From time to time desire came upon him when he thought of Torhild—he longed to embrace her great wholesome body as a man bleeding to death longs to quench his thirst. And he would be sick with impatience to place everything in her capable hands when he himself had to wrestle with matters that properly came under the care of the mistress of the house. He had renounced her because he felt he must, whether he desired her for himself or not.

But at the thought of Disa dwelling here at Hestviken, meeting him at his own door, of his having to listen to all that she said and and answer her—no, then he knew he would not—not if she brought him all the gold there was in Norway. He shuddered with aversion at the thought of having her sleeping here between himself and the wall through the long, sleepless nights. At such times he could not possibly bear to have an entirely strange woman close to him. Torhild—if she had been sleeping by his side now, he knew that whether asleep or awake her loyal heart would be full of care for his welfare; he would not feel ashamed with her, were his mind never so restless.

So it was: he often thought it hard that an instinct which he did not himself understand forbade him to fetch home the lowly Torhild and resume his concubinage with her. But his whole being rebelled if he did but call to mind that his best and most faithful friends sought to have him married to the rich and virtuous widow of Svein of Roaldstad.

He remembered having once thought that in the end it might turn out that his life would shape itself after the manner of this—happiness. When it began to dawn on him that Ingunn was not destined for a long life. At that time he had thrust such thoughts from him as infidelity. But then she *was* here, she was his wife, and behind every grey and evil day and every fresh misfortune, every fresh drop of bitterness that fell into his cup, he had known that he would rather have the life he had, with Ingunn, than any other lot without her.

But now she was gone. And it would cost him but a word to acquire Roaldstad and wealth, a healthy and capable wife, heirs to all they might possess in common, a firm alliance with the kinsfolk whom he liked, a powerful position in the district. And then Olav felt that rather than have all this happiness he would *die*.

The brightness had passed from Ingunn's memory since that adventure in London; it was as though he could no longer keep her distinct from the other. All seemed blind, unthinking, bestially stupid—that she had frittered away the happiness of both, that he himself had strayed from every path he should have followed, till he now felt as though his own soul were nothing but a little grey, hardened stone.

Since that night after the pilgrimage all the thoughts he had struggled with seemed to have turned to stones. He remembered them and knew them in a way—as the lad in the fairy tale recognized his friends in the pillar-stones outside the giant's castle. But they left him dull and cold. He knew that in this new calm that had come upon him he was a poorer man than before, when he had lived in fear and pain: beneath every stab of remorse and every longing for peace there had been something that was much greater and stronger than his fear: he loved Him from whom he fled, and even to the end he had secretly hoped that the hour would come when he could fly no more. Sooner or later, he must have thought, he would be reconciled with God—without its being left to him to choose. But he had been forced to choose and choose again. And so long had he chosen himself that he had lost even his love of God. But therewithal the fire and strength seemed to have gone out of his love for all else he had held dear in this world.

God, Jesus Christ, Mary—once he had only had to think upon these words for his heart to glow with fervour within him. Now it mattered nothing to him whether he said his prayers in church or at home, morning and evening, if others were by and it was the time, or whether he omitted to pray when alone. But this new indifference was as much poorer than his old torment as a heap of ashes is poorer than a blazing fire.

But Ingunn—were her memory never so faded and burned out, he would not cast it out to make room for new possessions. And as his life was now, he would neither own nor bring into it this happiness he was offered.

Olav Half-priest had once told him of Hvitserk's howe, the largest of the mounds here by the brow of the wood. It was before the Christian faith had come to the land; the race of Inggjald then possessed Hestviken, that stock of which his grandfather's grandmother had come, and the name of the chief was Aale Hvitserk. He had been a famous viking, but now he was in extreme old age. Then his enemies burned his homestead of Hestviken—this was the first of the three burnings that had laid the manor in ashes. Aale's sons cleared the site and had timber brought to build the houses anew, but Aale let his house-carls cast up a barrow, and on the day they set about dragging off the charred beams of Aale's hall, the old man went into the mound and bade his thralls close up the earthen house with stones.

Olav Audunsson remembered that he had shaken his head when his old namesake told him this tale—but at the same time he had thought him a doughty fellow, that same old heathen.

Now he lay in the darkness smiling a little at this thought. He had taken good heed not to speak of it to any priest, but he offered a Yule cup to the spirit of the mound and carried out a bowl of ale on the eve of other great festivals. Even Arnvid did so at his own home—'twas no great sin, said he, if one did but go quietly about it, without asking anything of the dead in return. Now maybe he ought to be more mindful of his offerings—like enough he would meet with his heathen ancestor in the end.

2

IT had chanced, while Olav was in England, that Eirik had received full assurance that he was true-born.

He had had to go up to Rynjul one day with a packload—cups and vessels that Olav had borrowed for his wife's funeral feast. Now they had a very snappish little bitch tied up in the yard there, and that day she had slipped out of her thong, dashed up, and bitten Eirik in the leg as he came in between the houses. Eirik kicked the bitch so that she rolled over on the grass howling. Torgrim rushed out of a door in a great rage:

"—afraid of a little dog like that—and kicking at a bitch—none but a child of bawdry such as you would do the like!"

Eirik had come into the hall, and Una was counting over her vessels; then the lad burst out:

"Una—those words that Torgrim said—are they *true*?"

"Are what true?" she repeated from among her wooden cups.

"Child of bawdry—that is the same as whoreson, is it not, Una?" whispered Eirik dolefully.

"Yes—why?" She looked up and saw the lad standing there, pale as bast, his narrow young face stricken with despair. "Holy Mary—what ails you, Eirik?"

"*Am* I that? Answer me truly, Una mine!"

Una Arnesdatter stood speechless.

"Ay, I guessed it long ago," whispered Eirik.

"*What* did you guess? Are you not ashamed—to say such a thing of your father—and your mother, who lies under the sod? Help us, what have you taken into your head now again!"

"You must have heard him say it, Torgrim—Father himself called me bastard once."

"You may be sure," said Una more gently, "neither of the two would have called you such bad names if you had been so indeed. Surely you have wit enough to see that 'twas only the word of an angry man."

"Then *was* Mother married to Father?" asked Eirik.

"You have no need to ask that. Olav kept the poor woman in good and honourable state so long as she lived. You can have seen naught else."

"He took the keys from her and gave them to his leman," muttered Eirik. "That was a year and more ere Mother lost her health."

"Say no more of that, boy." Una turned red with indignation. "You do not understand it. I will speak no ill of your mother, poor soul that she was—'twas not *her* fault that her kinsmen dealt falsely by Olav, still less that she was as she was, sickly and feeble-minded. None could expect a man to be well pleased with such a marriage as fell to the lot of our kinsman. Scarce had the Stein-finnssons got the rich heir into their power when they bound the little boy in bonds of betrothal to one of their own children; and then they cheated him of all he should have received with his bride; never has Olav had help or honour of that alliance, but he was forced to take the ailing woman, for they had trapped him into her bed ere he was fully grown."

Una talked thus for a good while and said what she thought of Olav's married life. She was faithful to her own kin and fond of Olav as though he had been her brother; but though she had always been helpful and kind to his wife, she had had but a moderate liking for Ingunn, and in her heart she had called her a worm.

Together with Eirik's first sense of boundless relief on knowing that none could drive him away from Hestviken, there came a smouldering indignation against his father. He might have spared himself these years of anxious insecurity—but it was his father's fault: so barefaced had he been in his evil life with that cursed jade Torhild that it was only natural Eirik should fear the worst. Wrong, wrong, wrong had his mother suffered under her own roof.

Eirik spent that summer at Hestviken. Every corner of the old walls, every crack in the smooth-worn, reddish-grey rocks had a face that met his loving glances with a look of gentle kindness. The strip of seaweed under his own rocks looked different from seaweed elsewhere. No other wharves or boats smelt so good as theirs. When he took up the oars in his own boat or put out his nets, his whole body was filled with delight—*he* owned them! He caressed every animal he met that was theirs. Eirik took an ear of barley and laid it on his wrist over the pulse so that it crawled up under the sleeve—this old child's game had become a sort of magic ceremony: it was *his* corn. He need no longer be afraid as he lived and moved among all these things—they would never vanish away out of his hands.

Eirik's memory of his mother had quickly faded. In her last years, when she never left her bed, she had already passed out of the boy's world; after her death he had soon ceased to think of her. Now that he was so indignant with his father, he felt an added resentment on his mother's behalf; his affection for her awakened, he often longed for her. He had been so fond of her as long as she was well and he could be with her—and his father had treated her so harshly and cruelly.

But it only needed a friendly word from Olav, and Eirik forgot all his bitterness. Afterwards he remembered it and was angry at his own weakness. But no sooner did the man show him the least indulgence, no sooner did Eirik see but a shadow of the pale, frozen smile on his father's lips as he spoke to him, than the son became insensible to all but his abject adoration of his father.

A short time after Olav's return from England, Eirik heard the rumours that he was to marry Disa Erlandsdatter. Up at Rundmyr they gossiped freely about everything.

Eirik's temper rebelled again. He would not have a stepmother. He would not hear of joint heirs in Hestviken. No strangers should come, bringing new customs or anything new. All should be his and Cecilia's, the manor and the wharf and the woods on the Bull and along the back of the Horse Crag, Kverndal and Saltviken. He knew every path there, he had his own places, outlooks, and hidden grassy hollows among the grey rocks toward the sea; his habit was to go there, simply to sit there alone rejoicing vaguely and obscurely in the possession of these hiding-places. The hunting in the forest, the sealing, the fishery, all this would one day be in his control. But the last and inmost thought, which always made him mad with passion—for he knew he had no power to hinder its coming to pass—was that one day another might come between him and his father. He even spun long fabulous dreams of the deed that would one day make him his father's favourite.

The seal-hunting wellnigh failed that year. And Olav lost a good new six-oared boat out in the skerries; the painter was cut one night, whether it was the work of an enemy or someone had stolen the boat. So Olav came home from sea in a gloomy temper, even for him.

Some days after, he had business that took him inland, and Eirik was to accompany him as far as the church; it was a Wednesday in the ember days, and Sira Hallbjörn insisted that all who could should attend church in the ember days.

The frost fog was thick that morning and left a film of ice on rocks and woodwork. Olav stood outside the stable door, while Eirik led out the horses and was about to saddle them. Olav was standing there, sleepy and dazed and fasting, when suddenly he turned to his son and said hotly:

"Will you not rub the bit before you put it in the horse's mouth
—in this searing cold?"

" 'Tis not cold," replied Eirik sullenly. " 'Tis only the raw
weather that feels cold."

"Hold your tongue! Will you teach me to judge of the weather?
If you had that scorching cold iron in your own jaws—"

Eirik snatched an iron rod that was stuck in the stable wall and
bit on it. His father pulled it from him and flung it on the rock.

"You see—you are bleeding!"

" 'Twas not that it scorched me—you tore my mouth."

"Be silent," said Olav curtly, "and have done now."

About midday some of the church folk sat in the priest's house
taking a bite of the food they had brought, before setting out for
home. The wound at the corner of Eirik's mouth began to bleed
again, and he told some of the other lads how he had got it; but he
said it was his father who had taken the bit and forced it into his
jaws.

Then he noticed that the silence which followed was heavy
with scorn.

At last a boy said: "Shame on you, Eirik—do you let your father
make a jade of you?"

Eirik look around, hesitating. He had meant to boast of what
had befallen him. When he noticed the scorn on the others' faces,
something seemed to shrivel up within him. So he would make
up for it.

"No. But indeed it were useless for me to stand up against him,"
he said, warming with excitement. "I can tell you, I pulled off the
halter and struck at him. But he has the strength of a troll, my
father. One time, while he was with the Earl, they made wagers,
how big a load he could lift. Father put his shoulders under the
bench and raised himself till he stood upright. Eight men sat on
that bench."

He was met with icy silence.

"Then says the Earl: 'If you can lift the table-top Olav Audunsson, it shall be yours, with all the silver that stands upon it.' My
father took the table and lifted it at arm's length."

" 'Tis almost like the story you told us last year, Sira Hallbjörn,"
said a young girl, with a giggle; "of that Christian knight who was
a captive with the Saracen earl—what was his name?" There was
a hearty laugh from some of the grown people.

Sira Hallbjörn was sitting apart on his bed. That day he was neither surly nor frolicsome; he seemed rather dull. He looked coldly at the maid.

"You remember, Sira Hallbjörn—at my brother's wedding?"

"I know no such story. Your memory is at fault."

But a little later, when folk were breaking up, the priest came abruptly behind Eirik Olavsson and took him firmly by the arm:

"What is your meaning with such talk—do you tell lies of your father?"

"Nay, I lied not, Sira," Eirik answered coolly.

"You lied." Sira Hallbjörn gave him a blow under the ear. "And now you lie to your parish priest. The Devil is in you, I believe. Be off with you now!"

At dusk Olav Audunsson rode up to the priest's door. He would not go in, he said, it was too late. Sitting in the saddle he handed Sira Hallbjörn the casket of letters and turned to ride away at once. Sira Hallbjörn came out and walked at his side as Olav rode at a foot's pace between the fences.

"Master Olav," said the priest hotly, "you should not suffer your son to assort with those folk you have thought fit to set up at Rundmyr. 'Twill do the boy no good, what he learns there."

Olav knew not what to reply to this. As he said nothing, the priest continued, repeating what Eirik had said of his father: "—he makes himself a mockery in the eyes of the whole parish, your son, by lying in this fashion—and lying so foolishly." Meanwhile they had come to the crossroads, and the priest laid his hand on Olav's bridle and held it as he looked up into the other's face. There was still a glimmer of daylight within the mist that was gathering again—Olav saw with surprise that the priest seemed greatly agitated.

"I cannot guess why Eirik should say that." Olav told him what had taken place between him and his son that morning.

"Ay, so goes it when the young have bad masters."

Olav frowned and puckered his lips in a sort of smile, but made no answer. Eirik hardly needed a master to teach him lying—that talent he was surely born with.

"Had any wise man counselled my father as I now counsel you," said Sira Hallbjörn, "then he had taken me away from the house where I was fostered after my mother died. I was a pious child while I was with her—she had vowed me to God while I was yet unborn. But then Father sent me to a foster-father, and he was of Lappish race—"

"Do there dwell Lapps in Valdres?" asked Olav; he felt he ought to say something.

The priest nodded. "I saw many a strange thing as I grew up, Olav. They are the most excellent hunters, the Lapps—and divers creatures are abroad in the mountains, both beasts and men—and others. Since then it goes ill with me to live elsewhere. I yearned not to return thither during the years I was in foreign lands, resorting to one school after another. But these folk hereabouts—they provoke me so that I lose patience—"

"So it seems." Olav could not forbear to smile a little mockingly.

"Ay," said the priest hotly. " 'Tis not good to dwell in these parts. You have no friends here either, Olav."

"So it seems," said Olav again. "But I know not if it be because — Maybe folk are no different here than elsewhere."

"Have you ever taken part in hunting reindeer?" asked Sira Hallbjörn abruptly—"at the old deer-pits among the fells? Have you seen the reindeer herd on the move—many thousand deer?"

"Nay," said Olav. "I have never seen a living reindeer."

"Bear me company some time"—there was almost an entreaty in the priest's voice, so eager was he—"when I go home to visit my brothers."

"I thank you, Sira Hallbjörn. Should the occasion suit, I would gladly bear you company one day."

They took leave of each other. The priest said once more:

"But keep Eirik from Rundmyr. If not, they will trick the lad into a share of their stealings—or father some wench's brat on him, before he is two years older. And you would be ill served with that, both of you, Olav."

Olav thought deeply over his talk with the priest as he rode down in the dark. He felt something like disappointment. Not that he had any quarrel with his parish priest—on the contrary; he was one of the few men in the district who had not yet been in conflict with him. But he too had thought there was some secret about Sira Hallbjörn—and then his being exiled, as it were, to this parish, outside all the positions and dignities to which he might be entitled by his high birth and his learning. So Olav had half expected that one day something or other would come to light about him. And now it seemed nothing but this, that Hallbjörn Erlingsson thrived ill down here in the lowlands and found it hard to be friends with their people, being headstrong and whimsical as fell-dwellers often are. No doubt it was little to his liking to have the quiet charge of a parish church and be at the call of any who had need of his ministrations.

Formerly Olav had instinctively sought the company of such men as he felt to be pure of heart and faithful toward God. Without thinking of it he had shunned the black sheep when he met them. Now he felt just as much at his ease among men who were less strict—who had the name, in any case, of being not too strict with themselves, though for aught he cared they might judge others strictly. In a way he was not displeased at heart to find some fault or other in a man, especially if it were a priest or a monk. Nor did he ever inquire into rumours now; he held his peace when the talk was of such things, but lent an ear, and that no longer with repugnance or sensitiveness.

He thought too of what Sira Hallbjörn had said about Eirik and it vexed him. But he did not care to speak to the boy about it —much better seem to know nothing. But he would have to forbid the boy haunting Rundmyr.

And he did so. But Eirik did not obey. Olav came to hear of it. Sometimes he spoke harshly to his son about it, but at other times he let it pass, as though he did not know Eirik had been there.

He had acted foolishly in letting Anki and Liv have Rundmyr. If they would only keep to what was his—that he could afford to wink at—but now there were murmurs abroad, folk found that there were light fingers at Rundmyr. At last Olav had to take Arnketil to task about it: "Meseems you two might live awhile on what you pick up at Hestviken." The man promised to mend his ways—but Olav was not so sure that the promise was worth much.

And now it might be difficult to be rid of them. When Arnketil came and asked him to hold their babe at the font, he had not the heart to refuse the poor simple man. Moreover he thought that if he agreed to be godfather to the boy, no one could suspect him of commerce with the mother. It never entered Olav's mind that, so far as he knew, no one had had such a thought; it was only himself who feared folk might hit upon this. There had been a hint of it when she had her first child—but then he was common talk over the matter of Torhild, and there are always those who are

ready to make a man blacker than he is. But by accepting the god-
child, he had now bound himself to support its parents.

To Eirik, Arnketil had been in some sort as a foster-father, so
it was not easy to part the lad entirely from him. And Liv came
out to Hestviken with her babe on her back—stayed there the
whole day, dealing out good advice to the serving-women and
talking of how everything had been done when she was in charge.

Torhild had turned out right in saying he acted unwisely in
housing such people so near to the manor. Olav thought of it with
a dull bitterness: that he could be so placed that he could not
bring in Torhild and profit by her sensible advice.

It was a vexation to Olav that Eirik forced himself thus upon
his notice and his thoughts. And again and again he came upon
this incomprehensible mendacity. Each time it was like a riddle
to Olav. He had told lies himself, hard and cold enough to split
rocks—he had not forgotten that—but then he had known why
he lied; he had lied because he was forced to it. But Eirik lied and
lied, and his father could never espy anything that looked like a
plausible reason—he did not lie for gain and he seldom lied for
concealment. Olav had seen that, though he had not been so care-
ful to note how seldom Eirik attempted to deny or to lie if he
were asked a straight question: the lad was quite ready to confess
even his worst misdeeds; falteringly, blushing and blinking, he
said how it was, if he were asked. So it was almost as though Eirik
made up these lying stories of his because it amused him—incomprehensible as such a thing seemed to Olav.

Year in and year out Olav's feelings for the child had swung
between a vague longing to be able to like this young being who
had been placed in his power—and dislike of this stranger who
was as a thorn buried in his flesh. Now at last they were coming
to rest for good. There were times when Eirik's incomprehensible
and positively high-spirited mendacity aroused hatred in Olav's
heart: as though the very lie he had taken upon himself as a yoke
were incarnate in Eirik's person, mocking him in the smile of the
fairy-like, brown-eyed boy.

Nevertheless there were other times when it was not so.

This second summer after his wife's death Olav had to attend
the Eidsiva Thing. He was short-handed now at Hestviken and

could not easily take any man from his work. So it came about that Eirik was to ride with his father.

Olav had little mind to this long journey, nor had he any great desire to meet his brother-in-law. He had not been north of Oslo in all the thirteen years since he had brought home Ingunn, except that one time when he fetched Eirik, and then it had been winter.

Now he took the summer road northward through Raumarike. It was fine, sunny weather, but warm for travelling in the middle of the day. So they found a suitable place near the road; Eirik unsaddled the horses and hobbled them. After their meal Olav and Eirik stretched themselves on the ground. The lad fell asleep at once.

Olav lay with his head on his saddle, gazing before him through the tissue of grass. The meadow was golden yellow with buttercups, flower upon flower, and round the little brown watercourse below were silvery tufts of bog-cotton. Beyond the brook blazed a mass of red campion in the shade of the alders. He looked at the flowers as though they were old acquaintances he had met again after an interval of years: it was true he noticed at home too when this grass or that came out, taking auguries from it of how the summer would turn out. But here as he lay idly watching the flowers blooming on land of which he knew not the owner, it was different—bringing back to him in some measure the tracts in which he had spent his youth.

Great silver-grey clouds shining at the verge welled up over the fir-tops and spread quietly and with wonderful swiftness over the whole warm blue sky—down on the ground not a breath stirred. Now they came over and put out the sunshine. Olav drew his cloak over his face because of the midges and slept.

In the course of the afternoon they came out of a forest and saw a great manor lying before them under the sinking sun. It looked like some great man's seat there on the top of its mound, with a little white stone church to the north of the group of houses, and the meadows surrounding it on every side. Eirik cried out with joy, so grand it seemed to him. Olav made no reply to his exclamation.

The bridle-path led up the hill and straight through the manor. This was no less imposing when one came up to it, with countless houses, new and old, in two rows by the side of the way, and every sign of activity and habitation.

When they had come down into the valley and were riding by the bank of a river, Olav asked Eirik: "Know you what that manor is called, Eirik?"

"Nay?" asked the boy eagerly.

"That was Dyfrin."

"Was it!" After a while Eirik said in a hushed voice, with strong emotion: "*We* should have been there, if we had our rights—is it not so, Father?"

"So it is." Olav rode in silence for a few moments. Then he asked with a sort of smile: "Which of the two manors do you like best, Eirik—Dyfrin or Hestviken?"

"Hestviken," answered Eirik warmly, without hesitation.

"Dyfrin is more than twice as large—you could see that?"

"No matter. At Dyfrin they have not the sea either—or wharves or boats. But 'tis galling to call to mind the injustice. Methinks a man who worked so much injustice to the landholders of the country as that Sverre—he could not be fitted to be king—"

"Some injustice must be done by every man who will gain his cause," replied Olav.

Eirik wished to hear of the old traditions—of Torgils Fivil and his sons and of the widow whom King Sverre gave to one of his men. Olav replied to his questions. But then they saw the road lying before them across a sandy plain, level and easy, and Olav urged on the horses; with that their talk came to an end.

Hallvard Steinfinnsson gave a hearty welcome both to his brother-in-law and to his nephew. With the passing of years Hallvard had grown very like his father, Olav saw, and he also resembled Steinfinn in his ways; he was merry, open-handed and not over-wise. He had the eldest son of Tora and Haakon Gautsson with him at the Thing. Eirik had looked forward with great joy to meeting his mother's kindred, but though they were so friendly to him, Eirik seemed unusually shy, and he kept close to his father at all times and places while the Thing lasted.

Quite unexpectedly Olav met his kinsmen from Tveit in Soleyar at the gathering: Gudbrand and Jon Helgessons with two sons and a son-in-law. Olav had met the men of Tveit only once before—at the time he was engaged in discharging the fines for the slaying of Einar Kolbeinsson, and then he had thought they gave themselves little trouble for a young kinsman. Now they were getting on in years, both he and the Helgessons, and it seemed late to take up the ties of kinship. But he exchanged words with them when they met. And on one of the last days of the gathering, when Hallvard had asked Olav to come and drink with him at his inn, he found the men of Tveit there; Hallvard had fetched them in to show courtesy to his brother-in-law.

Hallvard lodged in the same house Steinfinn had used when he came to the Thing. Olav could not recall it; he was not sure that this hall they now sat drinking in was the same in which they had betrothed him to Ingunn. Apart from that he remembered everything so clearly—Ingunn and Steinfinn and his own father —ay, he scarce remembered his father apart from that evening— and many of the guests' faces he could recall as though it were yesterday.

Olav was very taciturn the whole evening, but the others paid no heed to that; they drank, and at last they seemed entirely to forget that he sat there. But what chiefly occupied Olav's attention was Eirik—he kept so quiet and was utterly unlike himself as they were used to seeing him at home.

The lad sat on the outer bench together with the younger ones from Tveit. Olav looked at him: old feelings, by no means unfriendly, were strangely revived in him—during the journey Eirik had not chanced to do anything that might irritate his father. He sat there very quiet and well-mannered, talking easily in low tones with Knut and Joar. The dark-skinned, sharp-featured boyish face was beginning to put on a maturer look: the forehead was high and narrow under the shock of black hair, the nose was high and thin, hooked, or rather indented, from the very root down to the bridge; the mouth was prominent, with a pronounced curve in the upper jaw; when listening he was apt to show something of his front teeth, and they were very white; the two midmost were very slightly crossed. Nevertheless his face was far from ugly: he had a fine complexion, red-cheeked and browned by the sun, the lips bright red, the eyes unusually large and pale brown, so light that they made one think of amber, or bog-water in sunlight. Olav felt, as a fleeting quiver through his mind, that here he sat in company with his own kinsmen and brother-in-law, and he found little to say to them. And underneath the honest, open ties that bound him to the others, the ties of blood and of the law, he was joined to this slender, swarthy lad who sat like a stranger among the fair, red Tveit boys—he knew not himself how indissolubly.

Hallvard had wine, and so it was near midnight before the guests broke up. It was a half hour's walk down to the booth where Olav lay, and at the parting of the roads he stood awhile talking to some men who were going the other way. Then he walked on quickly with Eirik. The night was mild and so light that the moon seemed quite pale and faint. When they had gone some distance they heard the men of Tveit before them on the road—they were drunken and noisy, and Olav had no desire for their company. So he turned out of the path with Eirik; they strolled along the hillside, which was covered with great rocks and juniper and other bushes; a few dun horses grazed among the tussocks in the moonlight.

They came out on some little crags, and beneath them lay a great bog, which would be tiresome to go round; so Olav sat down to let the Tveit folk get ahead. But now it sounded as if they had come to a halt on the path just below here—they made no move, and Gudbrand vomited with loud retching, while the others formed a ring and made sport of him. Eirik lay on his stomach on the close-cropped grass, laughing quietly and mimicking to his father the words and noises that came up from below.

"Look at the moon, Father," said Eirik. The half-moon was near its setting now, floating on its back above the tree-tops in the west, with a few thin strips of golden cloud lying under it. Near it was a great star blazing alone in the pale blue sky.

"Ay," said Olav. "We shall have wind."

"It looks like a ship," said Eirik, laughing quietly at his own idea, "sailing on the sea—and the big star is like a dog running after the ship."

"Nay, Eirik"—Olav could not help smiling—"how can a dog run after a ship that sails on the sea?"

"Oh yes," said the boy eagerly, "they have left it behind—and now it runs along the shore, in and out among the headlands, barking and howling after the boat."

The boy's words reminded Olav of something—he had once heard or dreamed something like this about a dog that ran along the shore wailing after a ship that sailed away—a dog, or a man, that had been left behind.

He looked down at the lad's upturned face—quite pale it seemed in the twilight, and the wide-open eyes were dark in the shadow. It was as though the man in moving had tightened the invisible bond between them.

"Of the noise of cats' treading and the beards of women and the roots of the rocks and the breath of the fishes and the spittle of the birds—" it was a rigmarole he had known as a child, of someone who had forged a chain, and it was more pliant than silk and bound faster than fetters of steel—a wild beast was to stay bound in it till doomsday.

It was quiet down on the road. "Come," said Olav, and unconsciously he let his hand drop on the boy's shoulder, kept it there a moment.

They went down and found the path again. Of the Tveit folk they saw no more and reached without delay the booth where Olav had hired night quarters for them.

The bed was exceedingly narrow. Eirik fell asleep at once, and very soon he turned over in his sleep, so that he almost lay on top of his father.

In the narrow, uncomfortable couch, with the darkness around thick with the smell of men, Olav lay feeling the pressure of Eirik's thin, slender body, the warm scent of his skin and hair—without distaste, with an unreasoning sense of pity. Though only God and His blessed Mother could tell why he should have compassion on Eirik. He knew of nothing to make him pity his son, but it was as though the lad's very youth made him soft-hearted—though that is a fault one soon grows out of, thought Olav.

Olav got no proper sleep, but lay, as it were, rolling back and forth between sleep and waking like a piece of driftwood on the beach. But after an hour or two, when he heard some men moving in the other rooms, Olav gently withdrew from beside the sleeping lad and went out to see to the horses himself. He had not the heart to wake the boy.

3

THE FRIENDSHIP that had grown up between Olav Audunsson and his kinsfolk at Rynjul and Skikkjustad was declining again. Una had gone so far, that day in the spring when he sailed her home, that they could not honourably carry the matter farther. And Olav made no move. So they avoided each other. But that the people of Rynjul resented it Olav was well aware.

How his conduct was interpreted by his neighbours he had a chance of hearing one day when he met Sira Hallbjörn down on the wharf. The priest burst out in his abrupt way:

"A great gull you were, Olav, to take up again with that Torhild woman—she coaxed you into buying her wretched cot and, worse than that, you let her spoil a good marriage for you."

"What idle talk is this?" Olav's face turned red as fire. "I ask counsel of no one, either in buying land or taking a wife—in such things I do as I *will*."

"Pooh! You think so, I can well believe. You thought, no doubt, you had your will with her when she did as she willed. Torhild Björnsdatter is the wiser of you two. Beware now, Olav, that she make not another halter for you of her girdle."

Olav replied angrily: "Howbeit, this can be no concern of yours, Sira Hallbjörn, so long as I have not lain with her again. Belike I may take counsel where I will—I have not begged it of you!"

He turned his back and leaped down into his boat.

But afterwards a raging desire for Torhild flared up in him again—day and night, day and night. Simply to take her to him in defiance. If folk were resolved to meddle with his affairs, then let them have something to meddle with. And Björn—he had banned the child's memory, driven back his thoughts whenever they would go that way. Now it came upon him—was it worth the trouble? So many a thing had gone amiss with him, should he not after all take what good there was to take?

Waking and sleeping, he dreamed of his son. But behind the image of the little fair-skinned boy he saw the other fair child—Cecilia. For her sake he must stand firm and deny himself that which he desired. It would not be good for her to grow up in a house of which her father's leman was mistress. Not yet had he wrecked Cecilia's future, and he would not do so either.

Olav saw little of his daughter now. If she ran out into the yard to play and her father stopped to speak to her, Cecilia had scarce time to answer him. At night she slept with Ragna in Torhild's old house. But Ragna was only a poor serving-woman, unfitted to rear the daughter of a man of Olav's condition when the maid grew a little older. Moreover Ragna had all the household duties to perform and her own three children to herd. The eldest lay outside the house door all day long, drivelling and snoring and rocking his great head—the poor child lacked something of his wits—but the year-old twins were lively as kittens and could be seen creeping and crawling everywhere in the yard and across the thresholds.

Olav was at his wits' end to know what to do with this daughter, to have her brought up in seemly fashion. Maybe *this* would have been easier if he had married Disa—though one never knows with any woman how she will turn out as a stepmother.

And there was this Liv hanging about the place early and late— Cecilia clung to her—she remembered no mother else.

Then quite unexpectedly a way appeared out of these difficulties, it seemed to Olav. One day two townsmen from Tunsberg came to him with a message that Asger Magnusson lay dying in the Premonstratensian convent in their town and would speak with him. Olav had nothing special to do that day, and the wind was fair; so he sailed over at once.

It seemed strange to him that they should thus come up again in his life, one after another, the men he had known in his youth and for years had wellnigh forgotten. It was almost as if he had come out of the fairy hill—and as they say of those whom the fairies have carried off, so it was with him; he felt a stranger among these men and cared little for them one way or the other. Not that there had ever been any warmth of feeling between him and Hallvard Steinfinnsson or the men of Tveit. Asger in any case had been his friend: they were distantly related to each other, and when he was in Denmark he and Asger had associated not a little, though they had never had much to say to each other—this friendship was the only tie that had not broken of those he had formed in his days of outlawry. Apart from this the years with his uncle at Vikings' Bay seemed to Olav like a half-forgotten dream. But Asger had come hither to Norway with the banished Danish lords, and so they had been brothers-in-arms on the raids against Denmark. At the thought of those war summers Olav's heart rejoiced—he longed to see his comrade again. He caught himself feeling thus as he stood at the steering-oar keeping an eye on the familiar sea-marks. Asger was surely not so near dying as the townsmen said, 'twould not be like him.

But next morning after mass when he was taken to the upper chamber where the Dane lay abed, he saw at once that death could not be far off. Asger's great broad face was greenish grey beneath his red beard, and his powerful, rather hoarse voice had shrunk to a broken wheeze. And he said as much himself as soon as he saw his friend: " 'Tis all over with me now, Olav."

On a chest under the little dormer in the gable sat an old woman and a little girl. The woman stood up and gave her hand to Olav when he greeted her. Her appearance was such as to cause some wonder in Olav: she was a good head taller than he, broad-shouldered, thin and erect in her black weeds; outside her coif she wore a dark-blue widow's veil. The narrow face, white as bone, must once have been passing fair: her great blue eyes still shone beneath bushy, iron-grey brows, and the ridge of her fine hooked nose was glossy as ivory. But her cheeks were furrowed with long wrinkles and she had strong tufts of grey hair at the corners of her mouth. She was the mother of Asger's wife, and her name was Mærta Birgersdatter. Olav had never before heard of any living woman being called Mærta, but this one looked as though she brought no shame on her patroness, the good lady of Bethany.

She went out at once, and Olav seated himself on the edge of his friend's bed. Asger was now an outlaw both in Norway and in Denmark; he had had the misfortune to slay a rich man in his home district of Hising, where his wife had brought him an estate. And the slain man was a friend both of King Haakon and of Count Jacob. Nevertheless he had fled hither to Tunsberg; he was well known of old in the convent here, and so sick was he that they might well let him rest in peace while treating for his atonement, or die in sanctuary. For the Abbot maintained that this convent had right of asylum, though it was doubtful if this had ever been confirmed. But whatever might be the upshot of this, there was his mother-in-law and his child; would Olav take them in? Olav said yes at once and gave Asger his hand on it.

He had heard at the time that Asger had made a good marriage in the south. But now Asger told him that his wife had died three years before, and he himself had been broken in health of late years, after he had been shipwrecked one winter; he had suffered some inward hurt and since then he had been spitting blood and had little joy of his food.

"And yet you were not so broken but that you cut down Sir Paal in his shirt of mail?" asked Olav, and could not resist smiling.

Asger laughed and coughed weakly. No— It was the mother-in-law, Olav guessed, who had been most helpful in drawing Asger into these quarrels—ay, she looked to be the right one for that, and Asger had never been wont to sing small either. But the man was used to the ups and downs of fortune, and now he took his ill luck calmly. But his child's future seemed to weigh heavily on the father's mind.

Olav turned his eyes to the little girl sitting on the chest; he held out a hand to her. "Come hither, Bothild, my foster-daughter-to-be—shall we talk together, you and I?"

The child sat still as a mouse, and when the strange man spoke to her, she dropped her eyelids—she had thick black lashes. She was a little bigger than Cecilia—six winters old, her father said.

Olav saw that she was a most comely child—though she resembled Asger. She had the same broad face as he, a low, broad forehead, eyes far apart, and a short, square chin, but her skin was bright and clear, her forehead white as milk under the smooth, auburn hair that lay in two heavy plaits over her chest. When she looked up at Olav for an instant her eyes were a pure sky-blue. The lay brother who came up with Olav had given her a big apple, and there she sat clasping it untasted with both hands—she looked so still and timid, as though she understood how friendless and forlorn she was in the world.

Olav had never liked the smell of apples—it seemed to him mawkish or musty—and now it was mingled with the smell of sickness and bed-straw and fusty woollen garments. And the sight of the child's motionless grief stirred up a flood of vague tenderness and pain in Olav's breast. Memories of all the defenceless children he had seen in the course of his life, of mortal wounds inflicted on the weak and helpless, and every thought he had had of his own children, if they should be orphaned, of the child whose father he was, but over whom he could never have a father's right—all this passed through his mind like a stream of shadows. He went over to where the little maid was sitting and caressed her soft, cool cheek.

"Will you not look at me, Bothild? I mean you well. I have a daughter at home, Cecilia—you are to be foster-sisters and live together. How will that please you?"

Without a sound Bothild slid down off the chest and slipped under Olav's arm. She was away to her father's couch, nestled up to him, and took his hand in both hers.

"I will be with you, dear Father mine," she said miserably.

Olav picked up her apple from the floor and gave it to her.

Asger Magnusson opened his little bright-blue eyes wide, as though in great pain; his voice was feeble with helplessness:

"You must not take it amiss, kinsman Olav. I have given this daughter of mine her way more than was good for her." He put his arm about her and clasped the child's dark little head against his shoulder. "You must not think ill of her for this."

"Nay, nay." Olav sat on the bedstead and turned his eyes away. He felt quite abashed with pity for them both.

About a month later Olav received a message that Asger Magnusson was dead, but it was not till after Yule that he could sail down and fetch the old woman and the child. The Abbot told Olav that the dead man's goods had been seized, but doubtless Mærta Birgersdatter had saved no small store of movables in that great chest of hers. Since Asger when living had always proved himself a friend of the monks, the Abbot offered, if Olav would rather escape the charge of the poor child, to give him a letter to the lady Groa in Oslo, asking if she would take Bothild for the love of God—the little maid seemed well fitted to be a nun, for she was quiet and gentle, a winning child. Olav thanked him, but said he had promised the dead man to be to Bothild in the place of a father.

As Olav left the Abbot's chamber he ran straight on the child—she was on her knees in the gallery playing chuckie-stones. The weather was bitter and boisterous, sleet and snow blew in under the roof of the gallery; so Olav spoke to her, bidding her get up. Bothild did not answer, but obeyed at once. Olav took her by the hand; it was icy cold, and he rubbed her hands between his. He had occasion to go down to his boat, and he asked if she would go with him. Bothild nodded, and he led her down.

Her little hand lay so submissively within his that it made him fond: if he took Cecilia's it slipped away again at once; she could never walk quietly by the side of a grown person. But he could not get a word out of his foster-daughter beyond a faint yes and no.

He took Bothild with him back to the guest-chamber, and as he sat down by the fire to dry himself, he drew Bothild up on his knee. She settled herself there, leaning her head against his breast; such a sweet scent came from her hair. Olav lifted up her face and kissed her on the mouth—felt the living movement of the soft childish lips—she kissed him back. A warm, melting thrill went through him.

Eirik had often been ready to sit on his knees when he was small, but Cecilia always wanted to get down as soon as he had picked her up. And if it chanced that he tried to kiss his little daughter, he noticed that Cecilia did not like it.

For the last year Olav had slept in the hearth-room, in the bed that had been his marriage-bed. He slept better than he had done for many years, but even now he often lay long awake. At such times it was pleasanter to lie here than in the closet; there the daylight never penetrated, so that its air was always chillingly sour and musty, and there was always a cold, raw smell of oil and food that they stored in there during the winter. The great room smelt of men and smoke; even at night a hint of cosiness seemed to be given off by the hearth, where live embers were hidden beneath the ashes. A piece had been broken off the cover of the smoke-vent one night when it was blowing, and Olav had not yet had a new one made. When the moon shone he could see a corner of light on the parchment pane of the vent, and he could watch the dawn. Olav liked that.

Now he moved back into the closet; Mærta and the children were to have the south bed in the hearth-room.

Olav had expected Cecilia to scream and make a great to-do when she was told she was to sleep with the strangers instead of with Ragna, as she had been accustomed. But it turned out otherwise. He had come in to Hestviken late in the day, having taken

three days on the voyage from Tunsberg, as he had met with bad
weather and run for shelter. Bothild was more dead than alive
when Olav carried her up to the houses—she sat the whole evening on the stool where he had first put her down, feeling as if
she were still in the boat. Folk tramped in an out, carrying one
thing and another, and meanwhile Cecilia Olavsdatter hovered
about the strange little maid, and her big bright eyes were all
agaze under the tumble of flaxen curls.

No sooner had Mærta laid the poor exhausted little thing under
the bedclothes, and Olav said that now Cecilia must go and lie
down by her foster-sister, than she pulled off all her clothes in a
twinkling and jumped up into the bed. Soon after, Mærta came
with a pillow; she took hold of Bothild, who was already asleep,
to put it under her head. Instantly Cecilia threw her arm around
the strange child:

"You shall not touch her! This is *my* sister!"

It was a jest among folk in the countryside that now at last
Olav Audunnsson had got a heritage from his rich kinsmen in
Denmark: he had inherited a mother-in-law. They soon found a
name to call her by and dubbed her the Lady Mærta.

Olav got on well with the new mistress of his house. He was
spared further trouble with such matters as did not rightly come
under his control, and she seemed to be kind to Cecilia.

Galfrid Richardson owed Olav some money, and now he asked
him to accept in payment a handsome, well-trained falcon—Galfrid had bought her in the spring of an Icelander, but he himself
had little skill in hawking and wished to be rid of the bird. Olav
knew of old that it was difficult to mew these birds at Hestviken
so that they kept in good condition over the winter; nor had he
any horse now that would serve for hawking. Nevertheless he
could not control his desire to own this fine bird. He rode out
with her a few mornings, before the snow came. Most days he
got only black game, but once or twice it happened that he had
the luck to see the falcon hunt kites. When he came home,
warmed and cheered by the fine sight of the struggle in the air,
Eirik had the benefit of his father's good humour. When the boy
talked of catching young hawks in the spring and taming them
for hunting, Olav laughed a little—it was not so easy for an un-
practised hand, but he had known something of it in his youth and

he promised to help Eirik as well as he could. It was the lad's work to change the sand and keep the bird's cage clean. His father taught him how to handle the falcon, to slip on the hood and fasten the jesses on the legs. The man and the boy became good friends over this bird.

Then the kites left the country, and the snow came. Olav had set up a perch for the falcon within the closet and hung up some old blankets for a curtain. At night, when the walls were rough with rime and the coverlet over him was frosted with his breath, he lay listening for any movement of the falcon. He was anxious lest she might fare badly and be useless in the spring. Every day he examined her shanks and castings, watched whether she fed. He was still strangely happy in the possession of this treasure, so proud and wild and yet so frail and easily spoilt. He loved to feel the weight of her on his wrist; he carried her into the light and looked at her fine markings, the greyish bands and pale brown spots that showed in her white plumage. At night, when all smells were deadened by the cold, he thought nevertheless he could catch the rank scent of the bird of prey, and then he looked forward with longing to the spring, as he had not done since—he knew not when.

The deer had left the district after the last two winters, when wolves were rife.

As the new year wore on, Olav remarked several times that there was dissension in the house because Eirik set himself against Lady Mærta. Olav was very angry, for now he wished for peace —he corrected the boy with harsh words, but this seemed not to make him any better. Olav took it for granted that Eirik was to blame—so courteous a woman as Mærta Birgersdatter could hardly have expected the son of the Master of Hestviken to be so rude and childish an oaf.

Until now Eirik had never paid much attention to his little sister's doings. But on the other hand he had never been used to tease her; if now and then he turned to Cecilia, it would be to show her kindness and help her in her games. Now that too was changed; he was constantly in the way of the two little maids, provoking them and amusing himself by making Cecilia as savage as a young hawk. The other little girl simply shrank into a corner, dumb with misery.

One evening Olav came in from outside; he stayed in the ante-room awhile, getting out a chest of arrow-shafts and feathers—he intended to spend the evening making ready some arrows for fowling. He moved noiselessly, as had been his habit in all the years when he had had so much on his mind—he had come to hate noise.

He heard the children in the great room, Eirik and Cecilia—he was laughing and she was angry. Olav looked in. Cecilia was sitting before the hearth on the little three-legged stool that was her own. Tore, the old house-carl, had made it for her. She sat clutching the stool with both hands under the seat and her feet braced against the floor. Her mouth was slightly puckered and her eyes were round and staring; they were almost as blue in the whites as in the light pupils—she looked like a white, blue-eyed kitten crouching for a spring. Behind her stood Eirik. He put his foot under the stool and rocked it a little. Cecilia resisted with all her weight.

Olav came into the room for a lantern. Eirik left his sister, but no sooner was his father back in the anteroom than he began again. He dangled a red hair-ribbon—dropped it into the straw that covered the floor. Cecilia was to be quick and snatch it first, but Eirik was quicker still; roaring with laughter, he dropped astride on her stool.

His sister darted at him and seized his hair with both hands. She pulled it without making a sound; Eirik laughed and swung her this way and that, so that she fell into the hearth, put out her hands, and got hold of a log that still had some heat in it. Then she set up a howl and turned furiously on her brother, spitting at him so that it dribbled down on her little chin.

Olav came in, seized Eirik's hand roughly, and pulled it aside—the boy had got Cecilia by the hair when she tried to bite him. Her father lifted her up in his arms.

"So you pull little girls by the hair, I see."

"*She* pulled mine first."

"Nay, did she?"

Eirik turned red as blood. Cecilia remembered that she had burned her hand, and burst into a pitiable fit of crying. Olav comforted her, found some candle-grease, and smeared the burned place. Bothild came out of her corner and stood looking on.

Olav enjoyed being able to sit awhile with Cecilia in his arms and the other little girl at his knee. Eirik he pretended not to see. But when Lady Mærta and Ragna came in with the food and Mærta asked what was the matter, Olav answered: "Nothing."

Then Cecilia looked up from her father's breast. "Must not Eirik give me my horse now, Father?"

"Surely he shall give you your horse."

" 'Tis not her horse," said Eirik, red as fire again.

Then Mærta put in a word: "I gave the children a little wooden horse I found in Eirik's bed when we changed the straw for Yule. And now they have been quarreling over it for twelve weeks."

Olav smiled mockingly. "Is that wooden horse such a treasure, Eirik, that you will not let your sister have it?"

"Yes," replied Eirik defiantly. "Mother carved it for me when I was a child."

"Then you must let Eirik have it," said Olav. "Wooden horses I will give you, as many as you wish."

Later, after supper, Eirik came and asked if he might help his father with the arrows. Olav said he could. Once when Eirik could not get the feathers to sit straight, Olav paused in his work and looked at him.

"I cannot say you are very handy, Eirik."

This was not true; Eirik was deft and quick, it was only a fault in the wood of this shaft, which made the groove for the feathers too shallow.

One afternoon some days later father and son were down at the waterside salting auks. Olav flayed the birds; Eirik cut out the breasts, laid them in the kegs, and salted them. Now and then Olav dried his hands on the lappet of his coat; Eirik was tempted to do the same, but the salt stung his chapped and swollen hands so sharply that it was too painful even to touch the coarse woollen garment.

The south wind howled and beat against the wall of the shed; now and then a shower of rain poured down. Underneath the floor the waves splashed and gurgled, grinding the flakes of ice and breaking them against the rock. It was turning to foul weather. Eirik felt intensely happy at being allowed to stay here in the shed alone with his father and help him.

• • •

King Haakon came from the border round by the north to Tunsberg just after Easter. It was then rumoured in the country about the fiord that the peace with the Danish King was to hold for two years more. Folk were glad of this, for the first tidings that had come from the Kings' meeting there said that in the spring King Haakon would ravage Denmark with a greater war fleet than ever before.

But Olav felt no gladness when he began the work of spring. It was wearisome to look forward to a whole summer at Hestviken. He did not ponder why the days should seem much more dreary now, when at last he was rid of the lingering torment of a wife who was always sick. In those days time had hung heavily on him; now it went swiftly, though his mind was now filled with a never ceasing impatience. It was as though he had sold his soul and been cheated of the payment.

It was not in order to busy himself about this farm here on the hill by the creek—to sail out with his fishing-boats, to dig the ground, to visit the mill and go out to Saltviken—it was not for *this* he had finally silenced the voice that had urged and called to him so long. The secret spiritual conflict that for twelve years had been his whole life was like a web, woven by himself and One other. And he had acted like a woman who cuts down the tapestry from her loom, rolls it up, and hides it in a locked chest. To Olav it seemed as if he had thrown the key into the sea.

But he had not done so in order to have these calm days, wearingly alike, in its place. He had forgotten his doings in England and all the thoughts he had had there, better than he would have believed it possible for a man to forget such things. Nevertheless a dim memory flickered forth of that which had turned the scale: the song of the retainers and the salt, sweet taste of blood it brought back from his own brisk youth of outlawry, and he remembered the joy of grappling with foes of flesh and blood, footpads who used the knife in the darkness of the woods. It was as though these had been the bribes he was offered—no great matters, but enough to turn the scale in the hour when he was tempted to turn away from God for good and all, since it was so hard to return to the banner of his rightful Lord for a man who had become a traitor and a runaway. Thirty pieces of silver are not so great a sum as to have tempted Judas, had it not been for that bag of our

Lord's travelling-resources for which he would have had to account.

And at times the thought came over Olav this spring— He stood under the pale and boundless arch of the evening sky, still faintly yellow over the ridge on the western side of the fiord; the surface of the water beneath him loomed grey and restless, wrapped in an indefinite gloom where the darkness was gathering about the shores. Olav washed the rough dirt from him in the tub before the house door. Whatever he might turn his hand to, every day's work began and ended in his toiling up and down the familiar paths to the yard, creeping into his house, creeping to his rest within the closet. For an instant there came over him a temptation to do like Judas—he had such a hellish loathing of going in to the others.

Early in the winter, when the talk was of war, Olav had said that this year he would take Eirik with him on board. And so long as all men thought the fleet would sail, Eirik had been busy looking over all the things he was to take with him and exercising himself in the use of his weapons. But when the word came that peace was not to be broken, Eirik was yet busier, and now his talk was that if and if and if— It galled Olav every time he heard the lad's boasting.

Another thing that annoyed Olav was that Eirik was continually humming and singing. It had not mattered so much while Eirik was a child, he had had such a clear, sweet voice. But now that his voice was breaking he still sang as before; it did not sound well.

One noontide in the haymaking Olav sent Eirik home to the houses to fetch a rope. Time went on and on. A thunderstorm broke on the heights over Hudrheimsland; it was coming this way, the men worked hard to bring the dry hay under a rock shelter, and Olav grew angrier and angrier as he carried great armfuls of hay. He ran up to the farm.

In the yard stood Cecilia playing ball. She threw the ball against the wall of the storehouse and caught it in one hand; the other little free hand mimicked the action more feebly. Every time she threw the ball she tossed her fair head charmingly. Bothild sat on the ground looking on.

All at once Eirik leaped in between his sister and the wall and caught the ball. He ran backwards across the yard, throwing the ball into the air and catching it, Cecilia following and trying to get it back. Sometimes Eirik pretended to throw it to her. "Catch it, catch it—" and then he tricked her. Suddenly he threw it over the roof of the house.

Then he caught sight of his father. He picked up the ropes, which he had flung down on the rock, and handed them to Olav.

"Could you not find some that were rottener?"

"Nay, these are not rotten, Father," said Eirik confidently.

Olav put his foot in the hank, gave a tug, and threw away the broken ropes. Eirik was crossing over to the storehouse, when his father ordered him sharply: "Find your sister's ball and give it to her." He went himself to find a fresh rope.

In the storehouse all was in confusion; Olav hung everything in its place before he went out. He was making a loop in the new rope when he heard a disturbance in the dairy.

It was Mærta, who had given the little girls some curds and cream to taste; but Eirik forced himself in and wanted to taste the curds too. Mærta took hold of him and pushed him out.

Eirik shouted angrily: "You behave as if you were mistress here—'tis not *your* curds."

Mærta took no notice of him, but Cecilia made a grimace at her brother, finger in mouth.

Eirik was furious and shouted louder: " 'Tis not yours, I say, nothing is yours here in *our* house—even if my father allows you food and lodging, you and the brat you have with you—"

Then Olav was at his side.

"That is no courteous speech, Eirik. You must beg pardon of your foster-mother for it."

Eirik was obstinate and defiant; he turned red.

Olav flared up wrathfully: "Beg Mærta's pardon—kiss the lady's hand and do as I bid."

A flash of lightning cleft the black darkness over the fiord. Olav counted under his breath as he waited for the thunderclap. The peal rolled away among the hills.

"Be quick now, do as I tell you, and then come out to the hay."

Eirik did not move.

Olav let the leather thong run between his fingers; coldly and quietly he said: " 'Tis an age since you felt my hand on you, Eirik. But do now as I tell you, else you shall taste this." He gave the rope a little shake.

Eirik bent down on one knee and rapidly kissed Mærta Birgers-datter's hand. But at that instant Olav felt he could not bear to see the lad's miserable face.

The father took the coil of rope and set off at a run for the fields. He did not even look round to see whether the boy followed him. Abundantly as Eirik had deserved the humiliation, Olav hated having to force the lad thus on his knees before a stranger; he hated Eirik for it.

4

YET father and son got on together in a way for another year and more.

Then came Advent in the following winter, and they were killing meat for Yule.

Arnketil and Liv came out to Hestviken in the pitch-dark early morning; the man was to be butcher, his wife to help the women with puddings and the like.

It had snowed the week before, enough to whiten the fields, but with the new moon came mild weather, and that morning, as Olav came out into the yard, the fog was so thick that they could scarce find their way between the houses. Olav told the men they must rope the pig before they drove the toughness out of it—if it escaped them in this fog, it might not be easy to catch it again.

Olav stood on the doorstone, watching the torches lighting up the thick sea-mist; a moment later they only showed as faint red gleams in the downy grey darkness and then vanished. But soon after, he heard cries and roars and the squealing of the pig, and men came running over the smooth rocks of the yard. Something dashed past him in the dark, and Olav guessed it was the pig. He tried to jump in the way of it, but it was gone in the dense gloom, making eastward across the fields.

After it came the men with torches and brands through the mist, dark forms swathed in darkness. Olav ran on with them. Arnketil and Eirik stooped as they ran, lighting up the pig's tracks in the snow. Olav halted by the barn, and old Tore told him how it had happened. Eirik was to have held the pig, while Arnketil got on its back to ride it tender, and then he had let go.

One of the pigs that were not for slaughter had got loose at the same time. So this pig's flesh was to be effectually worked into softness before they stuck it. They could hear it through the fog.

Olav knew of old that Eirik was always squeamish on pig-killing days—but nobody *likes* them. And the lad was still as clumsy as ever when he had to lend a hand with a beast; it made things no better when he tried to conceal his shrinking with unbecoming flippancy and foolish jesting.

The house-carls came back. They did not think they could catch the pigs again until the fog lifted, and they cursed over the waste of time.

But an hour later Arnketil and Eirik returned with the pig—it had run itself into a drift of thawing snow. Olav went indoors again and lay down on the bench—it was the custom that the master of the house should keep away from pig-killing and only show himself in the yard when he brought out the ale-bowl for the refreshment of the butchers. He lay listening to the pig's shrieks—it was quite preposterous the time it took today before the life was out of it.

It was already daylight outside, stiff with grey fog, when Olav went across with Arnketil to the cook-house. On the snow outside it lay the pig's carcass split in two.

Under the cook-house wall stood Eirik and little Aasta, the youngest of the serving-maids; they were washing themselves in the water-butt, laughing and splashing each other. Eirik was not aware of his father for the fog; he made a dash at the girl and tried to dry his hands on her clothes—his conduct was not very seemly. Aasta screamed, but laughed still more and made no great struggle to escape the lad's forwardness, and Eirik made free with his hands under her kirtle.

The next instant Olav had him by the neck and flung him aside. Eirik had a glimpse of his father's face, grey and wild with fury—then he got a blow of his fist on the jaw which made him reel, his father caught him again, shook him, and hurled him backwards, so that he fell at full length in the snow.

"Be off, you foul trollop," said Olav to Aasta—she was standing there awkwardly. The girl slipped away. "Stand up!"—he gave Eirik a push with his foot.

Eirik rose to his feet and stood dazed before his father.

Olav said in a low voice, shaking with rage: "Do you think you can behave thus in your father's house—you and your bitch—in broad daylight, before folks' eyes—like a dog!"

Eirik turned red as fire. He too began to tremble with rage. " 'Tis not true—'twas only—jesting." His anger brought him to the verge of tears, and then he shouted: "May I not touch one of the maids here without you must needs think—that I shall deal with her as you did with Torhild?"

He raised his arms to fend off the blow—Olav threw him and was over him. He crushed the boy with his knees as he lay in the miry, blood-stained snow. He did not desist as long as he felt any sign of resistance in the body beneath him. Eirik lay limply, with his face half buried in the snow, as Olav stood up and left him.

Old Tore had stood watching Olav punishing his son. Now he knelt down in the dirty slush and tended the unconscious lad.

Later in the day they found the other pig that Eirik had allowed to escape in the early morning. It lay in the hollow behind the outhouses in a pool of slush, dead. Olav shrugged his shoulders when they came and reported the mischance. He clenched his teeth: he had *not* chastised Eirik too severely that morning.

No one saw any more of Eirik that day—nor was it noticed, so busy was the household. It was only old Tore who had seen Olav strike Eirik. The other house-folk remarked no doubt that there was discord once more between father and son, but that happened so often.

But at dusk, when Olav came in from outside, there was one standing in the anteroom; he followed the master into the empty hall and closed the door behind him. It was Eirik. A few logs were burning on the hearth—in the uncertain flicker Olav could see that the lad's face was bruised and swollen.

Olav seated himself on the bench. On the table lay a bannock and a tasty sausage, smoking hot. The man took a bite of the food, chewed and ate slowly—but Eirik stood erect and silent in the shadows.

"What will you?" asked his father at last, reluctantly.

"I wonder if you yourself believed what you said—" Eirik began, so calmly and naturally that his father wondered at him—and then felt a chill of remote misgiving: never had he heard the boy speak in this way. "If you think it so ill of me to trifle with the young maid—then you are not very reasonable, Father. But you are seldom reasonable or just with me."

Olav pushed away his food. He sat upright on the bench—a feeling of tension clutched at his heart. Then a cold clearness of vision came upon him, like acknowledging a defeat: Eirik was surely right.

The son paused for a moment. Then he spoke as before: "It is almost as though you had taken a hatred to me, Father."

But as the man on the bench still sat motionless, Eirik went on, more hotly, more like his usual self: "The way you treat us, one would almost think you had taken a hatred to your own children! You grant your son no honour and no authority—you keep me as a child—and I am in my sixteenth winter!" His voice had broken now, turning to a scream.

"I can see that *you* think so," said his father. And presently he added, with a touch of scorn: "Nevertheless you are very young, Eirik, to judge of your own worth."

Eirik turned and went out.

Eirik had already crept under the skins in his bed—so it appeared—when Olav came in that night to go to rest. The little girls were already asleep in the south bed, Mærta was still busy in the cook-house. But the next morning when the lady went to wake Eirik, she found nothing but a bundle underneath the coverlet.

Sticks and straw tumbled out when she took hold of the old cloak. Mærta was angry—she thought the boy had done this to make a fool of her. Olav stood by and saw it—for a moment he felt alarmed—absurdly, as he saw at once. He turned away in annoyance: what wretched child's tricks! The boy had not been in his bed that night, he wished to show he was offended; but such nonsense as this bundle! Then it struck the man: surely he had never gone to Aasta, to defy him? Ah, if that were so, he should have a beating he had never dreamed of.

He would ask no questions. But by the afternoon it was clear to the whole household that Eirik was not at the manor.

None of the boats was missing, and his horse stood in the stable. There was the same thick, wet fog again today—it was vain to search for the boy, nor could Olav spare any men to send out. But he wondered whither Eirik had betaken himself—to Rynjul or Skikkjustad or perhaps to that Jörund Rypa?

At night the wind got up from the south and it began to rain. In the course of the day the fields were all a mirror of ice, the air was filled with a roaring blast from sea and woods.

As yet Olav had not uttered a word to his house-folk about the matter. Lady Mærta tried to speak of it, but Olav cut her short. Now and again anxiety dragged at him. The boy could not have taken it so that he—surely he had not fallen over somewhere in the night and the fog? Thoughts crowded upon him, which he strove to drive away. It was unlikely.

He found occasion to see to the boats—took courage and looked under the sheds and the quay, went round the shore of the bay— all the while saying to himself: "Eirik is surely at Rynjul"—he had always been Una's favourite.

On Sunday he met both the Rynjul folk and those of Skikk-justad at church. After mass he fell into talk with Jörund Rypa's kinsmen. He saw at once that they knew nothing of Eirik's flight.

He went over to the parsonage. Several people had been in there to speak with the priest, and mass had been late that day, for the roads were almost impassable after the bad weather. Sira Hallbjörn had not yet tasted bite nor sup—he was pale about the nose from his long fast.

Olav told him his son had run away.

"Ay, 'twas not too soon," said the priest.

His ancient housekeeper came limping in with the dish of porridge; the men moved forward and took their places at the table. The priest and the deacon said grace, Olav stood silently waiting at the door. With a mute gesture Sira Hallbjörn invited him to sit down with them and break his fast.

Olav thanked him, but said he must go home. But he asked the priest to come to the outer door with him—he had three words to say to him. Sira Hallbjörn went out reluctantly.

"You know nothing of Eirik, do you, Sira? You have heard no rumour of where he is gone?"

"I—?"

Olav went out, angry. His horse stood outside in the rain, hanging its head; the water poured off its mane, running in streams among the darkened strands. It fell in a sheet from the cloak he had laid over the saddle and the horse's quarters when he put it on.

On the way he looked in at Rundmyr and questioned Anki and

Liv closely, making no concealment. They denied all knowledge of the matter, and Olav saw that they spoke the truth for once.

In the evening he asked Aasta—swallowed his pride and questioned the young serving-maid: "You can surely tell me, Aasta, whither Eirik has made off—since you two were such good friends?"

The girl turned red and tears came into her eyes. She timidly shook her head.

"But he came and said farewell to you, did he not, before he took himself off?"

Aasta broke into sobs. "There was no tie of friendship between me and Eirik, Master Olav." Eirik had only jested a little with her once or twice; Eirik was good-natured, wanton, but kind. On seeing her master's little crooked smile she wept outright and swore most solemnly that she never forgot the teachings of her honest parents, her honour and good name were without stain or blemish.

"Ay, if you let the young lads handle you as I saw that morning, you will soon find yourself without either the one or the other," said Olav sternly. "Now go and cry outside."

Then there was nothing left but to peer into his own despair. All day long Olav cudgelled his brains to find some credible explanation—what *could* Eirik have done? He had gone away in his great hooded cloak, his sword and spear he had taken with him. A little gold pin in the band of his shirt and a great brooch in the bosom of his jerkin, these and his finger-ring with a red agate he always wore; had he made for the town he might have provided himself with a lodging by selling one of these trinkets. He might have gone to Claus Wiephart or to the armourer's—or to one of the monasteries. Or, if he had been able to get carried across the fiord, to Tunsberg—likely enough the lad might have taken it into his head to seek his fortune where so many lords were passing to and fro. Between whiles Olav tried to fan into flame his first indignation at Eirik's flight.

But at night he lay awake—and then his thoughts would only dwell on what might have *happened* to Eirik. He might have lost his way in the fog that night, have fallen over the cliff somewhere. For the son of Hestviken manor was well enough known to many —it was incredible that he could disappear as if he had sunk into the ground or— Carried off, spirited away, spellbound by the powers of evil—now Olav called to mind all the stories Eirik had told as a child, about his intercourse with the folk of that world. There might have been some truth in it after all, even if he made up a deal of it. Or if he had been out on the fiord the second day after he ran from home—many boats' crews had not been heard of since that day. Nor were the roads inland so safe but that it might be dangerous for a young lad, well dressed and armed, with jewels on him, to travel alone. Northward, in the forests about Gerdarud, there were reports of robbers.—Or, or— For all that, Olav knew not a little of Eirik's fickle nature; he turned to melancholy as suddenly as to sport and dalliance. But he could not surely have taken his correction so much to heart as to throw himself into the fiord—

"Ingunn, Ingunn, Ingunn mine—help me, where is the boy?

"Jesus, Mary—where *is* Eirik?"

Olav rose on his knees in the bed with his head in his clasped hands. He leaned his forehead against the foot of the bed. "Not for myself do I pray for mercy. Holy Mary, I taught the boy these prayers myself when he was a child—be mindful of that now!"

But that was an age ago—he did not know whether Eirik remembered anything of them now. It was an age since he had thought of teaching the children anything of that sort. Cecilia never a word—that he had left to Mærta. It had come to this, that he *could* not and *dared* not. But, God, God! *they* must not suffer for it. He prayed God to take Eirik under His protection, he prayed God's Mother for his son, he prayed Saint Olav and Saint Eirik, as he had never been wont to pray.

Sometimes it made him a little calmer. For himself he cared not now, but for the young lad, Ingunn's son—

He never thought of Cecilia thus—that she was Ingunn's daughter as much as his.

He could not prevent the servants from talking of Eirik's flight. He himself said hardly anything, but he listened stiffly and intently—whether the others might have heard some news.

The southerly weather held. A draught of wind whistled through the church on Christmas Eve, levelling the flames of the candles in the lustrous choir whenever the storm came down with full force—the vault above was darkened, and then the heavy doors shook and the window-shutters rattled—as if the spirits of the tempest flung themselves with all their might against every barrier in their fury to thwart the sacred ceremony that was proceeding in the choir. There was a howling and piping about the corners of the building, a vast droning in the ash trees on the ancient burial mounds beyond the churchyard fence. Through the roaring dissonance of the storm the singing of the mass sounded strangely still and strong—like the smooth streak of a current in the midst of a rough sea.

The moment the silver bells chimed and the congregation knelt, while *Sanctus, sanctus, sanctus* resounded from the choir, it fell still. The candle-flames recovered themselves and gleamed erect; the painted images on the whitened walls of the chancel seemed to spring forth, shining in their blue and yellow and rust-red colours. Sira Hallbjörn's tall form, clad in pure white linen with the golden chasuble, appeared like that of an angel, descended straight from the heavenly visions of Saint John—a bearer of good tidings and a herald of God's judgment.

Then came a fresh gust of wind, crashing and roaring against the walls; the choir was plunged in gloom as the priest bent over the paten, whispering. The tolling of the bell in the ridge-turret over the people's heads was drowned in the raging of the storm.

When the congregation rose to its feet after the *Agnus Dei*, Olav Audunnsson remained sunk on his knees. Baard Paalsson from Skikkjustad, who stood by his side, bent down, trying to look into his face in the darkness.

"Are you sick, Olav?"

Olav shook his head and stood up.

After mass Olav and Baard struggled side by side across the green to the tithe barn. The great lantern under the roof swayed hither and thither. Everywhere in the shadows they descried the forms of folk who lay in the straw to take a short rest before the Mass of the Shepherds.

Olav unhooked his cloak and shook the rain from it.

"Are you sick?" asked Baard again. "You are pale as a ghost."

"No," said Olav. He went in and lay down in the straw, where some men moved closer to make room for the two.

"Nay, but I thought it," said Baard, "since you were not with Eirik. I saw how pale you turned tonight, and I thought maybe you had been unwell. Gunnar and Arne spoke of it; they thought it strange that you let your son travel thus alone, with only a token—"

"What mean you?" Olav managed to say.

Baard made no answer—he could not follow.

"Gunnar and Arne—is it Arne of Haugsvik you speak of?" As Baard said nothing, Olav resumed, as unconcernedly as he could: "'Twas not with my consent that Eirik left home—nor *against* my will either. He deemed he was old enough to shift for himself now—so I thought, let him try it. Then he took the road for Oslo," Olav ventured at a hazard. "He came through safe and well?" he asked when he received no answer.

Yes, he came through safe and well, replied Baard sleepily—it was the day of the storm. And he had been in good heart, said Arne, when the lad parted from them. But out at Haugsvik, when he came and asked for a place in their boat, he had told them there was an agreement between Olav and one of the great lords in the town that Eirik should enter his service in order to learn the trade of war and courtly ways. Nay, who his new lord was to be, Eirik had refused to say—that was his way, always such an air of secrecy.

Olav lay with his hands clasped under his cloak. "God, my God, I thank Thee—Mary, most clement, most kind, what shall I do to show my gratitude?" Memories of burned out thoughts stirred like ashes driven off by a puff of wind. Nay, that was all over— but he would give something to her poor, a cow to Inga, who had the leper son.

But as he rode homeward after the morning mass, in pouring rain—the wind had dropped now—his anger revived. Such conduct he had never heard of indeed—and there had been the usual bragging and romancing out at Haugsvik, he could guess.—A token, it occurred to Olav; what could that token be?—surely he had never taken something, his seal or seal-ring, for instance—run away from home as a thief?

He sat leaning over the table, silent and gloomy, scarcely noticing his house-carls, who fell on the steaming dish of meat. Now and then he recollected himself sufficiently to raise the ale-bowl, drink to them, and let it go round.

Afterwards he went in and turned over his store of treasures. But nothing was missing.

His wrath came and went in waves, died down and gave place to uneasiness. Eirik had made his way to Oslo—more than that he did not know as yet—and there was no saying what he might fall into there. There was no help for it, he would have to go and find out about his son, ill as it suited him to leave home at this time.

At last, on Twelfth Day, Olav met with a farmer up the parish who had spoken with Eirik in the town. He had been in to Nonneseter at Yule—the convent owned a share in the farm he occupied—and there he had come upon Eirik in the guests' refectory. He sat waiting while his master, Sir Ragnvald Torvaldsson, had speech with the Abbess.

The day after, Olav sailed in to Oslo. Inside the Sigvalda Rocks the fiord was frozen over. A great number of boats had been left at the edge of the ice, and there was not a horse to borrow at any of the farms about. So Olav let old Tore stay with their boat while he walked alone across the ice to the town.

He found Tomas Tabor and sent him out to the old royal castle at the river-mouth—Sir Ragnvald had custody of the place. But Eirik did not come to his father's inn the first day; the evening of the second day was wearing on and still Olav sat there waiting.

The travellers, as many as were at home, lay under the skins in their sleeping-places—it was cold. The hostess sat dozing by the hearth, huge in her sheepskin wraps; she was only waiting till it was time to rake over the fire and bar the door. Olav sat on his bed, with his hands hanging over his knees; his legs were like ice from the cold of the floor, and he was dull with waiting.

The woman got up to tend the two lanterns that hung at each end of the long hall of the inn. "Will you not go to bed, master?"

Then there was a knock at the door. It was Eirik.

Olav went a few steps to meet him and gave him his hand in greeting. They happened to come together just under the lantern. In a way the father must have noticed before now that Eirik had grown taller than himself and that shadows of dark down had begun to appear about his mouth, but never before had he been wholly aware of the change—Eirik was grown up. He was well dressed—wearing a plain steel cap, and under it a dark blue woollen hood that framed the narrow, swarthy face, making it seem yet narrower. His long cloak was brown and of good stuff; under it he was clad in a tight leather jerkin and he wore a sword at his belt, in token that he was now one of his lord's men-at-arms. Long iron spurs jingled as he walked.

"You will not get me back with you to Hestviken, Father," he said as soon as Olav let go his hand.

"I had not thought to do so either," replied Olav. "If you have taken service with a lord, you must know that I would not have you run from it before your time." To the hostess, who came up and asked whether she should bring drink for him and his guest, he replied yes, the best German beer.

"Nay," said Olav as they seated themselves on his bed; "I would have liked it better if you had spoken to me before you made off —but it is useless to talk of that now."

Eirik blushed slightly and asked with embarrassment: "You have business that brings you here, then?"

"My business is to give you what you need—you shall be provided as befits *my* son when you go out into the world." Olav pulled out of the bed a bag of clothes, a good battle-axe, and the blade of a thrusting-spear. Then he handed his son a purse: "Here are four marks of silver in good, old money. It is my will that you get yourself a horse as soon as you can—that you may be held of more account. It ill befits a man-at-arms to ride his master's horses like a serving-man of villein birth. More than that you shall not have of me, Eirik, so long as you stay abroad. You have chosen to be master of your own conduct—so be it then, and let it be such that you win honour thereby."

Eirik rose and thanked his father with a kiss of the hand. It gave him a warm thrill that his father spoke to him as a grown man; it was not often his father had addressed so long a speech to him. And yet there was a shade of disappointment—that this meeting did not turn out as he had pictured it to himself ever since Tomas Tabor brought him Olav's message: he had expected his father to be greatly angered, to threaten and command him to return; and then he would have made answer— But it seemed his father had taken his flight very calmly and had no thought at all of bringing him home again.

"Thanks, I am not hungry—" but, for all that, Eirik helped himself from his father's box of victuals and took a good draught as often as Olav offered him the tankard. At heart he very soon felt quite proud—it was an uncommon and almost a solemn occasion to be sitting here eating and drinking with his father at an inn and asking for the news from home—two grown-up men together.

"But how did you find out that I was here in Oslo, with Sir Ragnvald?"

Olav smiled his little pinched smile. "Oh—I find out most of what I *will* know, Eirik. When you have come to my age, perhaps you will have got so much wisdom as not to let men see all that you know."

Eirik turned red as flame—memories of all kinds of secret misdeeds, great and small, in the whole of his young life hovered through his mind and gave him a moment's insecurity. His father noticed it and smiled as before. But he went on talking calmly, gave his son good advice as to how he should conduct himself, now he was in a knight's service, spoke a little of his own youth.

The last of the guests came into the inn. The curfew rang from the church towers, and Eirik said he must go.

"I think to go home again tomorrow about midday—maybe I shall not see you again before that?" asked his father.

Eirik did not think he could come.

"Nay, nay." Olav went to the door with him. "Keep yourself well and in honour, Eirik. May God Himself and His blessed Mother be your protection." He kissed the young man on both cheeks and gave a little nod, as Eirik seemed to pause at the door —the lad had such a strange feeling at this solemn farewell, with the kisses of his father's hard, thin lips on his face.

Olav had business with Claus Wiephart next day, and the German accompanied him down across the common. Due south the sun's disk shone through the light frost-fog, gilding the surface of the ice. "Fine weather, Olav."

They turned into a narrow street between warehouses, which led to a strip of beach among the quays; from there the ice could be reached. From the common behind them came the noise of a band of horsemen, clanking of arms and harness. Olav and Claus had to cling to the walls as the troop thundered into the lane and rode past. At its head rode a short, thickset knight—Olav knew Sir Ragnvald Torvaldsson by sight. His men followed, one by one, for the lane was narrow. One of the horses was near being squeezed between two others, there was some confusion in the rank, and one or two horses reared. Olav saw Eirik among the rest; he sat erect and easy in the saddle—but he did not see his father, he had enough to do to manage his horse, which seemed very fresh. He laughed and called to the man ahead of him in the crowd of steaming animals.

"But—was not that your son?" asked Claus Wiephart.

"It was."

"Ay, time flies. Ere one is aware of it, one is an old man. How old are you now, Master Olav?"

"Forty winters."

"Then you are younger than you look, after all. Is it not four winters since Ingunn died? You are yet too young to let your beard grow—and to sleep wifeless on a winter's night."

"You will see, I will shave off my beard yet, Claus—and a wife I will get me too, if so be that such is my lot." Olav gave a little laugh.

Claus bade him farewell and went back to his warehouse. Olav walked out on the ice, where a path was marked on the gleaming, coppery surface. He saw the band of horsemen far ahead—they were making across the creek toward Akersnes, where the massive walls of King Haakon's new castle rose in the fine frosty mist.

Again he felt the thought of Eirik like a cord that drew his heart together—but now it was like envy, of the other's youth.

5

THE NEXT three years passed much more rapidly—time whirled away like smoke with Olav.

He had settled down. This was a life that Olav Audunsson had never before experienced. In his heart he felt its quietude as emptiness or as a loss. But if he had been asked what he *thought* of his life now, he must have answered that he was well content.

His affairs prospered in these years, and he bought some shares in farms in the neighbouring parishes—Olav never changed in this respect, that he put more faith in the land than in the sea. And he had better luck with his farming than ever before. When he first came to Hestviken, full of zest and courage, he lacked experience—and since then he had always been tied.

Nevertheless it must be said that there had always been prosperity at Hestviken. But now, under Mærta Birgersdatter's control, it was more noticeable. There was no longer any trouble with the serving-folk. The old ones stayed on—the foreman, old Tore, went about his work, quiet and cool-headed; Svein, the herdsman, Jon and Bodvar, the house-carls, remained unmarried all three; Ragna lived in Torhild's house with her children and was dairywoman, Aasta had put aside all wantonness and still enjoyed her honour and good name. Besides these there was a young lad and a half-grown maid. They went somewhat short of merriment and jollity at the manor, but these folk lived well; the mistress was just and fairly open-handed. Pauper couples who were maintained in the homesteads of the parish were glad when their turn came to Hestviken.

The master of the house said little, and there was no denying he depressed the folk around him; but this was only until they got to know him, his servants said—one grew accustomed to him. Olav was not badly liked by his household. He left Lady Mærta a free hand and was glad to take her advice in those matters which came under himself. The footing between them was almost as if she had been his mother—a very masterful mother, and he a compliant son.

Even at the hovel, Rundmyr, things were quiet. Mærta Birgersdatter had reduced Arnketil and Liv to order. He had become rather hunchbacked, wrinkled, and dried up; she was ever yeasty and exuberant—a child appeared in the cot every year toward spring. Some trifles were always missed—food, wool, or tow—when Liv had been about at Hestviken; but it had become a sort of right that she might take without asking leave, so long as she kept within bounds. Elsewhere she never pilfered now, except from Una at Rynjul. Arnketil had given up stealing since Mærta surprised him one evening; he was in one of the storehouses struggling to strike a light. "No need for a light here, Anki—I think you know the way."

The two little maids were growing; their beauty was noised abroad. They were now old enough to be present at feasts and gatherings—which were but few, for Olav held intercourse with none but the circle of nearest neighbours, who visited each other year after year. But the people of the parish saw the Hestvik maids at church. Olav Audunsson rode up first, and Bothild Asgersdatter sat behind on his horse with her arms round his waist—for Cecilia rode with old Tore; that was his right, and if they took *that* from him, he would not stay at the manor another day, he threatened jokingly. The two children were always richly and handsomely dressed when they came to mass—Lady Mærta gave them kirtles of dyed cloth, with gaily embroidered edges, and she bound their flowing hair with silken ribbons worked with gold.

In everyday life Olav did not see much of his daughters. He had built a women's house by the side of the old hearth-room house—Mærta thought that the women ought to have a house of their own, where they could work with their looms, their sewing, and the like: Cecilia and Bothild must now learn to use their hands.

The new house was a fine one: Bodvar was a skilful wood-carver, and he decorated it with much handsome ornament. It was not every month that Olav set foot inside the door of it.

But although he saw so little of the children, a pale, wintry sunshine fell upon his spirit from the two fair young lives that were growing up so near to his own frozen life.

It looked as if Lady Mærta had succeeded in taming Cecilia's hot temper—or she had grown out of it as she got more sense. Headstrong she was still, but she had acquired a calmer, rather sulky way. The house-folk laughed when the child gave a short, sharp answer—she was so like her father, they said, but they thought it became her well. She was so fair to look upon that, whatever she said or did, folk thought it suited her.

She liked Lady Mærta, that was easily seen, though Cecilia gave little sign of it in words or loving behaviour. In the same way she showed her affection for old Tore, for Ragna and her children—a tacit, steady loyalty through thick and thin. Only toward her foster-sister, Bothild, did she show a different, gentler and softer way; so far as could be judged by the manner of this calm, reti-cent little girl, she loved Bothild better than anyone in the world. But all at Hestviken took pains to be gentle and kind to Bothild—she still seemed a little forlorn; there was something about her that seemed to ask them to deal tenderly and cautiously with her. Even Olav showed his fondness for his foster-daughter more than his affection for his own daughter. If some chance prompting led him to fondle the children, it was Bothild whose hair he stroked or whose cheek he patted—as though it came easier with her, as she brightened up with joy at the slightest caress. If the children came down to the waterside to meet him or accompanied him out into the fields, it was Bothild he took by the hand and led, for he saw she liked it. She looked up at him at every word they exchanged, and her blue eyes were so demure beneath her thick auburn hair. Cecilia's bright, pale eyes looked the world straight in the face, wide awake; there was an air about her whole compact little figure which said she could quite well walk alone. She was his own child, Olav bore his love for his daughter within him as a safely locked treasure that he had no need to look to. His kindness for his foster-daughter he could much more easily pay out in small coin, as occasion arose.

There was not a thing about Cecilia Olavsdatter to recall her mother. The last shadow of a memory of Ingunn Steinfinnsdatter's vain and hapless life seemed to have vanished from her home. Sira Hallbjörn remarked this one day when he had come to ask for a passage in Olav's boat:

"I wonder if there be any in the countryside who remembers your wife but you."

He caught sight of Olav's face as soon as he had said it. Instinctively he turned his own away, as when he was hearing a confession.

"But you remember her," said Olav after a pause, almost inaudibly.

"You know, 'tis not many days since I last said a mass for her— it came into my mind just now—I remember all the years I saw her lying in the bed there— I had thought to see you, though, at the mass for the dead," said the priest.

"I had forgot it was that day—until the evening. Oh no," Olav added after a moment; "there cannot be many who remember her now."

One evening early in the spring some men had come into the house at Hestviken—they were folk from within the parish who had their landing-place on Olav's shore. They had come by water from a feast higher up the fiord, and the drink was still in them.

Olav and old Tore were sitting together, mending some gear; the other men had not yet come in, and the women were in the outhouses. Only the little girls were playing on the bench. Then Olav sent Tore to fetch ale for the guests, and for a while the talk went peaceably, about the wedding and such matters.

In the course of it one of the men said to Olav: "That Torhild you had a child by when she was here, she was at the feast too. She bade us bring greetings to Hestviken."

Olav thanked them and asked how things were with her.

Well, said the men; she enjoyed great respect in the neighbourhood and she was prospering. She had done so well with Auken that folk now called the place Torhildrud.

Old Tore asked eagerly for more news of Torhild Björnsdatter; he had always liked her so well. Then they talked for a time of her way of keeping house.

Olav listened, but took no part in the conversation, except to ask: "Had she the boy with her at the feast?"

The men said yes, he was a handsome boy, fair and strong—"no need to ask who is his father."

But as the men stirred up the remnant of drink that was in them, they grew first fuddled, and soon after two of them began to quarrel and threaten each other. At last Olav had to ask them to keep the peace or go out.

At that moment the two men came to grips. The little girls jumped onto Olav's clothes-chest and stood there. Then one of the men caught sight of them, turned that way, and tried to make game of them.

Olav got up, upsetting all he had on his lap onto the floor—he was going to part the two who were fighting. At the same moment the third man caught hold of the girls. Olav saw Bothild shrink away, with a little helpless whine of terror. Something flashed in Cecilia's hand—the child had drawn her little knife and struck at the man. Olav took him by the shoulders, put his knee to the small of his back, and forced him to the floor. Tore now came to his master's aid and opened the door. Olav took the stranger by the shoulders and middle and heaved him out through the anteroom into the yard. Then he ran back to deal with the others.

With many a crash against walls and doorposts, with roars and oaths, but no very hard struggle, Olaf and Tore got the room cleared of the strangers and the door bolted. They raged and bellowed out in the yard, kicked at the outer door and banged on the walls. Olav and Tore listened, laughing and panting as they put their clothes straight; they too had got some knocks, either from the drunken men's fists and heels or from striking against the walls of the dark anteroom.

Smiling, Olav turned to the children. Cecilia's round, milk-white face was still contorted with fury; there was a pale-green flash in her eyes. But Bothild was clinging to the wall, trembling so that her teeth chattered. When Olav touched her, she burst into a fit of weeping so terrible that her foster-father was quite alarmed. He drew her toward him, had to sit down and hold her in his arms while he tried to comfort her like a little child—though she was no longer a little girl, he felt, she was growing up now, thin and long of limb—twelve winters she must be. He stroked her head with its long plaits, telling her not to be afraid—though he knew of old it was of little use; she was always taken thus when folk came to blows and she was by, even though no one thought of doing anything to her. Whenever the bawling and battering outside grew louder, a twitching went through the girl's delicate frame.

Then Olav gently pushed her away, got up, and went out. At the same moment the house-carls entered the yard, and the strangers took flight.

Later, as they sat at table, and Cecilia was about to cut herself a slice of cheese, one of the house-carls cried with a laugh: " Your knife is bloody, Cecilia!"

Bothild set up a screech, but now Olav and the men could not help laughing at her timidity. They were enlivened by the little tussle earlier in the evening, and now they sat at their ease over the table with good ale and food and a brisk fire on the hearth.

Cecilia spat on her knife and wiped it on the inside of her kirtle, then she cut herself a good piece of cheese and laid it between two slices of bread—not a word did she utter.

Olav laughed.

"May I see that knife of yours—'twas a feeble defence that, my daughter!"

"Then give me a better knife, Father!" said the maid.

"That I will," replied her father, gaily as before.

After supper Olav fetched in the little iron-bound coffer in which he kept his treasures. The girls hung over his shoulders as he searched in it—not many times had the children been allowed to see what their father kept therein. They uttered a cry and asked a question as each thing was brought to light, and Olav, who was in a good humour this evening, let them handle the jewels and try them on. At the bottom lay four handsome daggers—Olav never wore them.

Cecilia snatched the longest. "Will you give me this one, Father?" She drew it out of its sheath.

It was a foreign weapon with a three-cornered blade, the handle and sheath finely ornamented with gilt rings. Olav took it from her, looked at it a moment.

"That is no woman's knife, Cecilia—'tis only fit to strike down a foe. This you will find more useful—" he handed her a big Norwegian knife with a broad, strong blade and a handle of carved walrus tusk.

"I would rather have the other," said the maid.

Olav considered a moment. " 'Tis not often you ask anything of me—take it then." He took up her thick flaxen plait—it lay in coils, so curly was Cecilia's hair. "You should not have been the *daughter* of this house, Cecilia, that is sure."

Olav heard tidings of Eirik once in a while. And as he grew accustomed to the boy's absence, the thought sometimes came to him: perhaps Eirik would never come home. And it might happen that he thought that were best. He must surely receive something in return for having sold his soul. If the fraud were wiped out, so that his race and his heritage were not falsified—then it seemed to him it would be somewhat easier to face death and judgment. His own life he had thrown away—by his own fault; he thought of it with a strange, clear composure—it almost gave him a kind of chilly joy to recognize that the injustice was his, God was just. He had never been able to understand how any man could find consolation in blaming or cursing God. And he himself was only *one man;* his fate could be no such great matter. He felt it a good thing to know that the world was safe in the hands of the gentle Christ, however many men might rise in revolt.

Cecilia's happiness—that he believed in firmly.

The same year, about midsummer, Baard of Skikkjustad and Signe Arnesdatter married off their eldest daughter. The bridegroom lived in the neighbouring parish, and Olav Audunsson was one of those who brought the bride home to his house, for he was her godfather.

A good godfather he had not been; he had paid little heed to the maiden—her name was Helga. She was of plain and modest appearance and had little to say for herself, by all accounts; but on her wedding-day she was fair to look upon.

At first Baard had refused to hear of this marriage; he had had many matters in dispute with the bridegroom—who was much older than Helga. But at the mid-Lent Thing this year an atonement had been made between the men and so Baard betrothed his daughter to Hoskold Jonsson.

Olav was strangely moved at the sight of the young bride—Helga Baardsdatter was so changed that she seemed to have taken on a new semblance. Others of the wedding guests had felt the same, he found—they spoke of it as they sat together on the evening of the third day of the feast in a little house apart, where quarters had been assigned to the older and more esteemed guests who attended the wedding. Olav had been placed high up, next after Torgrim of Rynjul, the husband of the bride's aunt; facing him sat Sira Hallbjörn in the highest seat.

From Hoskold and Helga the talk shifted to other women who had been notably fair and merry brides—or good and staunch housewives. The old men always thought that none of those now living could bear to be set beside the women they remembered in their youth.

Sira Hallbjörn leaned over the table, drawing lines with the spilt ale. He had been out of humour all through the wedding, tired and taciturn. This seemed to weary him.

"Do you mean to sit here all night prating of these dead women? While they lived, their husbands were as sick of them as are most men, I'll warrant. Methinks that fair companion of Olav Audunsson's is better worth possessing than all the rest together." He laughed weakly, being somewhat gone in drink. "Tell me, friend Olav, will you sell me that fair mistress of yours?"

Olav straightened himself abruptly, red and angry—he could not guess what the priest was aiming at. Torgrim of Rynjul did not see it either; he asked:

"What mean you, Sira?"

Sira Hallbjörn laughed as before, stretched behind Torgrim's back, and passed his hand over the blade of Olav's axe, which hung behind his seat. "She it is I mean—" he let his hand fall on Olav's shoulder.

Olav shook it off with a laugh of displeasure. "No, priest—lately you would have my falcon—and this axe is not—"

The axe Kinfetch rang—everyone present heard it. Its deep notes sang out through the room and slowly died away.

Sira Halbjörn leaped up and seized the axe. "Is she one of those that sing, your axe, Olav?" he asked excitedly.

"So 'tis said. But I thought she had lost her voice long ago—from old age." He took the axe from the priest and hung it back on the wall.

The men fell into a discussion, whether the axe had sung of itself or whether it was owing to Sira Hallbjörn's touching it.

Olav and the priest had looked each other in the eyes an instant —then they both laughed, alike uncheerful. It was as though they had discovered a bond between them—that the heart of neither was in this merriment.

Olav took his leave of the bridal gathering the same evening, but told his men they might stay till the next day and escort Mærta Birgersdatter and the children home.

The sky was covered high up by a thin veil of cloud. Under the colourless vault of the summer night the farms loomed grey with uncut meadows and strips of pale-green corn, as Olav rode along the path that ran through the belt of copse skirting the home fields. The world was asleep but for the harsh note of the corn-crake somewhere in the meadow.

He reached the hamlet by the church, and the horse moved more freely, eager for home. The church stood on a little height with its stone walls shining faintly and its shingle roof rising above the little window-slits. Olav turned his horse into the track that led to the church green. The stillness of night seemed to press upon him like a living thing, as the sound of the horse's hoofs was deadened in the rough grass.

By the churchyard wall lay some ancient burial mounds; the largest came right up to the fence, so that the old ash trees that surmounted it cast their shade beyond it. Olav dismounted and tied his horse to a rail near the gate of the churchyard. He must have no steel on him, he remembered—he took off his belt and laid it on the ground together with his axe. Then he went forward to the biggest of the mounds.

The very sound of dry twigs breaking under his footsteps—there was a thick carpet of them under the ash trees—gave him a chill feeling that raised the hair on his head. He walked over the mound, down to the churchyard wall, and mounted it. Within, the gravestones lay sunken in the summer growth of grass, which reached to the wall of the church. Olav gazed till black specks seemed to float before his eyes, and his heart beat so that he had a taste of blood in his mouth. But the feeling of dizziness was only as though the world swam around him; within himself there was calm, an undisturbed core. Nevertheless he involuntarily closed his eyes at the sound of his own voice, as he called clearly and firmly:

"Ingunn Steinfinnsdatter—arise!"

His horse out on the green gave a start, he could hear. He dared not turn and look that way; his eyes were fixed on the church wall, where he descried the gravestone close by the women's door. Cold and stiff in the cheeks with pallor, he called again:

"Ingunn Steinfinnsdatter—arise!

"Ingunn Steinfinnsdatter—arise!"

Again he had closed his eyes, but he *saw* it—the grey stone slowly lifting, the white figure of the dead rising up and shaking the mould from her grave-clothes.

He bent his head back, drew breath, and opened his eyes. There was nothing to be seen but the grey, mild night. Olav stared—as though this was more incredible than aught else. But the churchyard lay there asleep, with the sunken stones half-hidden by the long grass, right up to the grey wall of the church.

At last he turned, walked back across the mound, down to his horse. As he untied the reins he saw that the dun noticed something; he stood with his head raised, nostrils distended, laid back his ears, and started twice as Olav lay his hand on him—but Olav could see nothing. Then he got into the saddle and gave the horse his head—the swift pace did him good; the pressure of the air and the thud of hoofs overcame the sinister silence.

It was morning when he reached Hestviken; the clouds were faintly tinged with pink. When Olav had stabled his horse he went out on the rock to look at the weather—from habit. A little breeze before sunrise darkened the water of the fiord.

The living-room was empty and deserted. Olav went into the closet, flung himself on the bed without undressing. But as soon as he had closed his eyes, he started up, wide awake. He stared at the grey opening into the larger room—but there was no one.

Thoughts rose in him like bitter waters. She had once *promised* —if the dead may visit the living.

But now she was infinitely farther from him than before—the first year, nay, the first summer after her death he had felt how near she was yet, in the darkness that concealed them from each other. Now they had come so far asunder that she no longer heard him when he called.

As he lay, the solitude about him turned little by little to a kind of vision. He was up on a bare and rocky mountain-top, where some heather grew and the rocks were grey with lichen. Beneath him on every side lay forest, grey with rime, and in the hollows were pale bogs with frozen water-holes, but far away the grey, closed sky was merged in low, dark-blue ridges. He tried to send a cry out yonder, but knew it was useless. The vision faded slowly into a dreamless gloom of sleep, and he did not wake till Ragna came in at breakfast-time; she had wondered greatly, she said, when she heard from Svein that his horse stood in the stable, but not the others'.

6

IT chanced several times that autumn that Olav saw smoke on the high ground above Hudrheimsland. He paused in his work to watch it. It must be there that Torhildrud lay, as near as he could guess.

There came some gleaming blue sunny days, when the very roar of the waves against the rocks seemed permeated with light and wind. Yellow leaves flew brightly in the air, and space itself was widened, from the dark-blue, foam-flecked surface of the fiord up to the bright, wind-swept vault, where little shreds of white cloud raced along, infinitely high. And one day about nones Olav went down, took one of the smallest boats, and sailed across alone.

Today it was like a sport to lie sailing over the flowing translucent waves. The spray that wetted him through was gleaming white. The sky was so high up that he felt lost in this little boat among the waves, and every time the boat rose on the crest, he saw that the land on the other side had come nearer, plainer to the sight. He was almost in the mood of his boyhood, when he had run away from Frettastein to play in the woods.

On coming ashore he walked rapidly up the path to the hills. The wooded slopes here were already thinned; yellow leaves whirled and drifted, flying past him like showers of glittering light, dancing over the path. The rushing wind filled Olav with well-being.

Now his only wonder was that he had not thought of this years ago: he ought to have come over to see her, find out how she and the boy were doing. Not but what he could be sure she would hold her own, capable woman that she was. But he ought to have offered to help her, if she would accept his help—seeing that he was the father of her son.

He himself did not understand why it had once seemed so impossible to meet Torhild—as though their meeting could only breed new difficulties. For they were no longer young, either of them—but he had never thought of that before.

He came to the gate at the edge of the wood, followed the path between the cairns. There was much more plough-land now —stubble-fields. She seemed to have harvested all her crops.

Olav looked forward, but without excitement, to seeing her again, and Björn.

A dog began to bark within the house. The door opened—the dog came rushing toward him, yelping. Behind it Torhild stooped in the doorway, looking out.

He could not interpret the expression of her face, but it was somehow quite different from what he had expected. She accepted his hand rather half-heartedly.

"Are *you* abroad—over here?"

"Ay—think you that so strange?"

"Oh, nay. There may well be reason in it too," said Torhild quietly.

She invited the man in, bade him be seated, offered a bowl of milk—"ale I have none." Then she knelt down by the hearth, blew life into the embers, and made up a fire. "You must be wet and cold—will you not sit closer?"

Olav thanked her and seated himself on the stool she had pulled forward—for that matter, he had walked himself dry. "But warm your feet now," suggested Torhild.

From the bed came a faint sound of whimpering—an infant, he could hear. Torhild gave a rapid glance over her shoulder, but took no further notice; she hung a pot over the fire and poured milk into it. Meanwhile their talk was of the wind and the fine weather; it dragged somewhat with both of them.

"Björn is not at home?" asked Olav.

"No, he went with Ketil—they were to take a cow to the manor here."

"Ay, it has been told me how much you have increased your estate. You must have not a few head of cattle, since you till so many acres?"

"We have four that give milk and three young heifers—" The infant screamed louder and louder while Torhild was telling Olav of her cattle.

"*He* seems to be in great distress, though," said Olav with a smile. He was about to ask whose child it was, but remembered Ranveig, Torhild's young sister, and checked himself.

"It is a little girl," said Torhild, suddenly getting up. "I shall have to quiet her." With a rapid gesture she parted the folds of her kirtle and drew out one full, blue-veined breast.

Olav looked at her, his mouth half-open with astonishment. Then he bowed his head—his forehead grew hot, a blush spread over the man's face. He felt he could not look at her, had to keep his eyes firmly fixed on the floor. *That* was the only thing he had never once thought of, that it might turn out thus!

Torhild had seated herself on the step of the bed, with the child at her breast. Olav felt that she was looking at him; and he was angry with himself that he could not cease blushing. They sat thus for a good while, saying nothing. Then all at once Torhild spoke, quietly and in a clear voice:

"I would rather you said your business now, Olav—then I will answer you as well as I can."

"Business—I have no other business than that I thought—I would ask after Björn—see him and hear how he does—and you—"

Torhild answered, as though weighing every word she uttered: "I see right well, Olav, that you may think—that it was not for this you gave me the farm here—I was given Auken that I might support myself and the child over here. But as I told you, the work here is now double what it was when I came. And I hold it better to have a man here to help one than that I should carry on the farm alone with hired servants. Then you must bear in mind, I am now so old—Björn cannot have *many* brothers and sisters. Perhaps no more than this one—" she bent her face caressingly over the sucking child and pressed it to her.

As Olav was still silent, Torhild resumed with more warmth: "I considered it last year, before I gave him his answer—whether I should go over to Hestviken and speak to you of the matter. But then methought it was long since I had heard from you. But I see that you may think I have acted otherwise than was in your mind when you gave me house and land—though there never passed a word between us that I was not to marry."

Olav shook his head. "I knew not that you were married."

" 'Twill soon be a year ago," said Torhild shortly.

Olav rose, went up and gave her his hand. "Then I must wish you good luck." She shook his hand, but did not look up from the child. " 'Tis a daughter you have got—what is her name?"

"Borgny, after my own mother." Torhild took the child from her breast, gathered together the kirtle over her bosom, dried the little one's mouth with the back of her hand, and turned her face to Olav.

"A fair child." Olav felt he must say so. Out of the tiny red face the dark eyes, wondering, as is the way of infants, seemed to meet his. Then they slowly closed; she was asleep. Torhild remained sitting with her in her lap.

Olav thought that now she would surely tell him something of the man she had taken in here to be her husband. But she did not.

"Your brothers," Olav then asked, "were they at one with you in this?"

"You know, they have been used to that from childhood—if only I have them under my eyes, they listen to me."

Olav thought in that case she might have done better to keep at least one of them here, but all he said was: "Nay, 'tis like enough you should deem there was need of a man here now."

"Ay, as matters stood, I *had* to marry Ketil—he would not stay here longer on other terms. And had I not had his help all these years—he has done more than a man's work at Auken since he grew up. If I had let the lad go—hired another labourer—I could not be sure that he would not come to me one day with the same demand. So it was fairer to let Ketil take me and share the good fortune that is so largely due to him."

Olav made no reply. Then she said again:

"You remember Ketil? You saw him when you were here last?"

"Nay?"

"Ay, he was not fully grown then—"

It dawned on Olav: a half-grown lad with a foolish face—a foundling—who had been with Torhild at that time. Flushing deeply, without looking at her, the man asked: "Is *he* the one you have taken to be to my son in the place of a father?"

"Yes," said Torhild in a hard voice.

"Nay, I have never claimed to order your doings." Olav shrugged his shoulders. "And Björn?" he asked. "But maybe he is too young to have a say in this?"

"Oh no. He has known Ketil as far back as he can remember.—Here they come." Her pale, large-featured face softened and lit up in a little smile.

The door flew open—it led straight into the open air—and a gust of wind brought in the sound of young, laughing voices, a child's and a young man's. The smoke in the room swirled blue in the daylight. The boy had a windmill in his hand; he ran straight to his mother, beaming and shouting with joy. The man followed him, tall and fair; he said something as with a laugh he pushed back his ruffled yellow hair and wiped his face. Then they both caught sight of the guest.

Olav saw that Ketil knew him. He checked himself, became more reserved in his manner, and looked confused.

Torhild's husband was tall, rather loosely built, with big labourer's hands, which hung dangling to his knees, but his face was childish and rather foolish, with the long, low chin covered with fair stubble. Yellow, shaggy hair hung over his forehead. For all that, he was far from ugly.

Torhild got up and laid the child in the bed, saw to the pot. She signed to Ketil that he was to take his place in the master's seat. He did so.

The boy had remained standing by his mother. He was not tall for his age, but was close-knit, shapely, and strongly built. Olav saw that Björn took after the Hestvik race—curly hair, pale as bog-cotton, large eyes, clear as water, set rather far apart under fair, straight brows. His skin was white as milk, with a few little dark freckles over the root of the nose. He stood coolly surveying the stranger.

Torhild spoke to her husband, asking how he had fared in his errand at the neighbouring manor. Then they talked awhile of the weather and the crops; she tried to draw both the men into the conversation, but to little purpose. Then a young woman came in—one of the neighbors who came to help Torhild in the dairy; Torhild had not yet been churched after her childbed. Torhild asked whether Olav had a mind to go out with Ketil and look round the farm.

Björn went with them. He took his stepfather by the hand, and while the men went round the little farm, indoors and out, the boy grew talkative—he agreed with everything his stepfather said or added something to it. Hitherto they had borrowed a horse, said Ketil, but if their luck held a few years more—

"You must know, Ketil," said Olav, "that if Torhild thinks I ought to do something more for her—"

"I know she does not," Ketil interrupted. And Olav, meeting his eyes, saw that the young man did not always look such a fool. "We have shifted well enough for ourselves all these years."

They had eaten their porridge, and Olav said he must think of going down to his boat. Then he called Björn and bade him come over to him.

The boy came and stood before Olav, looking at him with the cool, watchful expression in his handsome, sullen young face.

"Do you know who I am, Björn?" asked Olav.

"Ay, I guess that you are that Olav of Hestviken who is my father."

Olav had drawn a gold ring from his finger. "Then you will accept this ring, Björn—a gift from your father?"

The boy looked at his mother and then at his stepfather. As they both nodded, he replied: "I will, Olav—I thank you for the gift!"

He tried the ring on, looked at it a moment; then he went over to his mother and asked her to keep it.

Olav took his leave soon after. He asked Torhild to go outside with him. It was dusk, and the wind had increased. The violent gusts bent the bare rowan trees so that their branches scored the chilly green of the clear sky, but thick masses of cloud were advancing from the south.

Torhild said: "Will you sail home against this wind?—we can house you tonight."

Olav said he must go in spite of it. He threw the flap of his cloak over his shoulder. "Since you are now married and have a child in wedlock—might it not be as well that Björn came over to live with me?"

He could not hear the answer for the wind, and repeated his own words.

"You must not ask me that, Olav."

"Why not? I shall not marry again—and I shall bring the boy up as befits my son."

"No. You too have true-born children. I will not have Björn go where he will be reckoned an inferior. Better to be the first at Torhildrud than the last at Hestviken."

"Eirik has not been home now for four years. We seldom hear news of him, and 'tis uncertain when he will come back."

"I know it. But there is Cecilia—and that foster-daughter of yours, and your kinswoman, Lady Mærta. Then you know that the name my brothers bear in those parts is not such as to bring the boy more honour."

"You are well instructed about my affairs," said Olav sharply.

"Such things are noised abroad, Olav, of a man in your station."

Then Olav bade her farewell and left her.

He tried to shake it from him as he walked down through the darkness and the storm. It was unreasonable to be so angry. Torhild had a perfect right to marry. But that was the only thing he never thought could happen.

It was true that she might need a master on her farm, and true what she said, that if she let Ketil go, the next foreman she took might make the same demand. But that she should choose this foundling of all others— He recalled Ketil's face, childishly young and fair, a tall, powerful lad—hand in hand with the boy, merry and playful both. The last time he took leave of her—it must be seven years ago now—it had been Torhild's wish that *he* should take her back.—No, he would not harbour such thoughts; it was servile to think basely of any, without certain knowledge.

Björn. It must be bitter as death for a man to lose such a son, if he had had one.

The roar of the surf filled the whole air—through the gathering darkness the breakers rolled, alive and white. The packed stones of the little pier were battered and ground together with a dull booming by the waves that broke over them. Olav stood for a moment looking out—the wind had shifted due south. For all he had to do at home, he might just as well have stayed at Torhildrud till the morrow.

He had never thought of taking up with her again—but still his anger seethed within him whenever he recalled what he had seen up there. He was so wrought up that it surprised himself.

He had known all the time that she should never more be *his* —but he had nevertheless had some sense of ownership, in knowing that she was there—

The seas broke right over him as he went out on the little pier, where his boat lay rocking on the lee side.

7

THE FROST came early that year. Week after week the weather held, calm and cold, with brazen dawns over dark ridges; the fields were grey with rime, lakes and bogs frozen hard. On clear days the fiord was dark blue and ruffled; then the light breeze died away, and the surface seemed to expand as it turned grey under the frosty mist that came and settled, raw and biting, on the country about Folden. One day the sky was sullen; there was a scent of snow in the air. In the course of the day a few hard little flakes began to fall; the snow grew thicker, rustling down with a faint, dry sound—toward evening it fell in great flakes.

It snowed for a couple of days, one evening the south wind got up, and then there was driving snow.

They had gone to rest early at Hestviken that night—it was two days before Lucy Mass.[1] Olav was waked by a thundering at the outer door; he heard one of the house-carls get up and go out. It often happened in such weather that people of the neigh-

[1] December 13.

bourhood, coming ashore late, asked lodging for the night at
Hestviken, so he lay down again; was sleepily aware of folk coming into the room; someone stirred the embers, rekindled a flame.
Then he was wholly roused by hearing his name called. Before
his bed stood Torhild Björnsdatter with a lighted splinter of pine;
the snow lay white on her hood and the shoulders of her mantle.

Olav raised himself on his elbow:

"In God's name—are you here! Is it Björn?" he asked hastily.

" 'Tis not to do with Björn. But Duke Eirik crossed Lake Vann
today—with five hundred horsemen, they say. He will be bound
for Oslo, to greet his father-in-law and return him thanks." [2]

"Where have you heard this news?"

Torhild thrust her torch into a crack of the wall and sat on the
side of his bed as she talked. Her brothers had had a share in a
fishing-boat this autumn, and now she had been with them out to
Tesal, to her mother's kinsfolk there. Thither some yeoman had
come that morning, who had fled before the Swedes—they were
ravaging the country, plundering both goods and cattle.

"God have mercy on the country people," said Olav. "They
cannot secure their cattle in the woods either, in wintertime."

"Hestviken lies out of the way," replied Torhild; "yet I have
thought, Olav, it were safer for your little maids and for the
women on our side of the fiord. They say there are German mercenaries with the Duke. So I bade Egil to put in here to Hestviken,
I would offer to take them home with me."

"You are faithful to me and mine, Torhild," said Olav gently.
"And thoughtful."

"I was well off while I was with you—and Cecilia is sister to my
son. But what will you do yourself, Olav?"

"Carry the news northward to Galaby."

Torhild went into the hearth-room to the house-folk. When
Olav came out to the others, he was dressed in a short homespun
coat, which showed the leather hauberk underneath, long woolen
breeches swathed about the calves; on his head he wore an Eng-

[2] Duke Eirik was the brother of King Birger of Sweden, son of King
Magnus Ladulas, and grandson of the great Earl Birger. Eirik had been betrothed in 1302 to Princess Ingebjörg, the little daughter of King Haakon V
of Norway. His ambition was to make himself master of the three Scandina-
vian kingdoms, and as one of the steps to this end he seized his brother
Birger and threw him into prison. Eirik's invasion of Norway, here de-
scribed, took place in 1308.

lish helmet with cheek-pieces and gorget. He carried his shield
and the axe Kinfetch in his hands. Torhild looked at him.

"Think you Reidulf would try to raise the yeomen to resistance?"

"That would be no bad plan," said Olav. "There is both the
Hole and Aurebæk Dale—narrow defiles between screes, where
the horsemen cannot move to either side. The Duke must have
thought he could trust to the black frost's holding till the change
of moon at least, but these snowdrifts will delay his march."

Mærta Birgersdatter said she would stay at the manor. If the
Swedes came, it was not impossible that she might find kinsfolk
and friends from the border country among them: "and then it
might be of use that I speak with them—that they deal gently
with your property. I owe you so much, Olav, that I would fain
do you a service in return, if I can."

"Think not of *that*," said Olav deprecatingly. It troubled
him vaguely that these poor women came and wished to show
their gratitude for the little he had done for their welfare—as
though it reminded him of old and half-forgotten things: of One
who had stretched out His hands to help him, but *he* had turned
away, ungratefully.

He bade Bodvar arm himself to go with him northward, and
went out to the storehouse together with old Tore. They put up
some sacks of food, for Olav thought that Torhild could not possibly bear the cost of feeding so many mouths for an indefinite
time. While busy with this he chanced to knock down his skis,
which stood in the store. He had used them little since he came
south—folk hereabout had given up ski-running a generation ago.
Now it occurred to Olav that they might be useful: the road from
the shore up to Galaby must be well covered with fresh snow.

Together with his men he carried the sacks aboard the Björnssons' vessel; she was not so very small, there were seven men in
her. While they were engaged, in the darkness and the driving
snow, in stowing sacks and boxes, the light of the lantern fell on
a big bundle that lay near the mast, well covered over, among
barrels and other goods. Wrapped in rugs and skins, Torhild's
children lay asleep; Olav had a glimpse of the boy's fair head.

The herring-boat put off from the pier, and Olav stood awhile
listening for her after the night had swallowed her up. The gloom
and the flying snow surrounded him like a tent on every side. He

could feel the hill behind him and the homestead under the steep black wall of the Horse Crag in the black night, and before him the pitch-black water swirled below the edge of the pier, the teeming snowflakes sank into it and were gone. He stood there with Bodvar and a strange lad who had been on board the fishing-boat; on seeing the master was armed, he had begged leave to join him.—All at once an unruly joy surged up in Olav—as though he were released from fetters; it was dark behind and dark before, and here he stood all alone with two armed men, utter strangers, and he knew naught of what the morrow might bring.

Bodvar leaped down into the boat and began to bale her out.

It was toward midnight when the three men from Hestviken reached Galaby. Through the driving snow they caught the smell of smoke beating down from the louver, and on reaching the door Olav heard that folk were still up in the hall—drunken men who were bawling and singing. He had to hammer on the door for some time before at last it was opened. He who opened it was a tall, thin man—he gave a low cry of surprise as Olav and his companions entered. Olav recognized Sira Hallbjörn.

"Are you come with a message of war, Olav—or why are you helm-clad, you and your men?"

"You seem to be a soothsayer, priest."

Olav looked across the room—two torches stood burning on the long table, and the eight or nine men who sat around it or lay sprawling over the board were drunken, all of them. Olav knew most of them—they were landholders from his or the next parish. Reidulf Jonsson, the Warden's deputy, had slipped down between the high seat and the table as far as his stomach would let him; his big head with its brown beard had sunk upon his chest. It was the youngest of his brothers who sat on the floor singing, with his legs stretched out into the straw and his head in the lap of another young lad who sat astride the outer bench, twanging on a little harp. The priest alone was almost sober. Sira Hallbjörn suffered from the same defect as Olav Audunsson: God's gifts did not bite on him; he was just as thin, no matter what he ate, and just as sad, drink as he might.

He stood tense and erect, listening to Olav's tidings. Olav had not remarked before that the priest's red hair had become strongly streaked with grey of late, and his narrow, bony, and freckled face was aged and wrinkled now. But he was still clean-shaven, like Olav himself—such had been the usage in their young days.

It was not many of the franklins that they could rouse to sufficient clarity to make it worth while taking counsel with them. They had come to Galaby for the settlement of a suit. "Baard, your kinswoman's husband, went home early," said the priest; "and ill it was that he did so. He was the man we had most need of as leader—Reidulf is little worth."

Olav said they must first send a messenger in all haste to the town, to the captain of Akershus—"but sooth to say, I have more mind to stay with you here—if you hold with me that it will be a great shame on us if we let the Duke march through Aurebæk Dale without trying whether perchance we may give him some trouble."

"Fifty men should be able to hold the pass a day long against an army," said the priest. "And the townsmen will gain time—if we gain no more."

Young Ragnvald was sober enough by now to take things in pretty clearly. He offered to ride in at once. The priest got out writing-materials; meanwhile Olav and some of the others went to the servants' room to wake the men there.

The snow had abated a little as the body of franklins made their way toward the church town, but every trace of the road was drifted over. The priest and some of the others rode; so they soon went ahead of the rest, who had to tramp on foot in the snow-drifts. Olav glided quietly and lightly on skis by the side of the horsemen; now and again he had to stop and wait for them. He was standing at the edge of a little clearing, when Sira Hallbjörn appeared out of the darkness. The priest reined in his steaming horse, leaned over to Olav:

"I have been thinking: we are two men here who can run on skis—what if we struck southward tonight and scouted?"

Olav said he had thought the same.

At the parsonage they came into a pitch-dark, ice-cold house —Sira Hallbjörn had been from home since break of day, and his house-folk were in bed. At long last he managed to strike fire and light candles. To Olav it seemed many days since he took boat at Hestviken; the night had been hard and long, the sail up the fiord, then on skis and into one strange homestead after another—it had all taken time. From within the closet Sira Hallbjörn called: would he not rest awhile before they set out?—but Olav said they could not afford to waste time. He packed in his scrip some frozen bread and meat and a ball of butter that the priest's servant brought him—remembered that he had left home without food or money, thinking he should be back before they took the field. But the very fact that he was now headed straight for warfare gave him an easy feeling.

Sira Hallbjörn stepped out. He wore a smooth, old-fashioned iron helmet with a big, hinged visor and a pitch-black canvas hauberk over the priest's blue frock, which he had kilted up; his sword hung in a leather baldric over his shoulder. In his hand he held a longbow such as the English and the men of Telemark use; the arrows rattled in their quiver on his back.

Olav could not resist saying, with a little smile: "You are arrayed to sing a man's requiem now, father!"

A tremor seemed to pass over the other's sharp, long-nosed face:

"*Tempus occidendi, et tempus sanandi*—you told me once, they taught you something of the scripture when you were at Hamar in your youth. Did he teach you that saying, the stubborn Lord Torfinn?"

"No. But so much do I know, that I think I can tell the meaning. A time to kill and a time to heal?"

The priest nodded; he bent his bow and strung it. " '*Tempus belli et tempus pacis.*' Solomon wrote that in the book that is called Ecclesiastes—'tis one of the bravest books in scripture. But take off your armour, Olav—'twill be heavy to run in."

Olav removed his surcoat and took off his hauberk. It was of elk's hide with thin iron plates about the waist to protect his vitals. As he folded it and tied the thongs he asked: "Are there more such sayings in the book you named—of war?"

" '*Laudavi magis mortuos quam viventes. Et feliciorem utroque judicavi, qui necdum natus est, nec vidit malo quæ sub sole fiunt*' —such are his words."

Olav shook his head: "That was too learned for me!"

" 'I praised the dead which are already dead more than the living which are yet alive. Yea, better is he than both they, which hath not yet been born, nor seeth the evil work that is done under the sun.' "

"Is such the wisdom of Solomon?" Olav slung the bundle of armour on his back, and the two men went out. Now it was snowing again so that the night flickered about them. "He must have said that because he sat too safely there in his castle of Zion and his days were too full of ease," said Olav, laughing quietly. Sira Hallbjörn laughed too as he ran and was swallowed up by the darkness; he had to go and find his skis.

They had the driving snow right in their faces across the fields and Olav had to exert himself so as not to lose the other's dark shadow in the flurry. Sira Hallbjörn went forward with long, supple strokes; the points of his skis sank deep in the heavy snow at each sweep. In the blind night he aimed blindly at gap after gap in the fences, where the gates were in summer. Olav wiped his face now and then and his helmet, on which the snow lay melting, sending streams of water down his neck, but he could not stop for an instant if he was to keep up with his companion.

Within the forest it was better. *Where* they were going Olav no longer knew, but the other seemed as sure as ever. Sometimes the firs stood so thick that their skis scraped the bare ground when they ducked under the snow-laden boughs. Olav recalled what he had heard said of the priest—that he was not afraid to hunt in another man's wood—but none cared to speak of it; Sira Hallbjörn raised strife enough without that. Likely enough it was true; the priest went forward as though he knew every turn of the way in spite of the darkness and the snow.

Once Olav recognized where he was—they had entered a narrow track with a steep wall of bare rock to the east of it and loose stones at the bottom, so Olav was afraid the skin underneath his skis would be cut to pieces, as they struck the bare rock so often. There was a faint gurgle of water underneath the snow. The weather had cleared; high up above the defile strips of black sky peeped out between light clouds, and a star twinkled. Folk shunned this pass after dusk:—any evening the troll's hound might be heard barking among the crags. Involuntarily Olav hailed the other under his breath.

"Are you afraid, master?" asked the priest with a little laugh as Olav came up to him. "Not even the troll will turn out his tike tonight."

"Not afraid either." Olav lifted off his helmet and let it hang on his back. "Only my head itches so; I am in such a sweat."

Sira Hallbjörn waited till the other was ready, then he set off again.

They went side by side over a flat white surface darkened by patches of water—it was oozing up now in the thaw. Sira Hallbjörn stopped for a moment, leaning on his staff and getting his breath.

"You are tired now, Olav?"

Above their heads the clouds were parting more and more, showing deep rifts of blackness and a few stars faintly shining. A deep sigh went through the snow-covered forest around the lake, and here and there the branches let fall their burden with a low gasping and rustling sound.

"Oh, nay. I feel I am not so good a ski-runner as I was in my youth."

"You are not used to finding your way at nighttime?"

"I went once from Hamar town to Miklebö in Elfardal—I have made that journey many times—but once I did the half of it by night and found my way—I knew not where I was going."

"Were you alone?" asked the priest.

Olav said: "I had company—half the way—with a young lad. But he was untried—had little skill at ski-running."

But Sira Hallbjörn asked no more. They stayed awhile longer to regain their breath, then the priest flung himself forward and they were off again. They plunged into the woods again and followed a watercourse—Olav had to go in the other's tracks, and they ran on and on. In a way he was pleased that the priest had asked no questions—and he felt it to be a good thing that he was beginning to be tired; more and more his body moved of itself. When he was gliding downhill he felt his heart beating less violently, and the breeze was cooling to his overheated body. A little shock of anger ran through him every time a branch caught in the load on his back and gave him a bath of wet snow.

He did not know how long they had been going, but at last the night began to fade away. It was in the grey light of early morning, with a sky again heavy with snow, that Sira Hallbjörn and Olav passed along the top of an enclosed field that sloped down to a cluster of farms in a plain. Olav was broad awake all at once— every yard was full of people, men in steel caps, armed with long swords, their horses close at hand. And thick black smoke rolled up from every roof—on one farm farther south a great bonfire was burning out in the yard.

Sira Hallbjörn stood watching, sniffing at the scent of smoke. Then he made for the alder thicket, creeping down gently and spying out. Olav followed, excited and wide awake.

They came to a rail fence. Before them a great white field sloped down toward the outhouses of the nearest farm. In front of the byre some armed men stood round two countrymen who were holding and flaying a slaughtered beast. Olav and the priest watched for a while.

"I declare!" Sira Hallbjörn laughed angrily. "They have forced him, Sigurd himself, to hold the beast, and 'tis his son that flays it."

Olav knew where he was now—these farms lay south and east of Kambshorn. The village was surrounded by forest, which divided it from the district to the east toward Jalund Sound. Olav advanced a little farther along the fence while he considered which way they ought to take in order to reach the more populous district under cover of the woods, so that they might have a sight of the Duke's main force.

Then he heard the twang of a bow-string behind him. He saw the arrow fly and bury itself in the snow behind one of the men who watched the flaying. Sira Hallbjörn knelt down on one ski and picked up another of the arrows that he had stuck in the snow before him. Olav turned abruptly and dashed uphill toward him. At the same moment the first bolt whizzed past him into the thicket, shaking the snow from the branches. The men by the houses rushed out into the field, but sank deep in the new snow. Then one of them fell. Sira Hallbjörn had shot a second arrow, but now he leaped up, and he and Olav fled together uphill over the pasture. One or two more bolts came whistling after them, but it was vain for the Swedes to give chase to the two ski-runners.

They halted a moment and listened—in a white clearing within the forest, where a few old barns stood.

"You shot unwisely, Sira Hallbjörn," said Olav with vexation.

"I have hit a longer mark ere now," said Sira Hallbjörn coldly; "but I sprained my thumb last night, so my first arrow went wide."

"It is not that I meant," said Olav impatiently. "But now we shall have small profit of our scouting—we have seen no more than we knew already. And 'tis most likely they will take revenge on the poor folk of these farms—"

Sira Hallbjörn's face flushed deeply with anger, the veins stood out like cords on his temples; but he received Olav's words in silence. And so they went on.

They now made for the highway, and early in the day they reached the southernmost farms of Saana parish. The folk here had already had news of the trouble, and as they came farther north they heard the church bells ringing. By the bridge north of the church they came upon a great body of countrymen, eager for news.

It was very mild and the sky hung low and grey over the level country, but the ice on the river was safe under the covering snow, so it would be useless to try to check the Swedes at the bridge. Moreover, many of the folk from here had taken their cattle with them eastward into the forest tract of Gardar; it lay well out of the way.

Sira Hallbjörn urged the men to go with him and join the countrymen farther north, all those able to bear arms. But it was easy to see that the people of Saana parish thought things were well as they were: they expected the invaders to march straight through their district without doing them great damage. And they even seemed not to wish that the Swedes would be thrown back—if they had the hostile army pouring over them, smarting under a defeat, it would be worse than all. "The rich townsmen, merchants and clerks, are better able to pay ransom than we."

Olav saw the priest was so angry that it would be imprudent to let him have a hearing. So he himself stepped forward and spoke:

"Good friends and kinsmen, see you not that if Duke Eirik get possession of the castle of Akershus, we shall have this hard master over us all for we know not how long, till the spring at least, and then he will fleece us all to the skin. He has with him three hundred German horsemen—we all know what that means—and he owes them pay. Much better were it that we meet him now and see if we can make him change his mind."

Someone suggested that surely King Haakon must come home now and defend the country.

"The King has his hands full with defending the border by the river. We franklins here about Folden had a name in old time of

166

being peace-lovers, so long as we were left in peace. Do you not remember how our forefathers danced more than once with their enemies on the ice outside Oslo?"

"They did not carry off the victory in that dance, Olav Audunsson," a man interrupted. "Know you not that?"

"They gained by it in the long run, for all that, Erling—'tis always worst in the end for him who dare not defend himself. And so thickly peopled is the country hereabout that we should be men enough to bring the Duke to another mind."

The end was that Paal Kurt of Husaby and the sons of Bergljot from Tegneby promised to follow with as many men as they could raise. Sira Hallbjörn and Olav then went on.

"Knew you not," asked the priest, "that the King sailed to Björgvin before Martinmas? Sir Helge and Count Jacob have charge of the new castle on Baagaholm with few men—"

"Better to let them think hereabout that they have our army at their back."

"Where have you heard that the Duke owes the Germans pay?" he asked again.

"Never have I heard aught else of dukes and mercenaries—" Olav gave a little laugh. "*Tempus bellus*, was it not so you said?"

"*Tempus belli*," Sira Hallbjörn corrected him, and laughed too.

Arrived in their own country, they heard that Baard of Skikkjustad and Reidulf, when he was sober again, had given up the plan of meeting the invaders in the Aurebæk Dale and had gone forward with more than eighty men to join the men of Aas; they had taken up arms. Folk judged that with the snow in this state the Duke could not advance farther the first day than Kraakastad or Skeidis, and so the country levies would wait for him a little to the northward, where the road runs under a little ridge, having on its eastern side some bogs that never freeze till after midwinter, as they are full of springs; there they thought they could decoy the horsemen out into the morass. Olav was not very familiar with the country inland, but the priest muttered and shook his head when he heard of this plan.

They reached the place as it grew dark. In a little hollow on the ridge the watchmen had made a fire. The scouts made their report, as they had agreed upon it—they both thought it useless to say that they had seen a little of the hostile army. They took

off their boots and hung them on poles by the fire, threw themselves down on beds of pine branches close to the crackling logs,
where some men had set up a sort of tent of blankets and cloaks,
and fell asleep, dead-tired both of them.

It was not yet full daylight when Olav was aroused as they
broke camp. He snatched his boots from the pole above the embers; they were toasted hard, but gratefully warm, for he was
chilled all through. He pulled on his hauberk over his coat and ran,
axe in hand, to the brow of the ridge.

Below him the rock sloped smooth and steep for thrice the
height of a man to the narrow road that skirted the bog. Farther
on, it swung onto the high ground. The slope was not very steep,
and the weak point of the position was that at the top of the pass
there was level and open ground on both sides—mossy ground
with scattered trees. Up here lay the men of Aas and Saana, a hundred or more. On the edge of the ridge stacks of timber had been
built.

From below, the muffled rumble of the advancing body could
be heard already, and the splashing of horses' hoofs in the slushy
road—he made out the leading horsemen to the southward; they
could ride three abreast here. Out on the bog dark clumps of men
could be seen running, where the ground was hard; they were the
yeomen who had lain at the little farms under the brow of the
wood in that direction. At that moment came the first shower of
arrows and javelins, but most of the men on the bog had aimed
too high, so that their shots flew over the heads of the horsemen
and struck the cliff—one fell in the heather about the feet of those
standing on the ridge.

"Too soon besides," said Baard of Skikkjustad with an oath—he
was standing just in front of Olav.

For all that, there was confusion in the ranks of the horsemen
on the road below; some of the horses reared or tried to break out
to the side. Those who rode in the van reined theirs in; there
were shouts to those behind and answering shouts. Then the
leaders spurred their horses; it looked as if they would ride on
without heeding the body of men on the bog. Great pools of
water had formed during the night, disclosing the danger of
attempting to pursue the attackers on horseback—nay, but some
of them were leaping out of the saddle, they would try a bout
after all.

So far as Olav could judge in the grey dawn, the mounted troop
was about an old hundred in number. They pressed on from the
rear; some horsemen were forced out to the edge of the bog. And
now the leaders had reached the top of the pass; there they were
met by the country levies, who received them with spears, axes,
and swords, and now the shots from the men in the bog began to
take effect—some riderless and wounded horses screamed and
neighed and caused confusion as they tried to break out of the
ranks, and the cries of wounded men rose above the clash of arms
in the pass.

Down in the road a loud young voice called out above the
tumult—a tall, erect man in knight's armour held in his horse and
called for a hearing. When the noise of the battle died down a
little the men on the ridge could hear that the knight was Norwegian. They could make out most of what he shouted to the
countrymen in the pass. In the stillness that followed Olav noticed that it had begun to rain.

The Norwegian knight called out that Duke Eirik had not come
to wage war on the people of the country, unless they attacked
him first. It was King Haakon who had broken treaties and agree-
ments both with the Duke and with the Danish King, so now they
might expect another raid on that land when summer came; and
he had made a pact with King Birger and would lead Norwegian
forces out of the country to support the Swedish beggar King
who wronged his own brothers. King Haakon had foully betrayed the man he had lately embraced as his son-in-law—and the
Duke sought no other aim here in Norway than to come to speech
with the King, but so basely had King Haakon outraged his own
knighthood, and so harshly and presumptuously did he rule in
Norway's realm, that Duke Eirik had found support with many
good and noble Norwegian lords, and they looked to it that the
people of the land would back their demand for a settlement.

"That is Sir Lodin Sighvatsson," said Sira Hallbjörn, "Bjarne-
fostre—a fox and a traitor like his uncle."

"Let go now," cried Baard along the line, and the men on the
ridge hurled down the piles of timber and stones. There was a
smell of scorched rock as the falling mass thundered over the
troop of horsemen below. Among the mass of tumbled logs Olav
saw horses' legs kicking in the air as the animals rolled; there were
neighs, cries, and shouts in the confusion and men struggled to

get out of the saddle and onto their feet—the road was a-crawl as when boys drop stones into a cup full of earthworms. Then he ran with the others along the edge of the rock and rushed out at the top of the pass, where the first troop of yeomen was now hard pressed and some men lay on the ground—and several of the horsemen had already hacked their way through, turned their horses, and attacked the Norwegians in the rear.

Olav had flung his shield over his back and wielded his axe in both hands, fighting among the steaming bodies of horses, while flakes of foam showered over him from the muzzles of the neighing and rearing animals. He seized hold of a bridle, warding off as he did so the rider's spiked mace with the head of his axe, pulled the horse down to its knees, and struck at the man so that he reeled to one side. Olav ran on past the overthrown horse and rider, and several of his own men followed him. He received a blow on the helmet which staggered him, but it glanced off and he kept his feet, fighting, feeling that this was an unequal struggle, men on foot with horsemen against them before and behind—the place was ill chosen. Now the Swedes broke through to the moor east of the road, where the opposing force was thin. Above the din of strokes and the noise of battle he heard a voice from there, shouting to the men to stand firm; it was that leader of the men of Aas whom he did not know. He could not see much on either side for the cheek-pieces of his helmet, but he realized that more and more of the enemy were riding round to the east over the moor—now the hottest part of the struggle was over there, and behind him his comrades were fighting with their backs to him and the others who received the advancing enemy. They had the bulk of the hostile force at their back now: the franklins' effort had collapsed, he saw that, and he yelled with the full force of his lungs, plying his axe like a madman. He guessed that the yeomen on the moor to the left of him were taking to flight, but the little band in the pass who were now fighting back to back, with mounted foes both above and below them, defended themselves with the frenzy of despair—no falling back, no falling back! sang the blows of their axes.

Then he saw down the road under the ridge a long line of advancing horsemen armed with lances; in the wretched grey light there was a gleam of wet on their steel caps and shoulder-plates, on the horses' armour—further resistance was useless.

He managed somehow to hack his way through to the steep side of the road, hooked his axe into a crevice, and got up. Before and after him his comrades climbed, scrambled, and ran—most of them had succeeded in getting up. A little way up the height he stopped and looked back. On the other side of the road the greater part of the country levies were in flight across the moor, pursued by horsemen, and they disappeared into the pine woods.

In the road, which was now much cut up, horses and men lay here and there, dark forms in the mud; some moved and some lay still, and on came the Duke's main force of steel-clad, heavily armed warriors, tramping and jingling—and the rain was now pouring down. Then Olav ran on along the wooded ridge.

Olav was making his way over a field, where some small houses lay, down by a brook. Before him he saw a man reeling as he ran; now he fell and lay still. Olav stopped as he came up to the man, lifted him, and turned him over. It was Baard's son-in-law, the bridegroom of last summer, he saw. Hoskold Jonsson pushed him away as though in stupor and sat half-upright, leaning on one hand, with drooping head; then he turned round and dropped down on his other side—like a child when one tries to wake him, Olav thought, turning over in his bed and going to sleep again. The snow was bloody about Hoskold. Olav gently raised the other and with some difficulty hoisted him onto his shoulders. It was heavy labour to trudge with him on his back through melting snow over the rough ground, but he got him into one of the houses and laid him down in a little room where two old women sat. Afterwards he could not remember what he had said to the women or they to him as he ran on in the tracks of some others, together with three men who had joined him by this hut. Now for the first time he noticed that he must have received a blow or a kick in the plate that covered his loins; it had made a dent that plagued him as he walked.

After a while he came up to a high, rock-strewn moor, where a number of the fugitives had halted. He flung himself down in the heather, leaning against the trunk of a spruce, and took some food—several of the men had bags of provisions and shared with the others. Baard was there and Sira Hallbjörn and four or five more whom he knew—in all, a band of something over twenty men had collected.

One of the men gave a shout, ran forward to a knoll, and looked out. Others followed him. From here a corner of Skeidis parish could be seen to the south. Beyond the forest a column of thick, black smoke rose up and spread itself in the heavy air. It was Hestbæk that was burning, said the men who hailed from that part. A little farther to the eastward they saw more smoke—the Duke's men must be taking revenge for the attack.

"You are sore stricken, Baard," said Olav in a low voice. Arne of Hestbæk, Baard's father-in-law and Olav's kinsman, was still alive, active and hearty in his old age. And now Olav had to tell Baard of his son-in-law, whom he had left behind, badly wounded, in one of the little crofts under the hill.

But Baard, the silent, good-natured franklin, only gave an angry laugh.

It was raining fast with a faint, rustling sound in the melting snow. The country where the farms were now blazing was ringed in by a thick, dark sky, which lay low on the black woods that closed the view. The men had crept in under the thickest trees, chewing food and sucking at lumps of snow as they talked together.

Now they could all see that an unsuitable place had been chosen for the attack. Aurebæk Dale would have been much better, with the narrow bridle-path between screes in the glen. But those whose homes lay nearest the forest there would have been loath to provoke the hostile army before it had left their district behind. Then it was said that the stacks of timber should have been saved till the mail-clad horsemen came up—and one man asked why the scouts had not reported that the force contained such a troop. Olav had just been thinking that had they known that, then —but it was Sira Hallbjörn's fault, so let him reply. But the priest said merely that these mercenaries must have lain at farms farther south than he and Olav Audunsson had been able to penetrate. The men cursed a little, others swore roundly: sure enough the Duke himself had been with that troop.

Then there was talk of what should be the next step. Most of the men were inclined to make for home and see how it fared with their farms.

Then Sira Hallbjörn spoke up: " 'Tis not to be thought that the Duke will be suffered to plant himself in Oslo without any trying to disturb him. If he sits down before the castle of Aker—he will scarce take *that* so soon; Munan Baardsson is neither a fool nor a coward, and he has a good following with him. It seems to me, then, that the best we can do is to make our way eastward to Eyjavatn and thence up to Sudrheim. Haftor, the King's son-in-law, and his brothers are brisk lads and the right ones to lead, if there be a levy. Haftor, I know, will scarce weep so sorely if he lose the chance of calling Duke Eirik brother-in-law—at Sudrheim they were but middling glad when the King betrothed to him the Lady Agnes's little sister."

Some young lads came climbing up from the wood, supporting among them an elderly yeoman who was bleeding like a pig. While some men, the priest among them, were tending the wounded man, one of the lads asked for Olav Audunsson of Hest-viken—was he here? At first Olav did not recognize the young man, but then he saw it was the lad who had leaped ashore from the Björnssons' fishing-boat and had gone with him to Galaby. Now the boy asked what Olav purposed to do and whether he might join with him. Olav said he might indeed, but he had not brought more with him than what he stood up in, and he for his part would follow Sira Hallbjörn's advice and betake himself to the Jonssons of Sudrheim, to see whether the men of Raumarike would try to drive the Duke out.

The stranger said that was to his mind. His name was Aslak and he was a son of Gunnar of Ytre Dal in Rumudal, but he had three brothers older than himself, and so his parents desired that he should enter a monastery. He had now been for three years, since he was thirteen, with the white friars at Tunsberg, for Father Sigurd Knutsson was his uncle. But he was not made for a monk —indeed, most of the time he had spent on one of the convent's farms at Andabu, and now he had leave of his uncle to return home.

"So when I heard of the raid and they spoke on board of putting in to Hestviken, and I saw you were in war-harness—uncle had spoken of you—you and he are friends, I think."

"Did Father Sigurd speak of *me*?" asked Olav, rather incredulously. "I have seen him, when I had occasion to go thither, but never have we exchanged many words—I cannot guess why he should speak of me."

"He said you were a bold man and had fared much in foreign lands—he told me you were fostered in his home country, at Frettastein, and had made your marriage there."

Olav made no answer to this. He never liked to hear of his young days or to meet with men from the Upplands who knew of him from that time. That Father Sigurd of the Premonstratensian convent had kinsfolk in that part of the country he had never known. But this seemed not to be worth a thought now. He asked Aslak where he had been during the fight in the pass and let the lad talk, but said little himself. He was rather tired too, and wet to the skin; he now felt his head aching from the blow he had had on his helmet, and his boots had rubbed the skin off his feet.

Soon after midday the party on the hill broke up. Most of them were going home—among them Baard of Skikkjustad; he wished to see to his son-in-law. But eleven men started eastward, led by one from Skeidis parish, who was to guide them through the forests to Eyjavatn. There were Sira Hallbjörn and Olav Audunsson, Markus and Simon, sons of Alf of Berg, and a stalwart young franklin whom Olav did not know; the rest were house-carls, and then there was this lad Aslak.

Within the forest a few more men joined the company, and there was talk of the fight; but none knew anything certain as to how many of the country levies had fallen or how many men the Duke had lost. One party of the horsemen had turned back, plundered and burned some farms, but they had not given themselves time to range far afield.

Soon all talking ceased. The little company tramped in single file up and down the woodland, over and around low pine-clad heights, in thick wet heather and sodden snow—on the tarns the slush was ankle-deep above the ice. And the rain poured and poured from a grey sky. At dusk they reached houses and cultivation; before them lay the lake, Eyjavatn, a wide grey surface under the darkening, rainy sky.

No one here had heard the least news of the troubles, and the people of the manor, where they asked shelter for the night, sent a messenger at once to the knight at Ormberg; war arrows were sent out and men went up to light the beacon. By next day they had assembled a band of over eighty men, who marched northward across the slushy surface of the lake on foot, on horseback, and in sledges.

8

THE FRANKLINS from outside were lodged at farms up and down the parish and lay there during the feast of Yule. In most places they were well received—the Raumrikings had a right good mind to march upon Oslo and give Duke Eirik a taste of their steel. But Sira Hallbjörn was invited to stay at Sudrheim—he was distantly related to Sir Jon Raud—and so the latter asked Olav Audunsson also to be his guest during Yule.

He occupied the manor with his youngest son, Ivar; the two others, Sir Haftor, the King's son-in-law, and Sir Tore, speaker of the Thing, were with the King at Björgvin. Sira Hallbjörn and Olav were assigned a bed in a fine house apart, where the two un-married sons lived, and Sir Jon had suitable clothes sent out to them.

Not for years had Olav kept Yule with so cheerful a heart. Messengers left the manor and came home with news: Sir Jon had his scouts abroad. The King's young kinsman, Munan Baards-son at Akershus, had received tidings of the raid in good time. The castle was undermanned, so he could not venture a sally, but he had beaten off the first attack. After that the Duke sat down be-fore the castle, but the long-continued rain forced him to break camp in the swampy ground about Aker and retire upon the town of Oslo. There he kept Yule in the old royal palace on the river-bank, dubbed his Norwegian friends knights, and held a tourna-ment—though it was said he had got an ague in the camp, so that he was often sick. He exacted a ransom from the country dis-tricts, nor did the townsmen go free, though he dealt somewhat more gently with them. The folk at Sudrheim laughed rather mali-ciously when they heard of it, for there had been no bounds to the affection the men of Oslo showed Duke Eirik before, when he visited the town as King Haakon's son-in-law to be. The Duke's army numbered three hundred German horsemen and a hundred and fifty Swedish men-at-arms, and his Norwegian adherents had among them a little over an old hundred of men, most of them armed after the fashion of squires.

Sir Jon Raud of Sudrheim was not so very old, but he was in bad health, so it fell upon his son, Ivar Jonsson, to lead the country levies, and he was courageous, prudent, and well liked by the people—but he was very young, just one and twenty. They kept their Yule feast at Sudrheim as usual, and here Olav met several men and women with whom he could claim distant kinship, going back to the time when his forefathers were in possession of Dyfrin. He was also related to the men of Sudrheim, it turned out.

"How can it be, Olav," asked Sir Jon one day, "that you have never cared to serve the King? 'Tis not right that a man of such good birth, substance, and courtly breeding should have no place among his bodyguard."

"I have served King Haakon when he called out the levies," replied Olav; "but you must know, sir, I was Alf Erlingsson's liegeman in my youth, and I swore by God and by my patron saint, when I heard the Earl had died in banishment, that never would I swear any other allegiance on the hilt of my sword, and least of all to the man who made him an outlaw."

"Then you are more loyal than most men," said Sir Jon, with a little sigh. He himself had known that Earl well, and after this he often talked with Olav of the gentle Lord Alf; and Olav felt he had not been drawn so near to his own youth and the time when he was free and light of heart—ay, not since he came home to Norway.

Sira Hallbjörn too was like another man, a sociable and kindly companion. He was in the war heart and soul and took part in all the Sudrheim men's plans. It was clearly far easier for him to mix with worldly lords and knights than with priests and countrymen. Sometimes he and Olav went hunting with young Ivar and his friends, when the weather suited. On the holy-days he said mass in the church, to the great joy of the people, for he carried himself nobly at the altar and had a clear and powerful voice, whether in speaking or singing—but the parish priest here was a bungler, and Sir Jon's chaplain was so old that he was in second childhood. He could still say mass, but he no longer knew people rightly; he often took Ivar to be Sir Jon, who had been his foster-son in his youth.

Sir Haftor's young wife, Lady Agnes Haakonsdatter, was at home at Sudrheim, as she was expecting her second child. There was already a son, and no doubt his kinsfolk had their plans for that boy, should the little Lady Ingebjörg die without heirs.

What Olav had heard of the lady's mother, King Haakon's

leman, had always moved him strangely, though most folk made a scornful jest of her. She was a yeoman's daughter from the fiords, and she had been Queen Ingebjörg's bath-house maid. One day when she had made the bath too hot, her mistress had struck her so fiercely that she left the bath-house bleeding and in tears, and there she was met by the King's young son, Duke Haakon. He spoke to the maid and asked why she was weeping so. Fair to look upon she was not, and she was much older than he, by a score of years at least; but before the year was out she had a child by the King's son. The Queen was sore displeased, but the Duke would not part from his leman, and when he took up his residence in Oslo, he gave her a manor in the hundred of Bergheim. Of the children he had with her, only Lady Agnes grew up. When he was to marry the German princess, he took his base-born daughter into his own house, but sent her mother to the convent of Reins; there she became a nun some years later. A pious and virtuous woman she had always been, and kind to the poor—but in the King's bodyguard they all thought she was ill chosen to be a royal leman, being small and pale, modest and shy with strangers; it was said she had often begged her lord to show mercy to such as deserved severe punishment. Lady Agnes took after her mother; she was small and wan, without charm, hard to talk to, but a gentle lady.

One day as Olav was sitting alone in the house, seeing to his weapons, a woman came in and went along the beds, lifting the coverlets and feeling the pillows. When she came into the light, Olav saw that it was Lady Agnes herself. He stood up and bowed, and when she came and gave him her hand, he dropped on one knee before the King's daughter and kissed her hand, thinking the while that she was more like a worn-out cottar's wife who was forced to keep up her toil until the very hour when she would be brought to bed.

"I wish to see if our guests are honourably housed here," said Lady Agnes. She sank upon a stool, and Olav stood before her with bowed head and a hand laid upon his breast; he thanked her, they lived well here in every way.

"You men from Folden can know but little of how it has fared with your homes?" the lady asked.

No, said Olav; they had heard no news from thence since they took the field.

"Then you have not had a joyful Yule?"

Olav could not help laughing a little—he had never drunk so good a Yule, he answered.

"But you know not whether your manor be standing or lie in ashes?"

"Hestviken has thrice lain in ashes, my lady," replied Olav as before. "If 'tis burned now for the fourth time, then I must even do as my fathers: take such fortune as God sends me and build it up anew."

"And what of your kinsfolk?" asked Lady Agnes.

"My son is with Sir Ragnvald on the border, and my daughters are with friends on the west side of the fiord, so I need not distress myself for them."

"Then you have no wife alive?"

"No, lady, this is the eighth winter since she died."

"Ah yes, then it must be easier for you, Olav, than for many men. One hears so many tales—the poor country folk in the south, God help them!"

"Amen, lady—but if He will, they will not have long to wait either, ere they be helped and avenged. Ill it is that we have not your lord with us, but Ivar has good will enough—"

"Oh, I know not," the lady sighed. "I cannot say I grieve so sorely either that Sir Haftor is away. Yeomen against German mercenaries—'tis an unequal struggle, even though the yeomen have numbers. And yet it is sad for me that my lord is absent from me at this time."

Olav looked down at the little wife; he thought her condescension somewhat uncalled-for and her words ill suited to a King's daughter, but he felt sorry for her. She had fine brown eyes like those of a hind, but other beauty there was none in her.

Nevertheless it was with a strangely keen pity that he heard, one morning a few days later, that now Lady Agnes lay in the pains of childbirth, and the ladies who were about her knew not how it might fare with her. Sir Jon and his kinsmen wandered about with gloomy looks, but what they must chiefly have feared was that if Lady Agnes should die, the strongest tie would be broken that bound Haftor Jonsson to the King, and if the child were lost, it would be one arrow less in their quiver.

But in the course of the evening a message came that Lady

Agnes had been delivered of a fine big son, and then there was joy: Sir Jon ordered in mead and wine, and the men drank to the welfare of the new-born babe. The grandfather had the elder boy, the year-old Jon, brought in, whom his kinsmen called the Junker among themselves—he was hailed and passed from man to man, and the franklins drank till they were under the table, like men, as Ivar said.

Next day the new-born son was christened by Sira Hallbjörn—Magnus he was called. The guests at the manor joined the kinsfolk with their offerings, and in the evening they held the christening ale with great merriment, but Olav could not but think of the young mother, whom all seemed to forget—one of her ladies had said she was very sick, lay wandering in a fever and wailing that Sir Haftor did not come in to her· they could not make her understand that he was in Björgvin.

But two days before St. Hilary there came word in the evening to Sudrheim that a levy of over two thousand men, from Lier and Ringerike, was marching on Oslo. The state of affairs in the town was that Duke Eirik had been dangerously ill during the holy-days, but now he was better and, for joy of that, his friends would keep the last day of Yule with wassailing. The men of Lier had had news of this, and they thought to fall upon the town that night.

Ivar Jonsson and his friends held a council at once, and next morning they set out with a body of over three hundred men, but the rest of the Raumrikings, who dwelt farther to the north and west, were to follow as quickly as they could: Ivar was afraid the men of Lier might forestall him and reap all the glory.

The men from Folden now mustered about fifty, and Olav Audunsson was their leader. It was he who had raised the yeomen for the first attack on the Swedes, and it was he who had sent warning betimes to the captain of Akershus. He himself had thought nothing of this till now, nor had he been among the leaders in the fight on the Oslo road; but here at Sudrheim he won credit for it, and it seemed to come about of itself that he was held to be the man of greatest mark among his company, the master of the ancient chieftains' seat of Hestviken and Alf Erlings-son's liegeman in days gone by. And here he himself thought it natural—as it should be, beyond that it concerned him no more.

The other three subordinate chiefs were much younger men, nearer in age to Ivar Jonsson.

As it was falling dark they reached the village of Tveit, below the Gellir ridge, and here they learned that the Duke had set guards at Hofvin Spital, at Sinsen, and at Aker by the church, but only a few men at each place, for it happened luckily that all these houses on the highroads belonged to Nonneseter, and the Abbess, Lady Groa Guttormsdatter, had protested with heavy threats against any injury being done to her dependants—nor would the Duke care to break peace with the masculine nun more than there was need. Everywhere in the ravaged districts the sisters' tenants had been let off more lightly than other farmers, whether owners or tenants; those who held their land of the Crown or of the nobles had fared worst. Sira Hallbjörn laughed when he heard it: there was no love lost between him and the Lady Abbess, for he had disputes of his own with her, but he too saw the humour of this. The priest accompanied Ivar in arms and armour.

After consultation with some of those who lived in the neighbourhood it was decided that the Raumrikings should move up into the forest before daybreak and conceal themselves there till the next evening. Then they would advance along the river Alna, surprise the guards at Hofvin on the way, and fall upon the town above Martestokker, at the same time as the men of Lier entered it from the west by way of the convent of nuns. The latter body would have to pass round by Aker church and over Frysja bridge, as the ice on the Bjaarvik was unsafe, and the lower reach of the Frysja was not yet frozen over.[3] Up here on the high ground it had frozen a little, and there was enough snow to enable the messengers sent westward by Ivar Jonsson to use their skis, if they kept to the roads and fields.

---

[3] This river (now called the Akers-elv) runs through some of the eastern quarters of the modern town of Oslo (Christiania). Its course lay some little distance to the north-west of ancient Oslo, cutting off the town, by land, from the fortress of Akershus, to the north of which was a marsh (where the city of Christiania was afterwards built). By water (or ice) the distance between mediæval Oslo and Akershus was comparatively short, across the Björvik (Bjaarvik), a small inlet at the head of the fiord. Akershus was newly built at the time of this story; the old royal castle of Oslo, which had been handed over to the Governor of the town and the clergy of St. Mary's, stood on the opposite shore of the Björvik, at the mouth of the little river Alna, which runs at the foot of the hill of Eikaberg.

They settled themselves in the farms of Tveit, Ivar and his captains, intending to rest there till near daylight. But shortly before midnight the door of the house was suddenly flung open, and in came one of the farmers with whom they had spoken earlier in the evening, accompanied by an old woman, his mother.

She lived in the town with her married daughter, and they kept an alehouse in a yard near the palace. The Duke's men had had word that a strong body of country levies was marching on Oslo from the west, and therefore they were making ready to attempt a storming of Akershus castle in the morning. The woman had watched her chance of slipping out of the town and bringing the message; for in Oslo it was whispered among the townsmen that the lords of Sudrheim were also engaged in raising men from the Upplands, but the Swedes believed nothing of this.

"There'll be another dance then, for the last day of Yule," said Sira Hallbjörn.

Now it was hard to know what course the Raumrikings should follow. Then Sira Hallbjörn demanded a hearing and said there were no more than two counsels to choose between: "—and neither is of the best. One is, that we set off at once and go west, the same way that our messengers went; cross the river by Sandakrar, fall on the guards at Aker farm, and then we must hold Frysja bridge tomorrow until the Lidungs [4] come up—if we can. Should the Duke have the luck to take Akershus, he can prepare a bloody bath for the yeomen's army coming from the west and buy his peace with King Haakon at whatever price he himself may offer—he and his Norse friends.—The other counsel is that we turn home again, up to Raumarike, and wash down our shame with the last of the Yule barrels at Sudrheim."

Young Ivar and his captains discussed the priest's counsel. It would be fighting on unequal terms, three hundred men, and of those not more than seven and forty mounted and armed after the manner of horsemen, the rest yeomen on foot, against the Duke's mercenaries and well-trained men-at-arms.

"What say you, Olav Audunsson?" asked Ivar. "You are the oldest and most experienced."

"I say the priest is right. There are but two courses open. Neither is good—but the first plan seems to me not so bad after

4 Men of Lier (near Drammen).

all. If we cannot hold the bridge, we can break it down and take refuge in Akershus."

Sira Hallbjörn reminded them that it was of great moment to prevent the Duke's getting possession of the castle. They must make ready to break down the bridge, as Olav said, and they had the church of Aker and the churchyard in their rear; that was a good position to defend if the enemy got part of his men across; and if they were driven back from the churchyard, they would have to take refuge in the church—that they could hold till the army from the west came up.

"Do you yourself believe what you said?" asked Olav as he and the priest were arming—"that the Lidungs can cut their way through to the church if the mounted troops reach the heights west of the Frysja?"

Sira Hallbjörn shook his head. "But we cannot return home without having ventured a brush. And it may cost the country dear, if Duke Eirik is to hold Akershus and treat for peace with his father-in-law that was to be—"

"Nay, that is so. Methinks this business has been somewhat brainlessly undertaken. But Ivar is young; 'tis worse to be heartless than brainless, and the heart is good enough both in him and in the men—no lack of fighting spirit."

"No.—Do you remember last summer at the wedding—when your axe sang? Now we shall soon see whether the warning was for you or for me."

"I have never heard that such weapons rang save for their own kin. But as things are shaping here, it looks most likely that it may mean both of us," said Olav with a little laugh; and Sira Hallbjörn laughed too—"Ay, it looks so indeed."

There was no moon, and the sky was strewn with stars. The snow was not deep enough to hinder the advance seriously; and now it was freezing a little. Olav Audunsson and Sira Hallbjörn rode at the head of the Folden troop—it was the last in the line. Olav and the priest had borrowed horses from Sudrheim, but Olav said he would fight on foot, for he was more used to that.

"If this frost hold a few days," said the priest, "the Duke will be able to bring mail-clad horsemen across Bjaarvik."

"Ay, we are late in moving," said Olav; "and lucky if we be not too late."

"At Sudrheim they would stay for the christening ale—and be sure these men from the west have had weddings and funerals and Yule barrels that must be emptied. But maybe we can yet drive back the Duke—as a repentant sinner drives off the Devil at his last gasp."

Olav said nothing. He looked before him, where the host of constellations descended to the dark line of the wooded ridge. It was strange to think he should have suffered so much all these years on account of *one* dead man, have pondered so sadly upon death and all that came after—but when it came to war and fighting, all such thoughts flew away and were as nothing. And so, no doubt, it is always and for every man.

Their guide could not find the ford over the river where the advanced guard had crossed; they had to go right up to a kind of pool, where boats lay. This delayed the Folden troop so much that it was already growing light as they came down again by a path that ran through the alder brakes on the right bank. The sky stretched above them wide and light, yellow as sulphur down toward the eastern hills, as they sighted the tower of Aker church above the trees, and below them, on the farther side of the Frysja, they saw the roofs of Fors, white with snow against the white ground. At the head of the fiord a mist lay over Akershus and the town, spread out in a thin sheet, above which rose the towers of Hallvard's Church and the gables of the old royal castle.

It looked more hopeful at the bridge than Olav had imagined —he had not passed this way since the King had built wooden towers at the bridgeheads. They were bigger than he had thought. The eastern one, on the Oslo side, was so much lower that the men on the western tower could shoot over it at an army advancing against Akersnes from the east.

Nor had Ivar been idle: his men were engaged in hoisting up stones and missiles into the barbicans, and in the middle of the bridge, where it rose highest, they were building a breastwork— some men were pulling down a few small cottages near the bridge, dragging out the logs and doors, while others loaded sledges with stones on the hillside and others again drove them down. So the men of Folden found work to do at once. From the Raumrikings they learned that the guards at Aker farm had been overpowered and cut down or made prisoner. Sira Hallbjörn at once secured two of the crossbows that Ivar had taken from the Swedes, for himself and Olav Audunsson—they both shot just as well with these weapons as with the longbow.

The day was already so far advanced that the Norwegians were saying that either the widow at Tveit had been doting, or the Swedes had given up the attack on the castle. The south-western sky was already afire above the forest on the Eikaberg ridge—the sun was just rising—when they heard the muffled beat of kettledrums just below at the brow of the wood under Fors. Their own work had been so noisy, and the falling water roared so under the bridge, that they had not heard the sound of advancing troops before. Now the rumble of many hoofs and the clanging of mail-clad men and horses rose and rolled toward them together with the undertone of drums.

The yeomen had been seen. A storming-ladder swung up above the bushes and shot down again: they were trying whether it worked in the grooves.

Olav flung his shield onto his back and dashed across the bridge with fourteen others, climbing over the obstacle in the middle. He had offered to take his stand in the foremost tower and had picked his party of young, strong lads who had a brisk look, to his thinking.

A boy came with them, bearing a banner—Olav knew his face from the streets of Oslo, but knew not who he was or how he had come here—and Olav answered, laughing: ay, let them set it up. It was a yellow banner with an image of Saint Olav on it—they had taken it out of the church; no doubt it belonged to a guild in Oslo.

The sun's disk shone in splendour over the top of the ridge as he stood on the flat roof of the barbican and saw and heard the enemy breaking out of the brushwood beyond the fields. The long mail-clad ranks advancing with a faint jingling and a subdued glitter in the cold shadows upon the white ground, the bright patches of the banners, the scaling-ladders and battering-rams that they car-ried—and now a horn rang out, and short cries were heard—Olav felt his heart beat fast: it was a hostile troop, but no matter, his joy at the sight ran down him like a deep draught of cold, strong ale.

He cried the watchword, at the same moment raising his shield aslant without thinking—old habits revived of themselves in every joint of his body. Simultaneously with the whirring of the two small catapults he had on his tower came the first shower of arrows and bolts from the western tower over their heads.

The men on the eastern barbican crouched down with their shields over their heads and looked out through the loopholes. Some horses had fallen, breaking the ranks and causing confusion.

"Have they only four ladders?" cried Olav to his neighbour, the boy from Oslo.

"They lost some under Akersnes."

A volley from the hostile army came flying, striking the wall of the barbican, rattling on the bridge behind them, but only a few shots fell on the roof, and none took effect. With exultant jeers the Norwegians picked them up. Now the ground thundered with heavily armoured horses. A troop of them were trotting toward the gate; they bore an iron-shod pole among them.

"What kind of playthings are these they use—do they think to take Akershus with the like of that?"

"You know they cannot bring their great battering-rams by this road," the Oslo boy roared back, "across the hill. They have reckoned on the frost—"

"Then they have been almost as bull-headed as our Ivar."

They shot the Swedes' own bolts back at the troop—they fell harmless on their defensive armour—set their shoulders to the pole, and raised the cauldron of boiling water up to the top of the parapet. As the first blow of the ram crashed against the gate, making the whole tower shake, the Norwegians emptied the cauldron upon the men below.

The shrieks of scalded men and horses, the thud of hoofs, and the jingling of armour were drowned almost at once in the din of a fresh troop that came up and thrust aside the sprawling mass of the first. "Go slow," shouted Olav to his men; "reserve your stones—" They had not too many of them and had to try to shoot straight down so as to prevent the attackers as long as possible from taking up the ram their comrades had dropped when the water came down on them. Meanwhile bolts and arrows from the archers in front rained down on their shields, and from the rear the shots of the Raumrikings in the western tower flew over their heads.

Olav saw one horseman who had been pressed too far out to the right—his horse slipped under him. Brought down on its haunches, it slid down the riverbank. Its shrill neighing rose above the din and the roar of the waterfall as it was carried into the dark, rushing water, with its rider hanging in the stirrup. The steep bank was covered with ice underneath the snow on both sides of the foot of the tower, and this was of great assistance to the Norwegians: the enemy could not send so many men at a time against the gate, and so far they had not succeeded in bringing up ladders. But it could not be long delayed.

A shout reached him from the bridge—eight or nine men were lifting baskets of stones over the breastwork and dragging them along. It had occurred to Ivar Jonsson that missiles might soon run short in the foremost barbican—thoughtless the young man was not. Olav's heart laughed with joy within him. Ivar had withdrawn his men from the breastwork and stood waiting with them in the western barbican, and this was right: it could not be very long before the Swedes broke down the eastern gate and reached the bridge. Ivar had had the parapet of the bridge thrown down at each end of the obstacle.

They had just had time to hoist up the baskets of stones when the first scaling-ladder fell against the parapet. So now it was the turn of the axes. It was a good thing he had brought up the basket-bearers, thought Olav, otherwise he would have been short of men for this work. Man after man they hurled down as they swarmed up the ladders. One or two of his own lay low, and the boards of the floor were bloody—but so was the snow at the foot of the tower—what snow there was left.

They could not hold the tower for long. Olav glanced up at the sun—the fight had scarce lasted half an hour.

Now the gate gave way beneath them with a crash, and it felt as if the whole tower staggered. Olav ran to the other side and looked down to see how things were going. The yeomen had dashed forward and manned the breastwork, Ivar in the midst of them. The horsemen could only advance two-abreast. The blows of the yeomen's maces and axes and the clash of swords rose above cries and the tramping of horses—for a while this might go well. More of the mounted troop, horse and man together, had gone down in the torrent; now the Swedes were sending footmen onto the bridge.

Sira Hallbjörn he saw on the top of the breastwork, slashing with his great two-handed sword; the priest fought like a devil.

Olav threw away the fragments of his shield; there were only splinters left between the iron bands. He grasped Kinfetch in both hands and turned to where the ladder had been, but now it was gone; it hung on a jutting rock in the hollow sheet of ice over the torrent, and they were bringing up another. Behind him his men thrust down the enemies who were trying to mount the inside ladder to the roof—they ought to have drawn it up.

Now Ivar and his men sprang over the breastwork and advanced over the bridge. They cleared it in a moment—for that time. And the Swedes drew back across the fields, out of bowshot.

Olav lifted off his helmet to cool himself a moment. There was refreshment too in the stillness, with the roar of the torrent, which had been drowned by the fighting. And now he found it was not only sweat that had made his clothes stick to him, for his elk's-hide hauberk was slit just over the body-plate, and bloody, but the scratch he had got was not a deep one, by the feeling.

A morion appeared in the opening—Sira Hallbjörn was climbing up the ladder.

"How many of you are alive? Go back now, you, and we fresh men will receive the next shock."

"There is not much here to receive a shock with, Sira Hallbjörn."

They saw men coming across the fields from the houses of Fors; they were carrying something.

"They will try to set fire to the barbican," said Olav. "We must hold out as long as we can."

"Ivar has placed combustibles within the breastwork," said the priest.

"Then it will end in the bridge being burned. After that they can stand on either bank and sing staves against each other," laughed Olav. "And then the issue will be better than we had looked for."

In the fields in front the horns sounded the assembly. Olav stooped and picked up the yellow Olav banner, which had been torn down, and set it up again—it was now stained with blood.

"Now we must show them what we can do with the crossbow, Sira Hallbjörn!"

The horsemen came on in close array, and in their rear followed men with fire-cauldrons, pots of pitch, and faggots. A bolt from Sira Hallbjörn's bow was so truly aimed that one of the fire-pots dropped on the ground and turned over.

Ivar Jonsson and his men had propped up the doors and wreck-age in the gateway. They stood behind with long spears, clubs, and cudgels with scythe-blades, and in their rear the bridge was filled with men, waiting to go forward as those in the front rank fell.

The third attack thundered against the gate and the shaking walls of the barbican. Once more Ivar Jonsson and his yeomen succeeded in beating back the assault, and the sullen little fire that smouldered at the base of the tower was put out by the men on the roof with the cauldron of water from the cold fireplace in the tower—no one had managed to keep the fire in.

Again the Swedes withdrew a little way, and the noise died down. From the barbican they could see the leaders ride round the ranks and come together for a consultation. Then all at once the priest cried: "Look!"

Olav turned and looked where the other pointed.

"Ay, now we can make an end and sing *Nunc dimittis*," said Sira Hallbjörn.

Teams of horses broke through the copsewood yonder—they drew the great catapults and heavy siege engines.

Ivar Jonsson ordered the horn to be blown. He stood on the bridge and called up to the men on the barbicans—his silken surcoat hung in strips outside his harness. They could do no more now but retire and see if they could break down the bridge after them.

Then came the sound of a horn from the hill behind them—in notes that answered Ivar's. A bright, resonant ribbon unwound itself in the blue and white light of the winter day. Olav turned round—up behind the churchyard fence the morning sun flashed on a close array of spear-points.

The shouts of joy from the little force about the bridge were met by a fresh blast of the horns. This was an ancient call—folk named it the Andvaka strain or King Sverre's dance. Little as Olav Audunsson was minded to praise old King Sverre, there was yet no tune he would so gladly have heard in this hour.

Sira Hallbjörn had laid hold of Olav's arm—the priest's hand was bloody. Olav saw with surprise that the other's cheeks were ashy white, his face was distorted in a wild luxury of pain:

"That is *our* horn! My father's, I mean—I should know it above all others. Then they must be here, my brothers—Finn or Eystein."

And as the horn sounded anew the Andvaka strain, Sira Hallbjörn joined in, singing in his fine and powerful voice the ancient stave that went to that tune:

> "*Cattle die,*
> *kinsmen die,*
> *last dies the man himself;*
> *one thing I know*
> *that never dies:*
> *the fame of each man dead!*" [5]

They took it up and sang with him, all those who knew the stave, while the Raumrikings tore down the obstacle before the first mounted troop—there were at any rate fifty men on horseback, armed after the fashion of the King's men. They rode across the bridge, and after them swarmed the footmen, country folk, but most of them handsomely armed. Olav saw Sira Hallbjörn running out into the fields by the side of a high brown horse, holding on to the saddle-bow—the man who rode it wore a closed helm and a fluttering blue silken surcoat over his armour.

What the new-comers meant to do he could not rightly guess; it looked as if they would try to drive back the enemy in open fight out in the fields. They had already surrounded the body of Swedes who were on their way to the bridge, and with the knights who led them at their head, the men from the west were now advancing, far off, against the main body who stood by the siege engines at the brow of the wood.

Ivar Jonsson had mounted the barbican with Markus of Lautin, one of his captains.

"Can they do that—drive back German mercenaries with a rabble of peasants—then anything may happen!"

"There must be two thousand of them at least," said Olav. They continued to pour down the hill below the church and across the bridge.

"And not one in twenty can get back over the bridge if they are beaten," said Markus.

---

[5] These lines are from the Eddic poem called "The Guest's Wisdom." The speaker is Odin.

The attack of the Norwegian knights had already broken down —two of them were dragged from their horses and carried away as prisoners. But the Lidungs simply went on—if one body was thrown back, another troop dashed forward. Time after time the German mercenaries rode into the mass, trampled them down, and used their lances, but the Norwegians ran in upon them from the other side, hammering at men and horses with clubs and axes, cutting and thrusting with hafted scythe-blades and spears. They had pressed up to the edge of the wood in great numbers and managed to hold the enemy there, so that his catapults were of little use against them; but neither could the men in the barbicans support the Lidungs to any extent—they were fighting out of bow-shot.

Before the bridge all was quiet. A few horses and men lay stretched in the brown and bloody slush, and one of the horses moved and struck out with its hoofs now and then. A young lad came walking toward the bridge, supporting his right arm, from which the blood dripped, in his left, and he jogged homeward with a curiously peaceful, solitary air, as though he were carrying something he had been out to buy.

But now the first groups of yeomen were being driven back over the lands of Fors. Olav grasped his crossbow; as he put his foot in the stirrup and drew it, he noticed for the first time that his body was stiff with tiredness.

Once more the flying Lidungs rallied in the fields, and once more the enemy rode forward. At that moment something struck Olav on the right cheek-piece of his helmet—there was a crash inside his head, and he fell backward into Ivar's arms. For a moment everything went round. When he stood up again and took his bow, he felt his mouth full of blood and pulpy flesh; he spat out blood and splinters of teeth and shot again with his crossbow.

Now the Lidungs had retreated so far that the Swedes could reach them with their catapults; stones and other missiles fell among the knots of men, and the first fugitives began to make, some for the bridge, others for the forest to the northward. Olav had stopped using his bow; he stood gazing intently at the conclusion of the fight, while all the time, without thinking, he had to feel with his tongue the sharp edge of steel that had penetrated his cheek and the broken molar in his upper jaw. But soon his tongue grew stiff and swollen and the wound filled his whole mouth like a bloody sponge. But he gave little attention to it as he watched the fight drawing to its end.

The horn of the Valdres knight sounded the assembly, untiringly, and once more the main body of the western men formed up just below the barbican. The Raumrikings in the towers had now been relieved by fresh men with bags and quivers full of bolts and stones. Olav tried to speak to those who had come up and stood around him, but it was no more than a blob-blob-blob and a croaking in the throat, with all the blood and spittle that filled his mouth. He could scarcely believe his eyes, but the Swedes were not advancing; it looked as if they were about to retire into the woods—had they had enough of the game?

Awhile after, he walked back across the bridge, as in a dream, so heavy was his head—amid the stream of strangers who were returning. But he had bethought him of his axe before going down from the tower; as in a dream he remembered striding over dead bodies that lay inside the barbican at the bottom of the ladder, and as in a dream he heard the shouts of the men who manned the towers, making ready to defend them again, if there were need. He had to make way for two men who were carrying a third by the shoulders and knees. Drowsily he noticed that the planks of the bridge were dark and slippery with blood, and he turned a little giddy at the sight of the black water that rushed under the bridge and thundered over the fall.

When he had come a little way up the hill toward Aker church he stopped and laid down his axe—he wanted to take off the helmet that pressed so painfully on his head, and it was horrible with this splintered steel among the torn and tender flesh of his mouth. A man stopped and helped him with it. The sweat burst out anew all over his sweat-drenched body, and the tears came into his eyes, before the other had got the helmet off him, and his cheek was gashed worse than before. The stranger offered to take him under his arm, but Olav shook his head, tried to laugh, but could not, for his face had grown so stiff and seemed enormous. Then the other picked up the axe and the helmet and gave them to him, said something, with a laugh, and went on. Olav tried to wipe away some of the blood that trickled down his neck, it made him so disgustingly wet underneath his clothes.

The sun was now high in the heavens, he noticed; it was past midday and had turned to the clearest and finest of winter days.

The tree-tops round the church shone against the blue sky as though it were springtime, but the light hurt his eyes.

He came up to a farm on the hill and went into one of the houses. It was packed full of men, but he saw none he knew. Several spoke to him when they saw his shattered face, but he could not get out a word. Some of them made room so that he could sit on the floor in front of a bench, and one who sat on the bench took his head in his lap, and then weariness overcame him. He did not really sleep, for the pains in his head increased, as though tearing out his very skull, and he felt himself growing chilled and numb, but he sank into a sort of lethargy.

Once he was roused from it—a bulky, elderly woman had told of him. A half-grown girl with solemn, staring eyes stood by, holding a bowl from which steam rose, and the woman dipped a towel, which was now stained brown, and washed the blood from his face and neck with lukewarm water. Dizzy and impatient with fatigue and pain, he had to submit to be helped up, so that he could sit on the bench—gazing the while with longing at the great blaze on the hearth, for he was shivering. The woman and a man stripped away his elkskin hauberk, peeled off his jerkin and shirt, which stuck fast to the skin; naked to the middle, he sat shivering as they washed him and tended his wound, a cut reaching upward to below the left nipple; and then they drew on his clothes again, which were now soaking wet.

He staggered to his feet and tried to go and sit by the fire, but a woman who was like Torhild took him by the arm and led him to a bed that had been made on the floor. When once he had lain down, it was good indeed to stretch out his limbs and lean his back and neck against the big sacks of hay. She who looked like Torhild spread a thin coverlet over him and offered him a warm drink, but he could not take much into his mouth and it was too painful to swallow. But soon he felt the warmth of the rug, and of a big, black-bearded man against whom he was lying, and the warmth was an unspeakable relief, though his head felt as if it would burst with pain.

After a while he was again roused from his doze; they wanted him to go out with them. He went. It was almost dark outside, the southern sky a greenish yellow; great white stars were shining in the frosty evening. Up by the church great red bonfires were burning, around which moved black figures—the stables and the church barn were crowded with men. The main door of the church stood wide open, and he saw that many candles were lighted in the choir, a flood of song welled out, but his companion led him past, to a group of houses.

He came into a room where many men were assembled—he recognized Ivar Jonsson and one or two from home. Some of them were busy about a bench, and on it lay a naked corpse they were washing. Olav stepped up and saw that it was Sira Hallbjörn.

He lay on his back, long and white, with his arms hanging down so that the hands rested on the clay floor with the palms upward. The left arm was broken, so that the bones protruded above the elbow. They were just washing the blood out of his grizzled red hair, and there was a faint crackling of broken bone—the skull had been shattered above the left temple. Beside the bench stood a bucket of steaming red water.

Ivar Jonsson came up to Olav. He told him in a whisper that they had found the priest's body in a thicket of briers close up to where the Swedes' catapults had been posted—half-naked and plundered: his arms were missing, as was his seal-ring and the gilt Agnus Dei that Olav remembered Sira Hallbjörn always wore about his neck.

His brother, the knight Finn Erlingsson, was among those the Swedes had taken prisoner, but his sons, Eindride and Erling, were here, Ivar went on to tell him. Olav looked at the two slight red-haired lads who stood by their uncle's body, and nodded. Ivar was still talking—there had been Lidungs, Ringerikings, and men from Modheim parish among the levies, and a little band from Valdres led by Sir Finn.

The dead man's face was grey and calm as a stone image. The men who stood by were discussing what the scars could be that the priest carried on his body: the left shoulder and upper arm were scored as though the flesh had been torn, and on the left pectoral muscle were four deep little pits; from there a silver-white furrow ran down across the stomach. But the scars were old, so it was hard to say what kind of wild beast he had been at grips with.

Olav knelt down together with some others, but his wound and his whole head ached so that he could say no prayer. When he rose to his feet they had dressed the corpse and moved it to the bier. Now Sira Hallbjörn lay like a priest, dressed in an alb and

an old chasuble, with sandals on his feet and a pewter chalice between his clasped hands: some of the priests of Aker church had
provided what was fitting for their dead brother.

Olav accompanied the bier as it was carried down to the church;
several other biers were already standing before the chancel arch.
But he had not the strength to stay and hear the vigil. The man
who had accompanied him to the mortuary chamber took him
under the arm and led him back to the farm where he had found
shelter; it was Little Aker, the other told him.

Bodily pain was a wholly new experience for Olav Audunsson.
Wounds and scratches he had known many a time, with smarting
and fever, but they had always been such as he counted for nothing—flesh wounds that healed rapidly and cleanly.

But this wound in his face was downright torture: a racking and
shooting pain in his skull and an intolerable aching in the jaw-
bone and in the root of the broken tooth. But worst of all was the
loathsomeness of it—his mouth was always filled with the foul
taste of matter from the wound.

Now and again he had high fever, and then it was as if the bed
he lay in rose up and up and his body felt flat as an empty bladder,
while something round and heavy that had been inside his head
rolled down over him, and visions hovered along the ridge of his
brows—creatures that were neither beast nor man, faces that he
recognized without knowing who they were. In particular there
was a beggar without feet who darted along at a terrible pace on
boards fixed to his hands and knees; it tormented him more than
anything when that vision came.

One night he saw Ingunn—she stood a little off the ground
against the wall at the foot of his bed and leaned forward over
him, so that her light-brown hair swept over her thin bare arms
and fell forward like a mantle. He thought she was clad in nothing but a shift, which was embroidered at the neck with little
green flowers, so that all the little coloured spots danced before
his eyes. Olav raised his hands to keep her from coming nearer,
for just in those days his wound was angry and stank foully; but
she sank down upon him like a wave of warmth and sweetness, he
was flooded as it were with the goodness of her—then he lost his
senses, fell into a kind of swoon.

In the morning he was able to spit out a whole mass of matter and splinters that had worked out of his jaw; the woman who tended him could wash the wound fairly clean, and he felt better. He was weak and cold, and as he could only lie on the left side, it felt as if the bones were coming through the flesh there, so tender was it. At the same time he was famished; he had hardly been able to swallow anything of what they brought and tried to make him drink.

They had been to see him almost every day, one or another of his companions-in-arms, but he had not been fit to pay much attention to what they told him. But this morning came Ivar Jonsson himself and some more; they could scarce conceal their exultation. The Duke had withdrawn from Oslo at daybreak; it was clear he had lost his relish for trying his teeth on the walls of the castle of Aker, sick as he was himself, and with three thousand men of the country levies posted on the high ground. And Munan Baardsson had received reinforcements and was thought to have put the castle in excellent posture of defence.

The Duke had not lost much above half a hundred men in the fight at Frysja bridge; of the yeomen two hundred had fallen, and many had got wounds great and small. But it seemed Duke Eirik thought this might be enough; he had looked for no opposition at all, counting rather that the greater part of the Norwegian nobles would be so discontented with King Haakon that they would make common cause with him.

After his friends had left him, Olav lay feeling how his whole being was now permeated by the pent-up joy and confidence that had lain in the depths of his soul all these long days while his body was one mass of pain and fetid humours and burning fever. In spite of all, this joy had lived within him the whole time like a glow on the hearth of a ruinous house. No pain could take from him the joy of having had the chance to stand up and act and fight for his home and his native soil against the strangers who poured over it. Even if it had availed nothing, that could not have undone the joy it gave him that they *had* risen in defence, he and his fellows in the countryside. But now that it *had* availed, he lay here feeling his tortured body as but a thin and passing scab on sound, healing flesh.

He was glad, deeply and cordially glad, as he had not been since he was young. During all his long years at home, while it seemed as if his life had so shaped itself that in other men's eyes he had

nothing to complain of—had he not prosperity, health, and peace?
—it had been with him in secret as though the snakes were striking
and tearing at his heart, as in the image of Gunnar on the door of
the closet at home. In his soul he had fought without hope, harried
by a terrible dread, against powers that were not of flesh and
blood.

He saw now it was not his suffering that destroyed the happiness of his life—a man may be happier while he suffers than when
his days are good. And sufferings that are of some *avail*, they are
like the spear-points that raise the shield on which the young
king's son sits when his subjects do him homage.

Some days later Claus Wiephart came with a sledge. He pro-
posed that Olav Audunsson should move down to his house and
submit himself to his leechcraft. Olav said yes to this—he could not
in any case stay longer at Little Aker. Claus tortured and plagued
him sorely at first, wrenched out the stump of his tooth, picked
out splinters of bone, cut and burned at the wound. Olav bore it
all with patience; nothing made any impression on this strange,
quiet joy of having fought and seen that it was of use. Not the
thought that Claus would surely see to it that he was well paid for
the cure, nor all that he heard of the Swedes harrying the countryside as they withdrew from the realm. He could get no word of
how things were at Hestviken—whether the manor had been
burned—but this touched him little. Had he had women and children at home, it would have been otherwise.

The grass was green in Claus Wiephart's garden, and great yellow buds were bursting on the trees, when at last Olav could make
ready for the homeward journey. The wound was now almost
healed and the skin had grown again on his cheek. The day before
he was to leave he asked Claus's leman if she would lend him her
mirror. He sat with it awhile, breathed on the bright disk of
brass, wiped it, and looked again at his own face.

His light hair had turned all grey, its curls were lank and lifeless, and his square, clean-cut face was furrowed and faded. The
right side was spoiled, the cheek so sunken that the whole face was
awry, and the great red scar had an ugly look; the mouth was also
drawn down a little on that side.

In a way Olaf Audunsson had always been aware that he was an
unusually handsome man. Not that it had made him vain, and in

his youth it had annoyed him if anyone spoke of it or if the women let him see that they would be glad to have dealings with him because he was so bright and fair. In an obscure fashion he had felt that his physical grace was itself a part of the tie of flesh and blood that bound him to Ingunn—since he had not yet been fully grown when they were mated. But it had been an element in his knowledge of himself that he was, once for all, a well-favoured man, rather short than tall, but strong and faultlessly built, without an unhealthy spot in his whole close-knit, shapely frame, fair and bright of hair and skin and eyes, as befitted the race from which he was sprung.

It was something of a humiliation that now this was past and gone, but he took it patiently, as a judgment, that now he must think himself old. Nor was he so many years from the half-hundred, so he must needs bow to it.

And so he came home to Hestviken one fine spring day, to green meadows and bursting leaves in the groves. The houses were standing, but all of them were empty—the Swedes had cut down and carried off all they found. In the byre stood a cow and a heifer that Lady Mærta had bought of Torhild Björnsdatter when she fetched home the children and the serving-maids.

But Mærta Birgersdatter was just as calm as was her wont, and Olav was just as calm as she, and they sat and talked together in the evening. But Olav said very little, for he spoke rather thickly, from the wound in his mouth, and it shamed him to talk. He was glad that the children *had* been fetched—Torhild Björnsdatter was the only one he was loath should see him, now that he was thus marred.

THE MASTER OF HESTVIKEN

Sigrid Undset's
ACCLAIMED EPIC

"Powerful, intense, and memorable . . . a triumph! . . . [Undset] combines a supreme identification with the manners, the morals, the feelings of a particular age and [with] an understanding of fundamental human character."
— *The New York Times*

THE AXE

Set in medieval Norway, a land torn by pagan codes of vengeance and the rigors of Christian piety, the first volume in this epic tetralogy introduces us to Olav Audunnson and Ingunn Steinfinnsdatter, whose youthful passion triggers a chain of murder, exile, and disgrace.

Fiction/Literature/0-679-75273-0

THE SNAKE PIT

After years of bitter separation, Olav Audunnson and Ingunn Steinfinnsdatter begin what each hopes will be a new life—but in Ingunn's past lies the shame of an illegitimate child and in Olav's past lies murder.

Fiction/Literature/0-679-75554-3

IN THE WILDERNESS

Bereft by the death of his wife, Ingunn, and haunted by the memory of his sins against her, Olav Audunsson leaves his estate at Hestviken on a journey of adventure, temptation, and repentance.

Fiction/Literature/0-679-75553-5

THE SON AVENGER

In the concluding volume, Olav, now in the last years of his life, must watch his grown children reenact the sins of his youth, with consequences even more fearful.

Fiction/Literature/0-679-75552-7

Available at your local bookstore, or call toll-free to order:
1-800-793-2665 (credit cards only).

KRISTIN LAVRANSDATTER
Sigrid Undset's masterful trilogy

"No other novelist has bodied forth the medieval world with such
richness and fullness."　　　　　*—New York Herald Tribune*

The acknowledged masterpiece of the Nobel Prize–winning Norwegian novelist Sigrid Undset, *Kristin Lavransdatter* has never been
out of print in this country since its first publication in 1927. Its
narrative of a woman's life in fourteenth-century Norway has kept
its hold on generations of readers, and the heroine, Kristin—beautiful, strong-willed, and passionate—stands with the world's great
literary figures of our time.

THE BRIDAL WREATH

The first volume of this masterwork describes young Kristin's
stormy romance with Erlend Nikulaussön, a young man perhaps
overly fond of women, of whom her father strongly disapproves.

FICTION/0-394-75299-6

THE MISTRESS OF HUSABY

Volume II tells of Kristin's troubled and eventful married life on
the great estate of Husaby, to which her husband has taken her.

FICTION/0-394-75293-7

THE CROSS

The final volume shows Kristin still indomitable, reconstructing
her world after the devastation of the Black Death and the loss of
almost everything that she has loved.

FICTION/0-394-75291-0

Available at your local bookstore, or call toll-free to order:
1-800-793-2665 (credit cards only).